THE FORGOTTEN

Cover photo: *Freeze*, a painting by Edward Zuber (1932-2018), a Canadian veteran of the Korean War who later became the Canadian War Artist for Korea. *Freeze* pictures a patrol illuminated by enemy starshell—if they don't stand perfectly still, they will be seen and draw fire. Used by permission.

THE FORGOTTEN

A Novel of the Korean War

ROBERT W. MACKAY

CANADA

*Publisher's note: This book is a work of fiction. Names, characters, places and
incidents are either the product of the author's imagination or are used fictitiously,
and any resemblance to actual persons living or dead is entirely coincidental.*

Cover art: War Art
Ted Zuber
Freeze
Accession number (ex. CWM 19710261-0123)
Beaverbrook Collection of War Art
Canadian War Museum

Library and Archives Canada Cataloguing in Publication

Title: The forgotten : a novel of the Korean War / Robert W. Mackay.

Names: Mackay, Robert W. (Robert William), 1942- author.

Identifiers: Canadiana (print) 20240382471 | Canadiana (ebook) 2024038248x |
ISBN 9781989689752 (softcover) | ISBN 9781989689790 (EPUB)

Subjects: LCSH: Korean War, 1950-1953—Fiction. |
LCGFT: Historical fiction. | LCGFT: Novels.

Classification: LCC PS8625.K396 F67 2024 | DDC C813/.6—dc23

Printed and bound in Canada on 100% recycled paper.

Now Or Never Publishing
901, 163 Street, Surrey, British Columbia, Canada V4A 9T8

nonpublishing.com
Fighting Words.

We gratefully acknowledge the support of the Canada Council for the Arts
and the British Columbia Arts Council for our publishing program.

The Forgotten is dedicated to the men of the Special Force

TABLE OF CONTENTS

"Let the bastards come."

~ Big Jim Stone, April 24th, 1951

PART ONE
"KOREA? WHO CARES?"
NOVEMBER 21, 1950

Chapter 1

Nineteen-year-old Charlie Black shivered in the cold November air that swirled in the cavernous hall of Edmonton's Canadian National Railway station, its windows dark in the hour before dawn. All night he had dozed off and on, slumped against his pack on the wooden bench, his .303 leaning against his leg.

The battalion was two days ahead of him. Not his fault, he assured himself, but they had left for the west coast while he did his best with his father. And then he'd missed the next troop train going west through a mixup by his aunt, who passed on a message to him and misinterpreted a phoned "1300 hours" as 3:00 o'clock. What he needed now was for the transport sergeant, Tuttle, to have come up with a ticket on the next train to the coast. Before he was listed AWOL.

Footsteps echoed. He pulled himself together and sat up. Grim-faced men, some of whom had thrown on suit jackets or topcoats over tieless shirts, hurried into the building. A harried young civilian with garters on his shirtsleeves was rushing by. Charlie intercepted him. "What's going on?"

"Out of my way!" The man didn't even look up from under his green eyeshade. He pushed past Charlie, a telegram clutched in one hand, and hurried down a corridor.

A man in a rumpled trench coat and sporting a fedora approached. "Where you going, soldier? You in the artillery?"

"Why, what's happening?"

The trench-coated man produced a pencil and notebook. "You don't know?" He transferred notebook and pencil to one hand, pulled half a cigarette from a pocket with the other, and stuck it in the corner of his mouth. "There's been an accident, kid. Two trains, head on. One of 'em full of soldiers."

Charlie was stunned. "What soldiers?"

"Dunno. Maybe dozens killed."

Cripes, Charlie thought. Soldiers killed? Were they Special Force, destined, like him, for Fort Lewis in Washington? They couldn't be Patricias, could they?

The man identified himself as a reporter with the *Edmonton Journal*. Charlie offered him his Zippo. "Where's the accident?"

"West, somewhere in the Rockies." The reporter lit his cigarette and looked at Charlie's lighter, fingering the raised crest before handing it back. "You're in the Princess Patricia's?" He answered his own question, glancing at Charlie's shoulder flash.

Just then a tall gray-suited man accompanied by a policeman entered the station. The reporter wheeled and followed them. Charlie sank onto the bench. Soldiers in a rail accident, in the Rockies? Surely not his Patricias. No, they'd be on the west coast by now. He spotted the eye-shaded telegraphist ducking into an office.

Charlie followed, carrying his pack and rifle. The man, a youth really, no older than Charlie himself, sat at a table. He wore earphones and had one hand on a morse key and scribbled on a pad with the other. He looked at Charlie out of the corner of his eye and nodded toward a chair.

"My God," the telegraphist said, tossing down his pencil. "A troop train ran into the Continental Limited. At least ten dead." He took off his earphones, set them down, and bent over, clutching his hands to his head. "Oh my God."

My God is right, Charlie thought. Who are they? He still wasn't sure his 2nd Patricia's weren't involved. But Canadian soldiers, in a train crash. He made his way back out to the main hall, keeping an eye on the army office door.

An hour later Charlie saw Tuttle, the sergeant in charge of the station's temporary transport office, unlock the door. Charlie collected his gear and went after him.

Tuttle was already on the phone, droplets of sweat on his brow in spite of the chill in the terminal building. He saw Charlie and turned on his swivel chair, his voice muffled the few times he responded. In a few moments he hung up.

"Christ," he said. "The train from Shilo, Manitoba, with the Gunners on board. Hit a passenger train that was coming east head on."

Charlie let out a breath, feeling relieved. Not the Patricias. But Gunners of the 2nd Royal Canadian Horse Artillery. A flash of guilt stabbed at him for his relief in the face of tragedy.

Tuttle passed on more details. The troop train had crossed the continental divide in the night, somehow ending up on the same set of tracks as the eastbound Limited. Both sets of engineers and firemen were killed instantly. Many soldiers dead or injured.

More calls came in, and Tuttle made some of his own, seeking details of rescue efforts. At last he turned to Charlie. "You still here?"

"I still need to rejoin my battalion, sergeant."

"Forgot to tell you in all the excitement. I have a ticket for you for 1500 hours. Day coach." He reached into a drawer and produced a ticket clipped to a copy of Charlie's travel order. He tossed them on the desk. "It's a waste of time. I just heard. The Patricias have new orders to sail for Korea early on the 25th. You'll be too late getting there. You might as well go back to Wainwright."

Charlie was dumbfounded. His whole being was invested in going overseas with the Special Force. First he was waylaid by the need to deal with his father, then he missed the Gunner's troop train. A lucky thing, for sure, the unimaginable horror of a train crash. But now the Patricias, instead of weeks of training in Fort Lewis, Washington, were headed to Korea early, at least according to Tuttle.

Tuttle was on the phone again. Charlie checked the time on the wall clock. His ticket was on the desk. He had just finished months of training at Currie Barracks and Wainwright, and he wasn't about to go back there. He snatched the ticket and left the office before anything else could go wrong.

—

At last Charlie was under way toward Vancouver and his battalion. He had an overnight seat on the Edmonton to Vancouver express, thanks to Tuttle. And thanks to him being distracted, and not actually ordering Charlie not to take the ticket.

One of the first on board, Charlie snagged a window seat. His day-car filled up, mostly men on business, with a couple of family groups in their Sunday best for a train trip. A portly man in a three-piece suit sat next to him, careful to leave space between himself and Charlie while he pulled some documents from a briefcase and examined them.

For the past three months Charlie had only known soldiers and the army, and felt out of place on a trainload of civilians. He might be on his way to fight in a far-off land, but the population outside the armed forces didn't appear impressed.

The hills west of Edmonton rolled past, the train puffing its way up toward the Rocky Mountains and the Yellowhead Pass. A blue sky with scattered clouds turned wintry, the clouds coalescing as the train moved west. The day faded into twilight and a dark, gloomy night that reflected Charlie's mood.

With every click of the steel wheels he was closer to his family, who lived in Surrey, British Columbia—not that he expected to see them for at least a year. Charlie Black had signed on and said good-bye early that summer, and for the first time since then he was alone. Not a recruit among hundreds undergoing training at Currie Barracks in Calgary, not a would-be rifleman in a tight-knit platoon in Camp Wainwright east of Edmonton.

Charlie's problems started when his dad, Bill, had made a surprise visit to Bill's sister in Edmonton, then suffered injuries in a car accident that landed him in hospital. When the battalion entrained for the west coast, Charlie requested a couple of days leave to see his father. His leave was granted, but his visit didn't work out so well. Then he missed his train after a confused message was relayed through his elderly aunt. Shoot—that in itself shouldn't be a problem; many of his fellow soldiers had gone astray for more than a couple of days and not suffered significant punishment. But now the 2nd Battalion Princess Patricia's Canadian Light Infantry was about to sail without him.

According to the original plan the battalion should be south of the 49th in Washington State at Fort Lewis, training for the Korean "police action," so styled by US President Truman and the Canadian newspapers. The Pats were part of Canada's Special Force, made up of new recruits like him, barely adults who'd missed out on World War Two; veterans who re-enlisted; and army regulars. Within weeks of the call going out there were 10,000 volunteers, keen to get into uniform. Those had been whittled down to perhaps 5,000 men and assigned to one of three regiments, his own being the Patricias. The others, the 2nd Battalion Royal Canadian Regiment and the 2nd Battalion Royal 22nd Regiment, hardly crossed Charlie's mind, busy as they were, training elsewhere, and—too bad for them—not Patricias. The three battalions together formed the 25th Canadian Infantry Brigade.

A couple of days before he enlisted, Charlie tried to talk to his dad. Bill often sat on the front porch on early-summer Saturday afternoons, but this Saturday in July he wasn't there. Neither was he in the kitchen where the scent of the morning's baking lingered as Charlie's mother and sister-in-law Jackie prepared dinner.

"Wanna play, Uncle Charlie?" Six-year-old Harry was setting the table but would drop that in a heartbeat to take him on in a game of checkers.

Charlie heard the confident tones of a CBC newsreader coming from the living room radio. He headed that way but smiled at Harry. "Get the board warmed up," he said. "I'll be back."

Leaving the kitchen for the living room, Charlie's eyes took a few moments to adjust to the dim room with its heavy curtains. Bill was in his chair beside the radio, a walnut-coloured monster whose handy upper surface was home to an open pack of cigarettes, an ashtray, and a glass with the remnants of a rye and water. Pushed to the back was a hand grenade mounted upright on a wooden base labelled PPCLI. When he was a kid Charlie had asked his dad about the grenade, whether it was still live or not. Bill had reassured him it wasn't. Charlie never did take a chance and pull the safety pin.

He perched on the coffee-stained couch opposite his dad, who still had a paperback in hand, but was listening to the news, an item about the American response to the latest developments in the Far East. Charlie's vision had adapted to the dim room, not that he needed his eyes to know that behind him against the wall was a glass-fronted gun cabinet that featured a Webley .455, a Lee Enfield .303, and a Savage .300. Bill had carried the Webley and a .303 in the Great War, and the Savage was a relic of his hunting days, long gone.

Beside the gun cabinet was a photo of Charlie's brother Jeffrey in battledress and helmet, a rifle slung over his shoulder. Jeffrey, who had followed his father's example and fought in a world war with Princess Patricia's Canadian Light Infantry. Jeff was a constant presence in spite of his death in 1944, six years earlier.

"Big day at the bank tomorrow, Dad."

His father folded his book and reached down to turn off the radio. "That so?"

"One-year anniversary." Charlie chuckled. "Maybe the boss will buy me a coffee."

"Didn't think it had been that long." Bill's eyes slid away, a glance over Charlie's shoulder, back down to the book on his lap. He picked it up, turned it over, and began to read.

Charlie's hands were on his knees, his fingers beating an irregular tattoo. He cleared his throat. "Mr. St. Laurent is ignoring the United Nations."

Bill turned a page.

"Think Canada will get involved in Korea, Dad?"

Bill kept his book open. "Korea? Who cares?" He looked at Charlie, his face shut tight. "You hang on at the bank, son. Keep your head down. This family's done enough, and so has this country."

Charlie's fingers stopped tapping and gripped his knees as he watched his father's attention return to his book. He sat a few moments, wanting to talk to his dad, really talk to him. Locked away, Bill was unable to get past the grief of Jeffrey's death, the loss of his first-born son.

Charlie was desperate to get his father's respect, and that desperation had driven him to the recruiting station and its promise of military service. In a moment of reflection, though, he had to admit to an urge to prove himself, to be a man among men. The Special Force might give him that chance.

All he had to do now was catch the Patricias before they sailed.

The steel wheels of his carriage clicked on the tracks. He looked out at the darkened foothills and shivered.

If he had caught a ride west on the artillerymen's train as scheduled he could have been killed or maimed. The victims of the crash were fellow soldiers, volunteers for the Special Force and the fight in Korea. Men like himself, with hopes and dreams and families of their own. He almost felt guilty, thinking how lucky he was, not to have shared the Gunners' fate.

Before leaving Edmonton he'd learned the death toll from the Canoe River Crash, as it was being called, had reached a dozen or more. A high price to pay, for a Special Force still to fire a shot in anger. A feeling of helplessness swept over him. If soldiers were dying in Canada, a country at peace within its borders, what would it be like in a far-off, foreign place, where the enemy was out to kill them?

Charlie shook his head. Three months of training had taught him a lot. How to survive in a shooting war. To rely on his comrades in his platoon, and on the leadership of his superiors. He'd be okay.

The train slowed, the darkening hills outside sliding by at a walking pace. Gliding silently but for the intermittent sound of the wheels on the tracks below, it came to a stop. A faint hiss of escaping steam reached Charlie.

The back door of the carriage opened and closed, and a man in a CNR Trainman's uniform walked past Charlie's seat. The three-piece-suited gent beside Charlie waved at him. "Why have we stopped? What's going on?"

"We're on a siding so another train can go by, sir."

"This is the Express. We have priority. I paid for priority, not to sit while cargo goes by."

"It's not cargo—well not normal cargo. It's a rescue train, bringing back injured and killed. Soldiers."

The man frowned, looking confused. "Soldiers?"

"Yes, sir," said the trainman, and walked away, resuming his trip forward.

The man glanced quickly at Charlie, avoiding eye contact. "Something to do with this Korean business?"

"Yes, sir."

The man asked a few more questions, but exhausted Charlie's limited knowledge of the train crash in short order. He sounded less arrogant as they spoke, but not for the first time Charlie was reminded that though Korea was by necessity at the top of the Special Force's list of priorities, it had faded from the civilian population's front of mind.

Charlie knew that sometime soon the rescue train would pass by, getting the wounded to medical attention and the dead to the proper authorities.

His lack of sleep caught up with him and he dozed, his head against the window.

When he woke his car was silent and unmoving. A train rumbled past on his left, moving fast. He couldn't make out any-thing through its windows—not a person, or stretcher, or doctor or nurse. The Express moved away at once, to the satisfaction of Charlie's neighbour, and of Charlie himself, very aware of the passing hours and the hundreds of miles between him and his battalion.

Much later, couplings banged as the train again jerked to a stop. The interior of the car was dim, passengers nodding and half asleep or leaning against their neighbour. Putting his hands either side of his face and pressing against the glass, Charlie could only make out vague shapes of rocks and trees. He stood and went to the washroom, where he splashed water on his face. By the time he regained his seat the train had started ahead and was picking up speed, wheels clicking on the iron rails.

He dozed, arms folded, head against the window. He sensed the train creeping along the tracks and opened his eyes. The cold car creaked, a dim light somewhere in the corridor. Charlie could see his breath. The man beside him stirred and muttered in his sleep.

At first it was pitch black outside, but the darkness retreated, conifers showing up tinged with light from somewhere ahead. The train edged forward, as if reluctant.

Charlie stared. The vague light brightened, solidified, and turned brilliant. Alongside the tracks was a fifty-foot-wide dark river. Scattered over both banks were the shattered remains of ancient wooden passenger cars, looking like toys, buckled and splintered, smashed by a giant fist. Yards further along were more cars, their frames wrecked almost beyond recognition, axles and steel wheels upended. Blackened wreckage, burnt foliage, boilers, fireboxes; the guts of a steam locomotive laid bare in the burning white light of floodlights powered by generators roaring in the background. The reek of burned petroleum and paint and wood permeated Charlie's west-bound car. He was transfixed by the scene and the thought of the horror suffered by those who had been in the midst of it, their bodies mangled and broken and scalded by steam from ruptured boilers. He recoiled from the window, only to find his eyes drawn back again to the horrifying remains of what had been a troop train with hundreds of young Canadians aboard. It took forever to get past the wrecks, then they were gone in an instant, leaving him wondering if he'd glimpsed hell itself.

He found it hard to believe anybody had made it alive from the Gunners' shattered train. How were such things decided? The 2nd Royal Canadian Horse Artillery had been bloodied. Charlie blinked, exposed, more desperate than ever to get back to his home in 7 Platoon, 2nd Patricia's.

—

Charlie stared, his eyes wide, as the speeding car crossed south across the Fraser River on the Pattullo Bridge, headed for the States. He was in his own back yard, just a few miles from home, but the landscape seemed trance-like and unreal. He had gone most of three days with little sleep, his train suffering constant delays between the site of the crash and his arrival in Vancouver. Even his fear of missing the ship could no longer keep him alert. His head bobbed up from time to time but mostly it rested against the barrel of his Lee-Enfield, propped upright between his knees. Crowder reached across from the driver's seat and shook his shoulder. Charlie blinked as he registered the car slowing. A large white structure loomed ahead.

"Peace Arch," Crowder said. "Better stow your rifle on the floor behind you."

A yawning border agent eyed the two uniformed men through Crowder's open window. "Business in the US?"

"Heading to Seattle. This man is due to catch an American naval ship to take him to Korea."

"ID."

Charlie fumbled in his pockets, having to go through them a second time, not feeling very sharp. He handed his identification card to Crowder, who passed it over to the guard, along with his own.

The guard sported a pencil-thin mustache, his uniform neatly pressed, cap square on his head. He looked at each card in turn, squinted at the two Canadians, one of whom was gritting his teeth with impatience. "Good luck," he said. "I hear bad things about the war over there."

Charlie thought he could make his own luck if they could get their ID cards back and drive off. The guard handed the cards over and waved them on. Charlie let out a pent-up breath.

Their army-issue khaki-coloured 1941 Ford sedan accelerated away from the United States of America customs and border control building, belching light blue smoke as it sped south on the two-lane highway toward Seattle. Charlie was in the passenger seat, right hand locked on the door handle, heart pounding. Behind the wheel Captain Crowder, or so he had told Charlie was his name, stared ahead. "Time now?"

Charlie glanced at his watch. "Nine-thirty."

"Nine-thirty, *sir*. Christ, don't they teach you Special Force guys anything?"

"Yes, sir!" Charlie held his breath until the captain once again swung his gaze back to the road ahead.

When Charlie had scrambled from the Canadian National station in Vancouver two hours earlier, rifle in hand and pack on his back, he still hadn't figured out the next leg of his trip. How to get to Seattle in record time? He didn't know anybody connected to the army in Vancouver. His father, the only driver in his family, was in the hospital in Edmonton.

A muscular-looking captain standing a few feet away beside an army sedan rescued him.

"Black?"

"Yes, sir."

"Get in," he said, waving him over to the Ford and sliding behind the wheel.

He gave Charlie just enough time to throw his pack into the backseat and dive into the front before accelerating away. "Name's Crowder," the captain said. "You want to rejoin the Pats, correct?"

He glanced at Charlie, who nodded, still catching his breath.

"You know the battalion is leaving for Korea today, not doing their planned training in Fort Lewis?"

"Yes, sir."

Charlie didn't know what he'd done to deserve an officer to whisk him through the border checks and speed him south, but he wasn't about to say or do anything that broke the spell.

A hundred-and-thirty miles to go, and two hours to do it in. At 1330 hours the USNS *Private Joe P. Martinez* would pull away from the Seattle pier, taking with her 800 US soldiers and the 900-odd members of the 2nd Battalion, Princess Patricia's Canadian Light Infantry. They'd be light one private if Crowder didn't keep the pedal to the floor and the Ford on the road, right side up.

Green pastures and dark green woods flashed past, with Captain Crowder barely slowing as they passed through small Washington State towns, taking a chance on local cops being otherwise occupied. Charlie was sweating in his woolen battledress, fidgeting, afraid he'd miss the ship and the war, or peacekeeping action, or whatever they were calling it now.

"I knew your brother, you know."

"Sir?"

"I recognized your name when Sergeant Tuttle phoned the local office and told us you'd be on the Express." Crowder looked at Charlie for an instant, then back at the road. "Jeff was a good soldier, sure earned his Military Medal. He was what—six years older than you?"

"Yes, sir."

"Must have been hell for your family. Like lots of others. Strange thing, when you think about it. Fine one minute, nothing left the next." He glanced at Charlie. "High explosive arty. Hit right where Jeff was standing."

Arty. Artillery. Jeff, obliterated in an instant. I wonder if the family knew that, Charlie thought, stricken himself. It was one thing in training to learn about the dangers of enemy artillery, and the blessings of having your own, but this was personal. Charlie felt sick.

Crowder didn't give him a chance to dwell on it. "How did you get separated from the battalion?"

"My dad was hurt in an accident in Edmonton. I took a couple of days leave, then was supposed to be on the train with the Gunners, but the message was fouled up and I missed it."

"Poor buggers. Damn good thing you weren't on board."

In Charlie's mind he could picture the wreckage at Canoe River, which only hours before he saw it would have been populated by the living, the dead, and the dying. He felt like the scene itself had screamed at him as he ghosted past on the train.

"You okay, private? You don't look so good."

"Yes, sir. I'm fine."

But it was complicated. He'd left his family behind when he joined the army, not without twinges of guilt. He was bored with his job in the bank, and the appeal of the Special Force promised an adventure, soldiering for Canada in a foreign land. With the approval of the United Nations! Jeff would have done the same.

The green open spaces of northern Washington State gave way to residences and commercial blocks as Charlie gazed out, anxiety growing as the minutes ticked by.

"Stand-to, private!" Crowder said. "Keep an eye out."

Seattle. Twisting streets along a waterfront, a grey day with a light rain falling. Long piers that stuck out into the harbour, huge ships loading and unloading, vehicles and stevedores everywhere. Rolling down his window, Charlie heard seagulls cry, and welcomed a few drops of moisture on his face. Crowder turned onto a pier and pulled up beside a couple of men who stood off to one side, smoking. "Seen a bunch of soldiers loading up?"

The men looked blank. One of them shrugged. Charlie looked at his watch: 1330 hours. What would he do if the *Martinez* had sailed? Was this the end of his great adventure, his mission to show his father what he was made of?

Crowder floored the accelerator, careening back to the main road and continuing south along the waterfront. Charlie breathed in air redolent of the sea: salt, fish, and creosote. The background roar of the busy port, with its clanking machinery and humming engines, drowned out the voices of the workers.

"What's that?" Crowder said, stopping the car.

Charlie heard it too. Mixed in with the clamour of men and machinery were vague strains of music.

Crowder drove ahead. The bow of a rusty freighter loomed ahead of them. Rounding it, they saw a long jetty with a huge grey ship alongside. A uniformed American band was playing *It's a Long Way to Tipperary*.

Beyond the band, at the seaward end of the pier, was a mass of khaki-clad men. "That'll be them," Crowder said.

They drove closer, and Charlie could make out the PPCLI shoulder flashes. Crowder drove past the band, right up to where the long line of hundreds of men snaked back and forth on the pier and stopped. Opening his door, Charlie sprang out and retrieved his rifle and pack from the back seat. The nearest soldiers looked at him, mildly curious.

Charlie shouldered his pack, picked up his rifle, and turned back to Crowder, who stood beside the open driver's door. "Thank you—"

"Do the same for any Patricia. Even 2nd Battalion." He waved Charlie off. "Good luck, private."

Charlie went in search of 7 Platoon C Company. Hurrying along the line of soldiers that wound back and forth on the pier, he was excited, recognizing some men but not yet his platoon. Noticing a couple of officers shaking each man's hand at the bottom of the plank, Charlie's eyes widened. They were none other than Lieutenant-Colonel Stone, who commanded the battalion, and Brigadier Rockingham, in charge of the whole Special Force.

After a frantic search he found the men of 7 Platoon, thirty or forty back from the front of the line. Leading them was their platoon sergeant, Smith.

He'd made it, and he let out a sigh of relief.

His section leader, Corporal Breton, stared at him, his eyebrows arched. "Charlie, where did you come from?"

Charlie grinned at him, thinking he had a story to tell his comrades. He stepped into the line behind Breton and waited his turn to shake hands with the brass and march aboard.

Someone tapped him on the shoulder. "Just a minute, private." He turned to see Sergeant Smith, who looked puzzled. "What are you doing here, Black? We heard you were in the Gunners' train crash, probably killed. You were listed among the missing."

"I missed the Gunners' train, sergeant, not my fault, I caught..." His voice trailed off, thinking it sounded stupid.

"Look, Black. The army wrote you off. It'll take them months to deal with the paperwork. Go away and get cleaned up, you look a wreck. Catch up when you get it sorted out."

Charlie had never before, in his short army career, contradicted a sergeant. "I'm fine!" He took a breath. "I'm trained, I—"

Smith held up a hand.

Charlie thought he saw a change in Smith's rigid, by-the-book NCO's face. Behind him, the line of men advanced up the gangplank at a steady rate.

"Okay, Black." Smith drew him to one side and lowered his voice. "Here's what you do. Fall in with 13 Platoon." He pointed to the tail end of the line. "Back there."

13 Platoon? There were only twelve platoons in the battalion, three to each of the four companies.

Charlie stood aside and Smith and 7 Platoon proceeded on board. Fifteen minutes later Charlie watched as the last of D Company shook the brigadier's hand and climbed up the gangplank. Behind them were twenty or so soldiers. With a start Charlie recognized a lance corporal everyone called Frenchy and a couple of other recruits he thought would have been dismissed and sent home by now. Was this 13 Platoon, barely a couple of undermanned sections for God's sake? What were they, all the misfits?

He shouldered his pack and moved into the line, shaking hands with Brigadier Rockingham and Colonel Stone, thanking his lucky stars they didn't yet know all their soldiers personally.

Welcome aboard, Charlie, he said to himself, and marched up the gangplank along with the men who perhaps lived up to the epithet the regular army pinned on the Special Force. The bums from the slums.

CHAPTER 2

Once on board there was another line, this one with a long enough wait to get through a door into the superstructure that Charlie set his pack down. The man he was following had blond hair and a round, cherubic face. He told Charlie he was from Winnipeg. "Mike Muller," he said. "Didn't see you before."

"I just arrived, told to join 13 Platoon."

"You must have pissed someone off." Muller grinned. "There's only twenty of us. Twenty-one now, I guess."

Charlie shuffled ahead, taking in the exotic world of a seagoing ship. He could see a lifeboat, held in place by a complicated-looking set of pulleys, cables, and cotter pins; a smokestack; guardrails to stop people from tumbling to the dock or the sea below. The cries of gulls overhead and the smell of unknown foodstuffs, creosote, and what he took to be the odor of the sea registered with a kind of eye-opening assault. Somewhat sobering was a large amount of rust that stained the superstructure and deck of the *Private Joe P. Martinez*.

The line moved. Each soldier was handed a card listing name, bunk number, and where it was located in the various holds by a corporal stationed just inside the door.

"Name?" he said.

"Black."

"Well, Black, I don't have a card for you."

"Somebody screwed up," Charlie said. "13 Platoon. Same as him." He nodded at Muller.

"Yeah, he's in 13," Muller said.

The corporal had a clipboard in one hand. "He's not on my list." He squinted at Charlie. "I don't recognize you."

"Typical army foul-up," Muller said.

The corporal looked again at his clipboard, as if it held the answer to the problem. He shrugged. "Okay, shoot, just follow along. There should be a couple of spare bunks in where the rest of the platoon is located. But Black, go talk to your platoon sergeant. Get him to straighten this out." The line shuffled ahead, and the corporal turned his attention to the next man in line.

Charlie followed Muller, stepping over a high sill into a short passageway, then onto a nearly vertical ladder that led down into the bowels of the ship. It was awkward going, his slung rifle catching on the treads, and his pack trying to peel him off backwards. At the bottom they turned and climbed down on to another ladder, then another, before coming to a stop three decks down.

A sweating corporal directed them to the area that would be their home for the next three weeks while the *Martinez* rumbled her way across the Pacific.

Bedlam ruled. High-spirited soldiers squabbled over who should have which bunk, which were stacked seven high, with hardly enough room in them to allow a man to roll over. Charlie followed Muller, coming to a couple of empty bunks near the deckhead. Muller claimed the one second from the top, and Charlie threw his pack up onto the upper one.

"What the hell are you doing here?"

Charlie looked over his shoulder to see Frenchy, the lance corporal. Frenchy was a man of medium height and wiry build, dark-haired, his face dominated by a prominent nose. A cigarette dangled from the corner of his mouth.

"Following orders, same as everyone else."

"Since when do you bunk in with 13 Platoon?"

"It's just for the time being, lance corporal."

Frenchy tilted his head back, avoiding the smoke from his cigarette. "You're a keener, Charlie." Frenchy took the cigarette between his thumb and forefinger, flicking it with his little finger, knocking off a quarter inch of ash. He waved it like a challenge in front of Charlie's face. "I don't get it," he said, eyes narrowing. "Must be a hell of a comedown, hanging out with us."

Couldn't have put it any better, Charlie thought. "I'll make do."

Frenchy glared for a moment, shrugged, and turned away. Charlie reached up and grabbed the edge of his bunk and took a deep breath, feeling like he'd just sidestepped a problem.

He sensed somebody close to him. Frenchy again. "Don't think you're any better than us, that's all."

—

Charlie had met Frenchy before. Back in Wainwright during their three months of intensive training, recruits were dropping like flies, the regular force army NCOs riding them, weeding out the men not up to the job. Charlie worked hard to be a good soldier, wanting to be as equal as he could to the World War II veterans amongst the volunteers. He kept his kit in good shape, boots polished, rifle spotless. He was turning into a good shot with his Lee Enfield, a rifle older than he was, almost identical to the venerable firearm in his dad's gun cabinet back home. Darned if he'd give the army an excuse to cut him loose.

After a long day on a cross-country march with full packs followed by two hours on the rifle range he stowed his gear in his locker and was about to head to the mess hall when a lance corporal he didn't know approached him.

"Hey, pal. Got a light?"

Charlie pulled out his Zippo and flipped it to the man.

"Where you from?"

"Surrey, BC," Charlie said. "You?"

"Montreal." He spoke with a vague accent.

Something clicked. He'd seen this guy before, a pushy sort. Everybody called him 'Frenchy'.

"Gotta go," Frenchy said, and turned away, wandering off.

Charlie hesitated, then followed. He caught up with Frenchy and tapped him on the shoulder.

Frenchy jerked around and gave Charlie a cold stare.

Charlie reached out his hand, palm up. Frenchy held his gaze for a moment before reaching into his battledress breast pocket. He retrieved Charlie's Zippo and dropped it into his hand. "My mistake," he said, and walked away.

Something about Frenchy rubbed him the wrong way, but Charlie shrugged it off. Frenchy was just one more soldier among hundreds in the battalion. He patted his pocket, feeling the lighter in there, reassured. A gift from Jeff, who had posted it from France when Charlie was far too young to smoke.

—

Down in the bowels of the *Martinez* Charlie looked around, taking stock of the men he might be stuck with in the short term. Muller, who had helped Charlie get by the corporal at the gangplank a short time before, seemed like a good guy. Frenchy, of course. He didn't trust Frenchy, based on the one minor incident. He recognized a couple of other faces but didn't know their names. Rejects, for some reason, not placed in the formal battalion structure. But here they were, and here he was, for now a member of 13 Platoon.

It wasn't easy moving around the crowded holds. Men wandered everywhere, exploring the ship that would be their home for the next three weeks. Charlie felt like he was in a strange place, one that he wanted to escape.

It was a couple of hours before he tracked down the members of the platoon he had lived and breathed with at Camp Wainwright. He bumped into Corporal Breton, his section leader back in Wainwright, who said, "Where the hell did you come from? We heard you were killed in the Gunners' train crash."

Charlie explained again. "I want back in 7 Platoon. There must be a slot for me."

"When the word went out they assigned somebody from the reinforcement pool, seems okay. How did you get aboard?"

"I just fell in at the end of the line," Charlie said, remembering Sergeant Smith said to forget they'd spoken.

Charlie's old platoon gathered around. "We're fully manned, up to scratch," Breton said. "You mean you're bunked in with 13? That's pretty rich." Breton shook his head. "You're the last guy I'd expect to see with that bunch. Have you talked to any of the officers, or the RSM?"

"I'm steering clear of them for now." The last person Charlie wanted to see was the Regimental Sergeant Major. His only direct contact with the RSM—the battalion's senior non-commissioned officer, and only one rung lower than God himself in the universal pecking order—was when he tore a strip off Charlie for walking across the parade square at Wainwright.

Charlie went in search of 7 Platoon's sergeant, Smith, to try again. He found the sergeant having a smoke on the upper deck along with two other NCOs. Seeing Charlie, he turned to talk to him.

"Sergeant, I have to get out of 13 Platoon. Can you get me back in 7?"

"Black, you're lucky to be aboard. Only in the Special Force, I tell ya. The First Battalion has twelve platoons, period. But the Second Battalion, we got a thirteenth. Guess the brass wants some spare bodies. Okay, I'll speak to our platoon officer, maybe he'll talk to the adjutant, help you out. You just keep your head down for now, stay with 13 until the army tells you different."

"But I had permission to go on leave, it wasn't—"

"I don't care about all that, Black. And neither does the army." Smith's face was set. "It was bad luck, getting added to the passenger manifest for the Gunners' train, then listed as missing, along with the others buried under the wreckage." Smith brightened. "Hell, soldier, live with it. You're on a sea cruise. Visit the fabulous Orient. Stay out of sight as long as you can, that's my advice."

Charlie felt blood rushing to his face. Smith was an old soldier, used to the army's strange ways, but Charlie wasn't. The sergeant had his platoon to look after, and Charlie was no longer part of it.

—

Charlie felt out of place and alone, his mood matched by the chilly November air. The *Martinez* was well clear of Seattle and into the Strait of Juan de Fuca. In the west the setting sun glowed orange-red, hanging in an open rim of sky between the clouds and the horizon ahead of the ship.

The seas were calm in these inland waters, the ship's motion barely discernible. A pair of American GI's stood at the rail smoking.

Moving up next to them, Charlie pulled out a cigarette and lit up. The nearest Yank glanced at his shoulder flashes. "Where in Canada you from?"

"West Coast, not that far from here. Never been aboard a ship, though. How about you guys?"

"We're both from Kansas, raised on farms."

"Never been on a boat, neither," said the other, taller man. "How long you in the army? We just got conscripted."

"A few months." Charlie felt like a veteran, though these boys weren't any younger than he was. Told him they had yet to fire a round in training. Hadn't even seen their weapons, which they understood were somewhere on board.

Good thing the Americans were winning the war, Charlie thought. Lucky for these boys, anyway.

Charlie had a vague understanding from newspapers and background briefings in Wainwright that North Korea had invaded the South back on June 25th. They'd succeeded in pushing the undermanned US forces of occupation and the army of the Republic of Korea almost off the Peninsula. But only two months before the *Martinez* sailed with the Patricias, General MacArthur landed US Marines at Inchon behind the North's army and turned the tide of the war. The United Nations forces drove the North Koreans all the way back to their northern border with China. The Canadian government had first anticipated the Special Force would be needed in the fight. Now, with victory within the UN's grasp, they wouldn't be needed as fighters. But Canada felt compelled to at least help out by providing peacekeepers. Not yet fully trained as infantry but close at hand at Fort Lewis, 2PPCLI received the nod and were now on their way.

Muller, the blond-haired and blue-eyed 13 Platoon member who had helped Charlie get aboard back in Seattle, joined them.

The taller GI spoke up. "We hear the fighting's almost over. The army and the US Marines are knockin' the shit out of the North Koreans."

"Yeah, crap," said Muller. "Guess the real war's over." He spat over the side. "I didn't join the army to be in some kind of a damn police force."

"You mean y'all *volunteered*?" asked the tall American.

"Yeah," Muller snorted. "Now it's a police action. Can you believe that? We spent the last three and a half months learning how to fight."

Curious about the Canadians' training, and why they wanted to fight in the first place, the GIs peppered Muller with questions.

Charlie wandered a few feet away. He hadn't figured on being part of some kind of a police force either; in fact, he ached for the chance to prove to his father he was as good a soldier as Jeffrey had been. 2PPCLI was only dispatched to Korea because the Canadian government assessed the risk to them was minimal given the Americans' recent military successes. If the war on the ground hadn't shifted in favour of the United Nations forces, Charlie and the rest of the battalion would be hustling around Fort Lewis, adding to their brief three months of training.

The *Martinez's* loudspeakers gave a burst of static, then settled back to a background hum. "NOW LISTEN UP. Cape Flattery is the land visible on the port side horizon. That will be your last view of America for a long time to come. That is all." There was a sharp click and the hum stopped.

Everybody on the upper deck moved to the port side. Through the fading twilight Charlie could see a hump-shaped, dark piece of land low on the horizon. Soldiers stood silent, six deep against the bulwark, rocking to the mild motion of the ship.

Charlie gazed at the distant corner of the United States. 'Last view of America' set him to wondering. Would every one of these Americans see home again? What little Charlie had gleaned from newspapers and radio over the last few months made it sound like there was a lot of killing going on, even if the UN was winning the fight.

It never occurred to him to worry about the Patricias. They were trained, and they were keen. A sea voyage was a new experience for Charlie, but the idea of it was not. He knew his dad had crossed the Atlantic by ship when he volunteered for duty in World War One. Jeffrey, a generation later, made the same trip over the same route to the European theatre of war for his part in World War Two. His father and brother had done their duty. It was his turn, on a different ocean this time, even if the Korean conflict didn't look like a real war.

He shivered. Cold air, he thought. Damp. Can't be nerves. No, Jeff hadn't come back from his war, but that was then, and he wasn't Jeffrey, as he had long-since concluded. His time as a recruit at Wainwright had been just the thing for him, giving him a chance to prove himself against other recruits, and even against some veterans. To himself he'd admit to a tiny bit of relief that he might not be facing an all-out war.

He just had to deal with the foul-up that landed him in 13 Platoon. Given the way the army operated, it might be his biggest hurdle.

—

"Hey, private. On your feet." Someone shook Charlie's booted foot. Charlie raised his head and saw Frenchy, looking officious.

Charlie was flat on his back in his bunk, trying to get some relief from the seasickness that had plagued him since the *Martinez* cleared protected waters. "What's up, corporal?"

"Sergeant wants you. Let's go."

He sat up, banging his head against the steel deckhead. Feeling stupid, he managed to land in the passageway without further mishap. Shaking his head to clear it, he hurried to keep up with Frenchy who made his way to the ladders and the upper deck.

"What sergeant?" he said to Frenchy's retreating back.

Frenchy carried on, not answering.

A muscular sergeant stood at ease waiting for them just inside the door to the open deck. Charlie stopped and stood at attention.

"So you're Private Black," the sergeant said. It wasn't a question. On his tunic was a World War Two service ribbon and others Charlie didn't recognize. He wore a well-trimmed mustache and appeared to be in his thirties. Charlie stood rigid, exposed under the sergeant's steady gaze.

"Follow me." The sergeant wheeled and led him down a short passageway past closed doors on both sides. Stopping at the last one, he knocked, shooting a brief glance at Charlie who pulled himself to attention.

At a muffled word the sergeant opened the door and gestured. "In here, Black."

Charlie entered a cramped space, no larger than a generous broom closet. Cardboard boxes took up half the space.

Behind a small desk sat a captain whose face was in shadow. Charlie stood at attention, swaying with the motion of the ship.

"Private Black."

"Sir." Charlie realized he was talking to the battalion's adjutant, responsible for administration and personnel. Captain Parker, the same officer who had intervened to let Charlie go see his father in Edmonton. And that hadn't turned out so well.

The captain had a document in his hand, something with an official look to it. "Sergeant Price tells me you've been hanging out with members of his 13 Platoon."

So that's who the sergeant is. "Yes, sir."

"I authorized you to take leave to visit your father. Bad luck for you, ending up on the Gunners' train. I have information here that you were killed in the accident." He peered at Charlie.

"I wasn't on the artillerymen's train, sir, I—"

"Never mind that." He tossed the document onto his desk. "The army runs on details, private. Recorded details. Paperwork." He glanced down at his crowded tabletop. "The question now is, what do we do with you? You can't stay here, you're dead!"

Charlie didn't think the captain wanted an answer from him.

"You've been taken off strength. I'll let the brigade staff know you're very much alive. We can send you back to Canada to get it sorted out. The *Martinez* will make a return trip a few days after we arrive in Korea."

"Sir, can't I join my old platoon?"

"Full up, private. Replacements pushed in already. You go back, get some more training once the paperwork is straightened out. Maybe you can transfer to one of the other battalions, re-badge to the Vandoos or RCR."

Charlie felt like the deck under him had opened up and was about to swallow him. "But—"

"Ten-shun!" the sergeant ordered, and Charlie backed out of the adjutant's office.

Charlie wondered what had just happened. He stumbled after Sergeant Price down the passageway. They exited the superstructure onto the upper deck.

"You'll be with 13 Platoon for the time being, Black. Until we get to Korea."

"Cripes, sergeant. I don't want to get sent home."

"The army works in mysterious ways." Price looked hm in the eye. "Things sometimes work out. Or they don't." Price dismissed him and strode off. Charlie turned toward the ship's side and leaned on the guardrail. He didn't know which made him feel worse, the rolling ship or the adjutant's decision to send him home.

PART TWO
"It's all Changed."
November 26, 1950

CHAPTER 3

At 0600 hours in their second day at sea Charlie woke. Hoping to beat the rush to the inadequate washplace, he climbed down from his bunk, grabbed his shaving gear, and made his way up, landing near the head of the line. His friend Muller joined him, and after shaving they got into another slow-moving line, this one for breakfast.

"They don't pick things up, we're gonna miss out," Muller said. "Frenchy said 0800 hours, on the upper deck. Sergeant wants us."

"I heard someone say there are 800 American soldiers on board. Plus 900 of us." Charlie looked around. Judging by the lineup at the galley, the *Private Joe* was carrying a lot more troops than she was built for.

Making it to the galley at last, Charlie held out his plate. A fried egg, a strip of bacon, and a charred piece of toast were deposited by a succession of three white-clad men reaching across a stainless counter. A fourth slopped on a scoop of some sort of runny potato dish.

"Hot damn," Muller said. "Can't complain about this."

The two of them squeezed onto a bench, with just enough time to eat and head out for the morning rollcall with the rest of 13 Platoon. Charlie wondered how this was going to go, unresolved issues of his presence in the platoon and fears about being sent back to Canada preying on his mind.

In a corner of the upper deck Corporal Turner, senior man in 13 Platoon's 1 Section, lined up his section facing the front, with him on the right-hand end of the line. 2 Section, with Frenchy on the end, fell in behind. Charlie took his place at the end furthest from Frenchy.

Sergeant Price was already there; he called the men to attention. Just like the day before, Price looked fit and capable, his uniform immaculate. Charlie hadn't figured out if he saw Price as an ally who could get him back to 7 Platoon, or an NCO who would back up the adjutant and look to ship him home.

A slim young lieutenant appeared and stopped a few feet from Price, who marched up to him and saluted. "13 Platoon, sir."

"Stand the platoon at ease, sergeant."

Charlie wondered what was coming.

The lieutenant stood in front of the platoon. "My name is Toogood, and I'm now your platoon officer." Looks harmless enough, and not more than a year or two older than I am, Charlie thought. 13 Platoon Officer—I wonder what he did wrong?

Toogood paused and took a moment to look from one end of the platoon to the other. "You'll see more of me during the voyage, as we learn more about what we'll be facing in Korea. Once we're there, you'll see a lot more of me." He turned to Price. "Dismiss the men. I want them gathered around."

Charlie and the rest of the platoon surrounded the lieutenant, crowding within a couple of arm-lengths. Toogood continued. "We're not sure what we'll encounter when we get to Korea. As you know, after North Korea attacked, South Korea and American troops stationed there were beaten back to a small area in the southeast corner of Korea, the so-called Pusan Pocket. But they've fought back. The Yanks, the Brits, the Aussies and ROK troops have pushed the North Koreans right up to the Chinese border. The latest word is that the United Nations command thinks the shooting is as good as done."

He glanced around. "Any questions so far?"

There were none, so Toogood carried on. "We're meant to be some sort of peacekeepers, working for the United Nations. The training we've all had so far will stand us in good stead, whatever the situation calls for. We'll continue training on board ship as long as the weather co-operates, and we'll adapt to what we find when we get there. The battalion has great leadership, with most senior officers and non-commissioned officers having World War II experience. They'll figure it out for us.

"I want to say a word or two about 13 Platoon. We only have two sections, not the normal three, which makes us smaller in numbers. And I've heard the rumours, too—that 13 Platoon is a bunch of rejects." He stopped talking and Charlie felt like Toogood was looking at him. A short pause, and the lieutenant carried on. "I don't see us that way. Every man here could just as well have fitted into one of the other twelve sections. We're going to be as good as anyone else, if I have anything to say about it. Whatever it takes, 13 Platoon will be ready. Carry on, sergeant!"

Price saluted, and Toogood disappeared to wherever it was officers spent their time.

Price dismissed the men but called Corporal Turner and Frenchy over. After a short huddle the two section leaders mustered their charges in separate corners of the deck. "Sports gear," Frenchy said. "Everybody back here in ten minutes, ready to go."

The men's clothing issue back in Wainwright included running shoes and T-shirts. As the men of the platoon scrambled to change and get back up on deck, Charlie thought about his circumstances. Literally at sea on board the *Private Joe*, as the troops called her. Stuck in 13 Platoon, an orphan platoon not in a company, adrift in the battalion. A platoon sergeant he didn't know, and an officer who was an unknown quantity. He gritted his teeth, threw on his sports gear, and made sure he beat Frenchy to the upper deck, ready for action. No reason to look for trouble by being late.

—

Frenchy drove them hard, and Charlie worked up a sweat. He could see Frenchy wasn't a trained physical training instructor, but he had been around long enough to pick up on useful calisthenics. The sun was out, the sky blue, with very little wind swirling across *Private Joe*. Even so, there were long rollers coming in from the south, and the ship responded with a slow sway from side to side. The section was kept at it by Frenchy for forty-five minutes, closing with jumping jacks. The men had been out of training for days, first on their train trip west, their brief sojourn on the west coast, and their time aboard ship. They huffed and puffed, while beside them a couple of unfortunate soldiers from another platoon brought up their breakfast over the side.

—

Under blue skies and scudding clouds *Private Joe P. Martinez* ploughed her way west. A Victory class cargo ship named after a US Medal of Honor winner who lost his life in the World War II Battle of Attu in the Aleutians, she had been converted to a troop-carrying role with a designed load of 1200-odd soldiers. About as long as one-and-a-half football fields and with a 60-foot beam, her gentle rolling allowed Sergeant Price to assemble 13 Platoon next to the funnel out of the wind. He checked they were all there, then gave them permission to smoke while they waited for a lecture on the characteristics of the Vickers Medium Machine Gun.

A tall, sturdy kid with light brown hair approached Charlie. He looked far too young to be going to war. "You with us now?"

"Not sure," Charlie said. They shook hands.

"Robert Powell. Where you from?"

"West coast, just outside Vancouver. A small town, Cloverdale." Charlie hadn't been home since he had enlisted, way back in August, and memories of home flashed across his mind. The farmers' co-op, the Legion, high school. It felt like a heck of a long way from the deck of the *Private Joe*.

They talked some more, and it turned out Powell was from Medicine Hat, Alberta. This was his first trip out of his home province, and his excitement at heading off to Korea seemed to rub off on all around him.

A six-foot angular man introduced himself as George Woodham, "Call me Woody, and this here's Dunstan." Dunstan was on the short side, dark haired with a round face. He nodded.

Frenchy had been talking to Corporal Turner of 1 Section, but now he walked over to the group around Charlie. "Cut the chatter," he said, "we have things to do besides gossip like my mother's sewing circle."

"What the hell's his problem?" Woody mumbled.

Sergeant Price arrived with a sergeant from the machine gun section, who soon hit his stride and delved into the intricacies of the water-cooled Vickers. Charlie found his mind wandering. He didn't want to be there, a member of 13 Platoon, but so far they weren't measuring up to their supposed 'misfit' characterization. There probably were rejects in the Special Force, but the project of recruiting and training had been very rushed, and the 13 Platoon members might not be better or worse than the rest of the battalion.

He looked around at them. Fair-haired Mike Muller had helped Charlie get on board and seemed like a good guy. Powell, Woody, and Dunstan. There were others, men Charlie had yet to get a read on. Rowe, who came from northern Manitoba, and Humphrey, a tall, skinny drink of water.

It reminded Charlie of one time in high school when he'd been moved from one class to another for some unfathomable bureaucratic reason. It had taken him a month to feel like he belonged. But here, he was torn. He didn't *want* to belong, and probably wouldn't get the chance anyway, if the adjutant had his way and sent him home on the *Private Joe*.

It took Charlie a long time to get to sleep that night. In those in-between moments, when his mind played tricks of its own, he wondered if he had made a huge mistake in even joining the army. No matter what he thought he might accomplish, he had gone against his father's express wishes. Too late to worry about that, he told himself. We're on our way across the Pacific Ocean, for gosh sake.

And what about Wanda? Wanda, dark-haired and dark-eyed, the only girl he'd ever gone out with, held in his arms. The last time he saw her, he had walked to her family home and she took a break from her Normal School homework. They talked in the kitchen, holding hands, Wanda's mother in the next room. They kissed, Charlie inhaling the fresh scent of Wanda's shampoo, the taste of her lipstick.

"Let's go see *Father of the Bride*, Charlie. Don't you think Elizabeth Taylor is beautiful?"

He sat up and reached for his coke. "What would you think if I was away for a while?"

"What? What do you mean?"

"Oh, I don't know." He avoided her eyes. "It's just, you know, maybe the bank isn't the right place for me."

"What do you mean, away for a while? You can just get another job if you don't like the bank."

"There's more to it than that."

"Like what?"

"I don't know. I'm in a rut."

She pulled back, gazing at him.

"You mean with me?"

"No, no. Not at all."

"What then?"

Charlie couldn't explain it. He should have given this more thought, planned what to say to make things clear. How he knew he was odd-man-out in his family, ignored or coming up short when they looked at him and compared him to Jeff.

"I joined the army."

Wanda's eyes widened. "You—"

"It's only for a few months." Charlie was babbling, his words rushing out of their own accord. "You know, the United Nations, Korea, the…"

Wanda jumped up and reeled away, until she came up against a corner of the kitchen table. She gripped the back of a chair with one hand, her other one going to her throat. "You joined the army? What's wrong with you?"

"Nothing's wrong with me," he said, his words belying the wish that he could sink into the ground and surface a mile away. "I'm not sure I want to be a banker, at least not yet," he stammered. "Maybe it's not for me at all." He felt like a fool, his thoughts bubbling to the surface. He was embarrassed and tongue-tied. Why couldn't he tell her that his life was flashing past while his friends did interesting things, his family stuck in a holding pattern? His hope that by enlisting, by taking Jeffrey's place, he'd get his father's approval, help him—and them—get back to normal? He could hardly explain his jumbled thoughts to himself, never mind to Wanda.

"How could you do this to... to us... to me?" Wanda sank onto the chair, wrapped her arms around herself and hunched her shoulders.

"Wanda, I—" Charlie wasn't even sure what he was about to say, but he was cut off as Wanda jumped to her feet and pushed him toward the front door.

"Just go home, Charlie. Go join your stupid army." She was about to slam the door shut behind him, but hissed through the remaining gap. "Don't worry, I'll find someone else to take me to the damn movie!"

What had he done? It was true he'd been surprised how quick and easy it was to join up; he had assumed there'd be days, maybe weeks of testing, physical and mental exams before he'd be sworn in. But it turned out he'd be on a train the next day, a train to the unknown in Currie Barracks, wherever that was, for heaven's sake.

Stumbling home, he berated himself for not explaining properly, for not talking to Wanda before enlisting. And for not coming to grips with his real reason for joining the army. He'd never prove himself to his father by sitting in a bank.

He had no letters from her to date. He'd screwed up with her, and now he was screwed up with the army.

Beneath him the *Martinez* rolled with a steady but unsettling motion, carrying him toward an unknown future. He'd be going home again, having accomplished nothing. He felt desperate. Calm down, Charlie, he thought. Calm down. Was there a way out? Could he turn things around? Even 13 Platoon could be a better option than going home.

Lieutenant Toogood—what kind of name was that, anyway? But he looked competent, and as far as Charlie could tell most of the privates were okay. Frenchy was the worst thing about the platoon. Their NCO, Sergeant Price, was an old guy in his thirties but seemed to know his stuff. And what was it he said? Something about things working out?

—

Training sessions continued over the next days. In one class Lieutenant Toogood delivered a lecture on the battalion's organization to the platoon and outlined what the various headquarters personnel would do during a typical wartime operation. On completion he turned the men over to Sergeant Price.

"Frenchy, take your section to a clear spot on the deck and put them through a half hour of work," Price said. "I want to see them sweat."

Toward the stern on the upper deck was a large enough space for the ten men of the section to spread out. The weather was cool, and the *Martinez* displayed only a mild roll. Charlie coped fine, out in the fresh air. He backed away from the others to get enough room, happy to be doing something physical.

"Okay, boys," Frenchy said. "Arms up, shoulder height, small circles at first and slowly get bigger, follow me." He put them through a series of stretches and warm-ups.

Charlie concentrated, enjoying it.

"Black! Quit gazing around." Frenchy glowered. "Ten push ups and make it quick."

Charlie dropped face-down to the deck while Frenchy counted aloud. Charlie did the ten and jumped to his feet.

"You guys are looking awful smug. Ten more, all of you."

"What's your problem?" Muller said, toes and palms down on the deck in the push up position.

"I haven't got a problem, but you will if you give me any lip," Frenchy said, looking at Charlie the whole time.

Continuing to work them hard, Frenchy led by example for a time, then paused for a moment. "You. Black. Twenty jumping jacks—go!"

Charlie's chest was heaving. It had been a couple of weeks since he'd had any sort of workout. He struggled, working hard, not about to give the lance corporal any excuse to ride him. He finished the twenty reps and looked at Frenchy, thinking to himself, *showed you!*

"I don't like your fuckin' attitude, Black."

"Tough."

Frenchy covered the ten feet between them in a heartbeat and stopped face-to-face with Charlie. "I don't need my rank to take care of you, private. The next time I tell you to jump, you damn well leap."

Charlie lurched back a half-step, braced himself, and pushed Frenchy with both hands. Frenchy batted his arms away and, head down, rammed a shoulder into Charlie's chest. Charlie grabbed Frenchy around the neck with his left arm. Frenchy drove him back, slamming Charlie into the bulkhead. Charlie swung his right fist and caught Frenchy with a glancing blow as he pulled loose, Frenchy's nose streaming blood.

Charlie tried to catch his breath as Frenchy closed in again, crouching, darting a feint to Charlie's jaw and lashing a quick jab at his midsection and another to his groin. Charlie doubled over, and Frenchy caught him with a knee to the face before he hit the deck.

In agony, crouched face down on the steel deck, Charlie braced himself for another blow. It didn't come.

"Jesus, you guys. Save it for the North Koreans," Muller said.

Charlie had a limited view, but he saw a set of boots arrive on the scene. Big ones.

"You boys getting along, I see." Sergeant Price chuckled. "Clean yourselves up before any of the brass sees you. Frenchy, see me right here, an hour from now." He walked away.

Charlie got his feet under him and lurched upright to lean against the bulkhead. He felt like he might throw up.

Muller stood between him and Frenchy, whose eyes blazed, his face red and blood-streaked He caught his breath. "I knew lots of guys like you back in Montreal, Black. Think you know everything, think you're too good for us. Well this is just a start, mister, unless you fuckin' shape up."

CHAPTER 4

A day later 13 Platoon gathered on the upper deck once again. Sergeant Price counted noses, and when he saw Lieutenant Toogood approaching, called the men to attention.

"At ease, sergeant. Gather around."

The twenty-one men of 13 Platoon relaxed their posture and moved into a semicircle around their platoon officer. Charlie tried to read Toogood's expression. The lieutenant looked like a man with something to say.

"It's all changed, men. The situation in Korea has taken a turn. As you know, we left Fort Lewis early because the UN forces had chased the North Koreans all the way to the Yalu River. We were meant to be peacekeepers, the fighting over."

He paused, and Charlie heard the wind moan as it swept through the ship's rigging.

"The Chinese have sprung a trap. They infiltrated the high ground and got the jump on the UN forces. They're in the war, and they're in it in a big way. The Americans and Brits and Aussies are pulling back, and they're going to need all the help they can get. So forget this peacekeeping stuff you heard about and get ready for action. We're soldiers again."

—

"Damnit, boys," Frenchy said. "Maybe they need 13 Platoon after all, eh?"

Yeah, even 13 Platoon, Charlie thought. *But where the heck am I going to be?*

"It's a war again," Muller exulted. "Hot damn. We're gonna get our chance after all."

Powell chimed in. "Wouldn't want all that target practice to go to waste, right?" Charlie thought he looked nervous in spite of his words. Who wouldn't be?

Charlie stood off to one side, watching as the boys thumped each other on the back and declared they could hardly wait to get into the action.

While the excited chatter continued, Charlie couldn't help thinking about the early days when training started at Currie Barracks, in Calgary. They had doffed their civilian clothes and wore khaki for the first time. Under the direction of the training staff they'd wrapped their civvies in brown paper and tied them up with string. Those brown paper packages were waiting for soldiers to reclaim when their enlistment was up. How many wouldn't get picked up, and be mailed to next of kin?

Dunstan punched him on the shoulder. "We're going to war, Charlie."

Charlie whacked him back. In for a penny, in for a pound, as his mother sometimes said. He had signed up for a war. And, hell, what's eighteen months to young guy in the overall scheme of things? Even if the Chinese are shooting at you.

And if they were going into battle, surely the army wouldn't send him back on the *Private Joe's* return trip to North America? He shook his head.

Sergeant Price didn't look all that elated, just his usual self. He'd been talking to a thin corporal that Charlie didn't recognize, but now he spoke to the platoon. "We've got a job to do, and nothing's changed from that." He spoke quietly, and 13 Platoon gave him their full attention. "Guest lecture. Pay attention to Corporal Ronson here. He was a Patricia in the war. He demobbed after, went back to school and studied history. Now he's here to educate us."

The corporal looked over the hill, at least in his late twenties or early thirties. "What the sergeant left out is that bad things happened to me. I had the distinction of being captured by the Germans in Italy." He spoke with a slight accent that Charlie couldn't place until he mentioned he'd joined the army from rural Nova Scotia. He flashed a rueful smile before launching into a half-hour discussion about how to behave as a prisoner of war.

Price had a question. "That's all well and good, corporal, but we're not dealing with the Germans. What can you tell us about the North Koreans?"

"You're right to be concerned. When it comes to North Koreans, whatever they know about prisoners they probably learned the hard way from the Japanese when they were occupied in the last war and even before that. You would not want to have been a prisoner of the Japanese. When the Canadian Army landed in the Far East in 1941 they weren't properly equipped or trained. The result was a quick defeat by the Japanese followed by years in prison camps for those that survived the battle. You've probably seen pictures in newspapers of the result. Starvation, torture, killings." He took a breath. "I have no reason to think the North Koreans would treat prisoners any better."

Charlie spoke up. "What about the Chinese?"

Ronson shook his head. "New ball game. I was briefed before we left Seattle, when it looked like the war was nearly over, and all we had to worry about was some sort of patrolling to keep the peace. Now it's the Red Chinese beating up on the Americans and the rest of the UN forces." He scratched his head. "What we do know is that the Chinese have been fighting wars for years, so they're probably quite good at it. They have a huge army. If they capture you, stick with name, serial number, Canadian Army. You have a duty to try to escape if captured." He flashed that rueful smile again. "Overall, don't get captured."

The last thing on Charlie's mind was getting captured. But it was a sobering hour. He had signed up for what the UN called a 'police action,' which was actually a war according to the army. Then it was downgraded to 'peacekeeping,' a non-war. Now it had swung back again. As Sergeant Smith said, 'If you can't take a joke you shouldn't have joined,' and Charlie felt like the joke was on him. Anyway, it was hard to get concerned about being captured when he might be shipped home.

—

On December 2nd the *Martinez's* upper deck was crowded with US and Canadian troops as she neared Pearl Harbour. Perfect, thought Charlie, looking at the palm trees that lined the shore and the green mountains in the distance.

Muller came up and stood beside him. "Hell, Charlie. No grass-skirted girls in sight, but if we get off this rust-bucket of a ship..."

A bustling US Navy tug nudged the ship into her berth. One of the *Private Joe's* crew pointed out the wreckage of the *USS Arizona*, a battered black mass of steel that protruded from the calm waters of the harbour. The Stars and Stripes still flew above the remains of the battleship, sunk by the Japanese on December 7th, 1941.

Only nine years before, but it seemed like a lifetime ago to Charlie. That had been a real war, fought by real men, men like Jeffrey. Charlie wanted to be a hero. But that didn't stop him from being nervous now that the moment was approaching.

Evidence of the military and industrial might of the United States sprawled in all directions. Long lines of trucks, jeeps, and artillery waited to be loaded for shipment to the war zone. Barracks and military buildings stretched for miles. Dozens of warships and transports lay at anchor or alongside. Surely, Charlie thought, with the Americans in the lead, the communists would be flattened in short order. Then he remembered the US soldiers he had talked to on board ship. They had not yet been issued rifles, never mind used them, even on a range. And they, along with the Patricias, would soon land in Korea.

The troops seemed to get their wish when they were ordered ashore, but they hadn't earned any R and R yet. Charlie and the rest of the men staggered as they stepped off the gangplank, the land swaying after a week aboard the *Martinez*.

13 Platoon followed Sergeant Price and the rest of the battalion on a route march through the maze-like naval dockyard.

"You'd think we'd get to go off for a beer somewhere," muttered Humphrey, looking skinnier than ever after missing a lot of meals.

"Maybe we still will," said Powell.

Dream on, thought Charlie. The long column of marching men wended its way between buildings and lines of heavy equipment he assumed was, like them, on its way to Korea. Where they approached exits from the dockyard, or roads that might lead to exits, American military police and shore patrol personnel in jeeps and on foot watched them. American conscripts on a stopover before Korea might be inclined to go absent without leave, given a chance to avoid shipping out to a war zone. But the MPs could have stayed home when it came to the Canadians. If a route march on their way across the Pacific helped keep them in shape for war, they were all for it.

"What's that, a hospital?" Frenchy was looking at a white-painted two-story building forty yards to their right. A well-tended lawn sloped down from the structure to their road.

"Yeah," said Muller. "A lot of purple hearts up there."

"What's that mean?" Jimmy Rowe asked.

"It's a US medal," Frenchy said. "You get wounded in the American army, you get a purple heart. You get wounded in the Patricias, you get patched up and sent back into action."

Rowe frowned. "Doesn't seem fair."

That's a hospital for sure, Charlie thought. In front of the building a dozen or so men sat in wheelchairs or on benches, crutches propped against the wall. Some of them smoked, while others just gazed at the troops marching by. They sported white bandages, slings, and casts that dazzled in the bright sun. The chatter typical of the Patricias on the march died away. Charlie couldn't help looking at the unsmiling faces of the wounded men, grim reminders that war had consequences.

—

Eight hours later sunny beaches and palm trees were the last things on Charlie's mind. Around him the *Private Joe* swung like a pendulum, and Charlie's stomach was in revolt. He was welded to his bunk.

Somebody gave his foot a shake. "C'mon, Charlie," Powell said. "I know you're alive, I see you breathing. I'm going up for a smoke."

A smoke was the last thing Charlie wanted, but fresh air might help. He roused and lowered himself down from his bunk, following Powell up the series of ladders that landed them on the same level as the open deck. They came to a door that was clamped shut. Hanging from it was a wooden sign proclaiming the upper deck out of bounds.

Charlie looked around. No officers or NCOs in sight.

Powell grasped the locking lever and yanked on it. The door was grabbed by the wind and swung open, jerking Powell across the sill. Charlie darted after him, and together they slammed the door shut and dogged it down behind them, laughing.

The wind was fierce, the deck canted over. Moving to shelter in the lee of a deck house, they stumbled across Frenchy and Muller, cigarettes cupped in their hands.

Frenchy, the last man on earth he wanted to share space with. Frenchy's eyes narrowed and flicked across Charlie. Charlie pressed himself up against the side of the deck house, the four of them strung out in a row, Charlie at one end and Frenchy at the other.

Offered a cigarette by Muller, Charlie shook his head. Nobody said anything, the smokers and nonsmokers alike staring at the horizon. Lost in his thoughts, Charlie wondered if this is how his journey would end. Huddled with the rejects of 13 Platoon, destined to be shipped home after a miserable voyage in an American ship, his tail between his legs.

The ship's broadcast system clicked on and repeated an earlier message. "All personnel are reminded the upper deck is out of bounds. No access to the upper deck."

"I'll be damn glad when we get off this boat," Muller said, and Powell added, "Amen to that."

"I can think of a few reasons why we're not in the navy," Frenchy said with a half grin, and Charlie agreed with him for once. Maybe there was a side to Frenchy that he hadn't yet seen.

The smokers flicked their butts into the air, where they were caught by the wind and swept away. Charlie followed the others back into the superstructure.

—

Three days later Charlie found himself standing in line for food, a line that was shorter by the day. Many of the soldiers were now sprawled on their bunks, unable to find the strength to move, still confined below decks. Charlie felt ill, but so far had been able to eat in spite of vomiting every few hours. He was happier whenever he could pull himself out of his bunk. Water somehow seeped into the hold where the platoon was bunked, and it sloshed from one side of the ship to the other with every roll she took. Some miserable soldiers, if they managed to get food down, shortly puked it right up and over the side of their bunks where it joined the watery mass of liquid cascading across the deck. The bulkheads and sides of the ship streamed water, whether from leaks or just condensation nobody knew; what they did know was that their temporary home resembled a clammy, sodden prison.

There was nowhere to go once he ate, the ship's crew enforcing the upper-deck-out-of-bounds rule. Charlie made his way through the dimly-lit space to stand in the narrow passage by Powell's chest-high bunk. "You still with us, Powell?"

Powell's hair was matted to his head, the pallor of his face all the more startling for the freckles that stood out in bold relief. "Yeah, I'm still here. Sure wish I wasn't, though."

Just then the ship gave a particularly hard roll combined with a fore-and-aft pitch. Charlie tightened his grip on the side of Powell's bunk and hung on. The water on the deck washed across his boots. Men mumbled and cursed, when a frightening metallic groan silenced them. Powell raised his head. "What was that?"

"Dunno—sounded like the ship itself, for cripes sake."

The *Martinez* rolled the other way and pitched again. The deck quivered beneath Charlie's feet. A feeling of weightlessness made his stomach heave. He clamped his jaw tight. After a few moments the ship stabilized and he eased his way up to his own bunk and wedged himself in, his cold feet encased in their stinking boots. For a moment his mind pictured the hundreds of fathoms of dark, cold water beneath the thin hull of the Victory ship, long past due for the wrecker's yard, if the rust on her hull meant anything. God, he thought, get us through this. He had to grin to himself, invoking Him all of a sudden. What the hell. Get us through this, God, and Korea and the Red Chinese won't scare me one bit. Just don't send me home again in the *Private Joe*.

CHAPTER 5

Six days out from Pearl Harbour, Charlie was grateful that his stomach had at last adapted to the *Martinez*'s ponderous but unsteady passage. Standing in the never-ending lineup for food with Powell, he dreamed about something solid to eat. For the first day or two the food had been alright, but it seemed the ship wasn't built to handle the 1700 men on board. There were only two meals scheduled per day, and the lineups never disappeared. On top of that Muller had told him the American GIs, who were scheduled to eat ahead of the Canucks, got the pick of what variety of food there was.

Powell read his thoughts. "Yeah, been like this for a few days. Frenchy says we're running out of food."

Frenchy says. Frenchy says. Even Charlie could figure that out. He and the kid from Medicine Hat had joined the lineup for a meal. When they made it to the head of the line the cook slapped a couple of spoonfuls of something—spaghetti, maybe? onto his plate.

He and Powell sat on one of the benches bolted to the deck, their food on a table that was likewise fastened down. Charlie lost his appetite as he contemplated his pasta. Powell, still a growing boy, polished off his plate. "Still hungry, Charlie?"

"Starving."

"Come on." They scraped their plates and dropped them in a basin for pickup by the dishwashers, then headed down toward the bunk space. Before they went down the final ladder Powell turned toward a door off to one side that Charlie hadn't paid any attention to before. Opening it, Powell stuck his head in, looked around, and turned back to Charlie. "Come on in."

Dunstan and Woody were sitting on wooden crates draped in a khaki-coloured tarpaulin. At Woody's feet was an open tin can, a heavy pocketknife beside it on the deck. The can was labelled Hawaii's Best Pineapple Slices.

"How do you like your pineapple, Charlie?" Woody wore a generous smile. "Fried, stewed, baked... or straight out of the can? Oh yeah—that's the only way we serve 'em!" He handed Charlie an unopened can and the knife.

Charlie slashed a large X across the top of the can, pried back the jagged pieces, and fished out a pineapple ring with the knife. The juice ran down his fingers as he bit into the fruit, the sweet flavour coursing down his throat.

"Where did this come from?"

"Frenchy checked out a storage locker. Found a whole load of containers, had a look at them. Turns out they're all pineapple, the cooks must have forgotten about them. We helped him winkle them out, passed a bunch of them around to the troops. You can live like a king down here—as long as you like pineapple."

Frenchy again. Cripes, Charlie thought, he's going to dominate my life until I get sorted out with the adjutant and out of this 13 Platoon mess. A few mouthfuls of pineapple were okay in the meantime, even courtesy of Frenchy.

—

At long last the weather broke. Blinking like owls, the troops emerged into dazzling sunlight. White clouds gusted overhead and gulls circled. The *Private Joe* still rolled like a punching dummy at a six-year-old's birthday party, but the wind was dying and a million points of light glittered off the blue-green seas.

Charlie had made his way to the upper deck, where he was surrounded by boisterous soldiers revelling in the fresh air and sunshine.

Muller had something in his hands, Dunstan and Woody peering at it. Charlie walked over. It was a fish, less than a foot long, its streamlined silver body stiff and unyielding as Muller prodded it with a forefinger.

"Where'd you get that?" Woody said.

"Found it right here. It's a flying fish, one of the crew told me."

"Ah, BS."

"It's true, Woody," Muller said. "Sometimes they fly too high, and land on deck. Then it's too bad for them. One last flight for this guy," he said with a laugh, and flung the fish over the side.

They were still two days out of Yokohama, and information sessions and physical training would start again the next day. For now the men were left alone. Charlie felt like the odd man out, not only barred from his 7 Platoon but stuck with 13. For now. Until he was sent home. It made him want to puke all over again, never mind the seasickness.

—

On December 13 Charlie got a look at the Far East at last. He gave his boots a last flick with a rag and hurried up from below to join the rest of 13 Platoon where they were falling in on the *Private Joe's* after deck. The chilly air carried the acrid reek of Yokohama Harbour. Gulls wheeled into sight only to disappear in the low mist that seemed to hang just above the ship's mast.

Sergeant Price eyeballed them. "One last reminder," he said. "You're due back on board at midnight tonight. Don't get in trouble ashore. Neither the US Navy Shore Patrol nor the military police have any sense of humour. You get in trouble you could end up in the crowbar hotel and miss the ship when we sail." He peered at Powell and flicked the flap on his battledress jacket pocket. "Do that up."

Powell fumbled with his pocket as Price continued. "If you have to hang out with whores, for God's sake use a safe. If you don't have any, pick some up at the gangplank on your way ashore. You're in uniform, and I don't want to hear any bad reports about 13 Platoon. All clear? All right, then, ten-shun! Dis-miss."

The men filed toward the gangplank. Charlie kept one hand on the guardrail as he walked down the steep incline to the jetty, taking in his first impressions of the Orient. Low sheds and warehouses lined the shore. The smell of bunker fuel and diesel exhaust mixed with other unidentifiable odours. Cranes creaked and banged as they swung overhead, unloading ships alongside the jetty. Military vehicles came and went: jeeps, trucks, and khaki-painted automobiles, driven by men and women in various uniforms of the U.S. forces. In the background was the hum of a large city. I'm a long way from Cloverdale, he thought, as he and Powell checked out through the waterfront gate and flagged down a taxi.

Humphrey and Frenchy ran to join them, Charlie wishing Frenchy would get lost. All four of them crammed themselves into the cab, much to the apparent annoyance of the driver, who muttered under his breath but jammed the car into gear. The tiny vehicle pulled away, swaying dangerously with its load of prime Canadian beef.

"Beer! Women!" shouted Frenchy.

An early afternoon sun was unable to burn through the still Yokohama air, but it turned the haze that hung over the city a dull yellowish colour. Charlie peered out the front window over Powell's shoulder as the cab zipped through traffic, running up behind vehicles at a great speed then slamming on the brakes. Charlie was unprepared for the fact that the Japanese drove on the left, not the right, which made the trip extra harrowing. At times the driver cut through alleys, tromping hard on the accelerator and shooting out into traffic again.

"Anybody know how to say 'slow down' in Japanese?" Powell drawled from the suicide seat.

"Guy thinks he's a kamikaze pilot," Frenchy laughed. "This is nothin'. A friend of mine drives a hack in Montreal. You should see the traffic there."

Charlie braced himself with one hand on the back of the seat in front of him, just in case. The taxi swerved around a corner, tires screeching, and slammed to a halt outside what looked like a bar. 'Soldiers and Sailers Wellcome' proclaimed a red-lettered, hand-written sign above the door.

The men piled out, and Frenchy took charge of paying the cabbie. "You guys owe me."

Charlie, Powell and Humphrey waited on the narrow sidewalk. From the bar came wisps of tobacco smoke and the odours of cheap perfume and stale beer. Rising above the city's hubbub was the twanging voice of Wilf Carter singing, "Hey, good lookin'..."

Charlie looked back at the cab; Frenchy's face was darkening, as he leaned against the driver's door with one hand and gesticulated with the other. Finally he pulled out a roll of greenbacks and peeled off a couple, handing them to the driver before turning to join the others. "God damn it," he said. "We should have settled on a price before we climbed into the damn taxi."

"Thought you'd know that, Frenchy, you knowing all about cabs," Charlie said.

"Give it a break, you guys," Humphrey said. "We've got better things to do than watch you scrap."

The cab pulled away as an ancient Japanese man emerged from the bar. Behind him was a middle-aged, tiny woman, who pulled on Charlie's sleeve. "You come in now," she chanted in a singsong trill. "Plenty beer. Plenty girl. You like!"

Frenchy pushed his way to the front of the queue as the Canadians were herded through the narrow door into the bar.

Charlie felt like a giant next to the Japanese girls that swarmed around him. The women swept the Canadians to bar stools, where they perched like khaki eagles amongst cooing pigeons. Charlie glanced at Powell, who looked confused but happy.

"You big man—want big drink." Charlie had to concentrate to figure out what the girl was saying, what with the blasting, scratchy music, her halting English, and the noise generated by a table of American sailors a few feet away.

"Sure. A beer."

The man behind the bar plunked an amber-coloured bottle down in front of him. Charlie took a gulp. It was cold, and it tasted close enough to Canadian draft that it was okay. And so were the ones that followed, in fact they were better than okay. They got better and better, as the girl holding his knee transferred her hand to the inside of his thigh, increasing the pressure while following every word he said with adoring eyes.

Charlie had to go to the washroom. He swayed to his feet, feeling giddy, reminded of the multiple beers he'd drunk. Powell, Frenchy and Humphrey all had attendant Japanese girls. As he pushed himself away from the bar, his consort guessed his errand and pointed toward a doorway at the back of the room. He had to walk by the table where the boisterous US sailors sat. Their table was covered with bottles, empty and full. Most of the Yanks had beers in their hands and girls on their laps.

A hand whipped out and grabbed Charlie's arm. A sailor, gob cap pushed back on the top of his head, pulled himself to his feet.

"You guys Canadians?"

Charlie blinked. "Yup. What of it?"

"Don't let these broads fool you. They aren't prostitutes. They're B girls." The sailor belched. "Bar girls. They get paid for every beer you drink. Come with us—we're going where there's some real action."

"Sure," said Charlie, game for anything. "Back in a minute."

"Better make it snappy. If the Shore Patrol happens by, we're long gone."

Charlie walked toward the back door, being very cautious, his sense of balance unaccountably absent. To the left was a small room that featured a hole in the floor with low raised platforms either side in the shape of a human foot. The troops had been warned they wouldn't recognize a washroom when they saw it. Yet another door looked like a back entrance to the bar.

Charlie made use of the primitive facility. When he finished he leaned on the doorframe so he wouldn't fall over while he wrestled with the buttons of his fly. As he was making his way back to where his fellow soldiers were with the girls, he was startled by a series of piercing whistles. The table of American gobs rose as one and ran toward Charlie and the back door. Hard on their heels was a pack of blue-jacketed US Navy Shore Patrolmen, whistles abandoned in favour of truncheons which they swung with great gusto at the heads of the retreating sailors.

Somebody ran straight into Charlie and the two of them crashed down in a flurry of flying legs and arms. More sailors stumbled over them. Charlie managed to look up just in time to see a billy club chopping down at him. There was a thunderous blow to his head, and he lay back, clutching his hands to his scalp. Warm liquid trickled between his fingers. He groaned and rolled onto his hands and knees.

Someone grabbed him under the armpits and pulled him up. "Holy cow, Charlie," said Powell. "You're bleeding like a stuck pig."

Charlie blinked. He saw a sailor in handcuffs being hustled out the front door by a shore patrolman. A table lay on its side, broken glass everywhere under foot. Humphrey grabbed a rag from the bar and gave it to Powell, who clapped it onto Charlie's wounded head.

"What happened?" Charlie croaked.

"Seems our US buddies were AWOL. Their ship sailed without them this morning." Powell snorted. "They knew they were in big trouble, and when the Shore Patrol came in they made a run for it."

"They might as well have waved a red flag at a bull," Frenchy said. "And you got in the way."

"C'mon, boys, let's get out of here," said Humphrey.

Charlie felt woozy. Powell continued to help him along, and Charlie held the rag firmly to his head. Somebody handed him his beret.

They went out to the sidewalk, where a Shore Patrol truck was stopped. One of the American sailors was standing glumly beside it, supporting one arm in a pose Charlie thought meant a broken collar bone. His face was bloody. A burly Shore Patrolman pushed him up into the back of the truck.

The Canadians made their way down the narrow street until they came upon a taxi. They piled in, with Charlie in the front seat. His head hurt, and there were bloodstains on his uniform that showed black in the dim light. His head still spun from the blow to his head or the beer, or maybe a combination of the two. What did I do to deserve this, he thought. His ruminations were interrupted by Powell. "Christ. Those bloody Yanks. They were out to break heads."

"They damn near did," said Charlie, lifting the rag from his head and looking at it, fresh blood showing. "They probably did a lot worse to their own guys when they caught them."

The four of them lapsed into silence. Charlie was shocked by the ugly reality of the bar brawl. He and his comrades had trained to fight an external enemy, not each other. The sheer violence of the Shore Patrol against their comrades shook him up.

"Very impressive," Frenchy said. "Wounded already, and we're not even there yet."

Chapter 6

The *Private Joe* bumped against the Pusan dock with a gentle lurch as dockworkers secured her berthing lines. Charlie, pack beside him on the upper deck, arms folded on the top of the bulwark, waited for the order to disembark and looked down at what appeared to be a human body floating between the pier's pilings.

He wasn't surprised. He had come onto the upper deck a couple of hours before as the ship glided toward her South Korean destination and had seen several corpses in the water.

This one was face down, its clothing a nondescript grey similar to the tunics and loose trousers worn by the civilians he could see from the ship. He couldn't tell if it was a man or a woman.

Muller dumped his gear beside Charlie's to stand beside him. "Christ," he said. "This place stinks." He caught sight of the floating body. "Jesus. Isn't someone going to fish him out?"

Nobody among the teeming mob of American servicemen and Korean civilians on the pier looked like they'd give a thought to an anonymous corpse.

Charlie tried to square his own family's ongoing consciousness of Jeff's death with the callous scene. Was this a casualty of war, missed by a Korean family? "Maybe there are too many bodies," he said.

Earlier that day, December 18, the sea had been dark with an oily sheen. The *Martinez* rolled gently as she approached the gray-brown city of Pusan. An early-morning address from the adjutant reminded the men they were stepping into a war zone, with the entire Korean Peninsula under threat of the Chinese, the North Koreans, and communist guerrillas roaming the countryside. The Americans and their allies had been routed from their high-water mark on the banks of the Yalu and forced back across the 38th parallel, close to where they had been when the war began.

The war raged on, and the Patricias could expect to be in the thick of it as fast as they could get ashore and up to the sharp end.

Two hours later 2PPCLI marched through the city. Their American guides led them on a circuitous route, winding between battered buildings on streets cratered by shellfire. Few structures were more than a storey tall. Civilians, almost all women, children and old men, watched in silence, their faces expressionless. A grey sky pressed down on them, accentuating a nauseating smell.

Charlie looked around at the shattered city. The "Pusan Pocket," the newspapers had called it when the North Koreans had it surrounded. It still looked battered, its people shellshocked.

Muller was just ahead of Charlie; he dropped back a little and spoke over his shoulder. "So, it looks like it's true, eh, boys? We're gonna get to kick some Communist butt."

"Keep the chatter down, Muller," growled Corporal Turner. "And keep the ranks closed up. Or I'll kick *your* butt." Turner, senior man in the platoon's first section and senior to Frenchy in the second, liked to remind everybody of that fact.

"You and whose fuckin' army," Muller muttered under his breath.

The march through the city was physically easy, the men only burdened with rifles and small packs. All around them the low buildings showed increasing signs of enemy bombardment, with blackened walls and missing roofs. Jeeps and trucks hurried in all directions. More than once the column of men gave way to honking American transport. In quieter moments Koreans could be heard talking to each other but they became silent as the men passed. There was a layer of smoke over the city, the air reeking with the smell of wet ashes, wood smoke, and unfamiliar food. And something else, a smell that intensified as they moved toward the outskirts of town.

Frenchy took a deep breath. "Phew," he said, blowing out. One of Lieutenant Toogood's briefings on board had pointed out that Koreans, like many in the Orient, fertilized their fields with human waste.

The men's route took a turn and led up a hill. Charlie was sweating when they paraded into a fenced, abandoned school-yard. The building looked intact.

Sergeant Price held up a hand and halted 13 Platoon. "Listen up. This is where we'll be located for the next week at least."

"Good deal, sergeant," Frenchy said. "A roof over our heads and a floor that's solid for a change."

"Dream on, corporal. When you're dismissed, you and Black go draw tents from a six-by-six around the back of the school-house. Ten men to a tent." He grinned. "Sergeants and above are quartered in the schoolhouse, along with headquarters staff. If that's all right with you, Frenchy."

Frenchy looked annoyed, but said, "That's jake with me, sergeant. The sooner we toughen up the better."

Charlie was still energized, relieved to be off the ship. He and Frenchy left their gear with their platoon mates and walked around the schoolhouse to where a 6x6 truck was tended to by a couple of US GIs. The vehicle had a canvas top behind the cab, and the ubiquitous white star on the doors. They drew two tents and lugged them back to the platoon's assigned corner of the schoolyard. They were as far from the schoolhouse and the brass as they could get, which was fine with Charlie.

—

"Private Black!"

Charlie was in his tent. He froze in mid-motion, his hand halfway to his mouth with a forkful of cold ham from a tin of C-rations. He hadn't been hiding out, but he wasn't trying to dis-tinguish himself from the pack, either.

"Here, sergeant." He stood, crouched, and, pushing the tent flap open, went out.

Price was walking away. Charlie followed, fearing the worst. Stopping and turning to face him, Price glowered. Charlie came to attention.

"What's this crap about 7 Platoon, private?"

"That's my platoon, where I was, ser—"

"That's where you were. It's not where you are."

Charlie hesitated. He'd talked to a couple of his pals in his Wainwright platoon, hoping against hope that maybe somebody had broken a leg or fallen overboard. No such luck. "I thought—"

"That'll get you in trouble every time, private. Try a bit less thinking and a bit more doing what you're told. You're in 13 Platoon."

Price turned and walked away, leaving Charlie to pull himself together. What had just happened? Had he been reprieved, no longer to be sent home? He wasn't sure, but it sounded like it.

Neither Sergeant Price nor Lieutenant Toogood could tell them how long they'd be in their schoolyard tents. Rumours raced at the speed of light around the encampment: they'd be on the front line in days; they'd join up with Brits, with Australians; they'd relieve exhausted American troops. In the meantime they were kept busy with routine cleaning, keeping their gear in good shape, and—happy days—receiving mail from home. A long letter from Charlie's mother included the news that Bill was home, but still a semi-invalid, his bones healed but complications remaining. The letter was tucked inside a parcel containing knitted socks—because what infantryman couldn't use socks, not to mention the matching scarf? There was also a letter from his sister-in-law Jackie, who passed on community news and included an update about Harry's prowess in grade one. Harry signed his own name.

Charlie shuffled his letters, hoping he'd somehow missed one, but there was nothing from Wanda. During the months of training in Alberta he had written several times. He had to admit his letters were hurried notes he threw together in off hours between training and visits to the canteen where he and his friends in 7 Platoon took advantage of their beer ration. She hadn't responded. In spite of that he stayed with it, writing again in more detail. Just the act of writing helped overcome the feeling of being in a strange and dangerous place. He told her what it was like in Korea, and that he didn't expect to see *Father of the Bride* any time soon. Not that he wanted to see Elizabeth Taylor, he went on, because Wanda was a lot prettier.

Charlie was still writing his letter when Powell dropped down and sat cross-legged beside him, his mail in his lap. Powell gave a quick glance to one letter before crumpling it and jamming it into a pocket. Another letter he folded and tucked in a different pocket. A package about the size of a shoebox remained in front of him. It had been secured with heavy wrappings of string which Powell slashed with his pocketknife. "From my brother," he said. Powell tore away the wrapping to hold up three pairs of socks marked with Eaton's labels. Something fell out of the socks into his lap.

"What's that, Powell?" Frenchy said from the other side of the tent.

Powell's freckled face blossomed into a happy smile. "Here's to my brother," he said, holding up a bottle of Wiser's Special Blend rye whiskey.

"You gonna keep it all to yourself?"

"No, Frenchy, I'm not. Grab your cups, boys."

He poured them each a tot.

"Here's to you, Powell," Charlie said, and raised his cup.

"2 Section 13 Platoon," Muller said. "The pick of the bums from the slums."

Charlie finished his letter to Wanda, feeling warmer about life in general.

Powell managed to save an appreciable amount of his whiskey for himself, even after providing tots for his section. In short order he was red-eyed and unsteady on his feet. Charlie talked him into crawling into his sleeping bag.

Frenchy told Sergeant Price, who told Lieutenant Toogood, that the kid had turned in early, tired after a long day.

—

Overcast and cold, Christmas Day had been brightened by turkey and all the trimmings, courtesy of the US Army. Afterward, Charlie sat in the tent wiping nonexistent dirt off his rifle when Muller appeared, looking glum. "So much for all the action we were going to see," he said. "This show is gonna be over before we get into it."

"What are you talking about?"

"I picked up a rumour that Big Jim arranged for us to have another six weeks of training, if you can believe it."

Charlie had mixed feelings on the subject. He was here for action, but if the colonel, "Big Jim" Stone, said they needed more training before joining the push against the enemy, that was okay with him. The rumour mill said casualties were high among the predominantly American UN forces and their allies.

What had meant a lot more to him was that *Private Joe* had sailed for Hawaii on its next round trip to North America and back with more soldiers for the Korean campaign—and he wasn't aboard.

Two days after Christmas a long line of American Troop Carrying Vehicles appeared outside the schoolyard, exhaust smoke rising in the cold air. Packed up and ready, the Patricias climbed aboard. They were due to move some fifty miles to a small town called Miryang. 13 Platoon rode seated on benches either side of their vehicle's cargo space, a canvas cover overhead. The convoy of TCVs ground its way north on a rough gravel road. They stopped at one point and inched forward, eventually reaching the site of the problem. An American Army jeep had broken down and blocked most of the road.

Progress was so slow that Sergeant Price had time to swing down from the passenger seat of the vehicle and talk to the jeep's driver. A moment later he climbed up onto the TCV's back bumper and spoke to the section. "Bad news," he said. "General Walker's been killed in an accident. Head on crash between his jeep and one of these babies." He slapped the tailgate beside him.

"He's—he was—the general in charge of us, right?" Charlie said.

"Yeah, we're part of the British Commonwealth Division, which is part of the American command structure. So, yes. He's also the guy that okayed Big Jim's request for more training for us."

"Lots of ways to die even if you don't get shot," Frenchy said.

Charlie and his section swayed in unison with the lurching of the TCV. "I'm gonna have a square butt," Dunstan said.

"Beats walking, you ask me," Frenchy said. "Take a ride whenever we can. Bet we'll be hoofing it soon enough."

A couple of hours later Charlie was glad to jump down from the truck and shake out his muscles. He joined the rest of the section as they looked over their new home, a tented camp beside the Miryang River. They were in the midst of an orchard, the trees all around in a grid pattern. And even better, it was well away from the nearest rice paddies with their attendant smell of night soil.

CHAPTER 7

Two days later Charlie and the rest of the platoon hiked to a level spot on a hillside overlooking Miryang. In the distance he could make out the river where it flowed past the small tent city that housed 2PPCLI. The day was chilly and overcast and the men could see their breath. Their attention was focused on Sergeant Dick Swann, a decorated World War II vet that Charlie hadn't seen before.

The stiff-backed sergeant looked around at the semicircle of twenty-odd men, a bit of a smile lurking under his thick moustache. "So you're the famous 13 platoon," he said. "You know, or should know, that there's no such thing as a 13 Platoon in a regular battalion."

Glancing past Swann, Charlie saw Muller roll his eyes.

So did Swann. "You, private. Take this." He unslung a sub-machine gun from his shoulder and held it out to Muller, who stepped forward, took the weapon, and held it muzzle down in his right hand.

"Is it loaded, private?"

Muller transferred the weapon to his left hand and pulled back the cocking lever to inspect the chamber. There was no magazine fitted, the breech empty. "No, sergeant."

"What's it called?"

"Sten gun, sergeant."

"Rate of fire?"

"500 rounds per minute."

"That's right, private. Give it here." He took the Sten gun from Muller. If he had hoped Muller would be taken down a peg or two by being singled out, he was mistaken. He looked at Charlie. "What's it fire?"

"Nine-millimetre, sergeant."

"A very basic weapon," Swann said. "Produced by the million in World War II."

The battalion had some exposure to the Sten during their basic training at Wainwright and a couple of them had the opportunity to fire one, although their training stressed and concentrated on their bolt action Lee-Enfield .303s.

"Who gets to use it?"

"Noncoms and above," Charlie said.

"Just a word to the wise," Swann continued. "If you get offered one to use, I suggest you stay with your .303. If an enemy sniper sees a member of a section with a Sten, he knows who's in charge and who he should take a shot at. A lot of junior officers have the good sense not to use one."

The sergeant gave a brief smile, apparently at the thought of junior officers having good sense about anything. "There's something else about the Sten. See that pit over there?"

Someone had dug a hole roughly a yard square over at the edge of the clearing. From where he stood Charlie couldn't see how deep it was.

"Magazine holds 32 rounds," Swann said, as he pulled one from his tunic pocket. He waved it at them, then jammed it into the side of the Sten. "When you fire the Sten tends to rise, so you hold it like this." He had the Sten at waist height, right hand on the pistol grip and left hand on top of the weapon, the magazine resting on his left forearm. He pointed the weapon at the hole in the ground and squeezed the trigger. A short burst of bullets threw up bits of earth where they hit. Charlie's ears rang.

"There's something else about the Sten that's very important. If it's not on safety, and you've cocked it or fired it and there's another round in the chamber…" He ostentatiously held the Sten in two hands, took a step toward the hole, and lobbed the gun at it. As if in slow motion Charlie saw it fall six inches short, the magazine hitting the hard earth. The Sten fired with a shattering roar, and kept firing, bullets zipping and ricocheting in random directions, the men scattering. The weapon bounced and fell into the pit where it emptied its remaining rounds.

Charlie froze in the act of flattening himself on the ground. For a moment there was an ominous silence. Jimmy Rowe, the kid from Manitoba, lay on the ground, doubled up and groaning. Swann rushed to where the man lay, looking stricken himself. Rowe's hands were clasped on his left shin, blood seeping between his fingers.

Charlie supported him around the shoulders while Swann and Powell eased Rowe's fingers loose so Swann could pull out a knife and slash at the wounded man's trouser leg. He tore it open to the knee, exposing a neat round hole in the front of Rowe's shin. There was very little blood visible there, but there was more from a jagged wound in the calf muscle. Swann produced a field dressing and wrapped it in place.

Rowe was pale and starting to shake in Charlie's arms. "How bad is it?"

"You, lance corporal, plus one other—medic and stretcher, fast!" yelled the sergeant, looking at Frenchy, who grabbed Woody by the arm. They charged off in the direction of camp.

Rowe looked like he was going to pass out, his eyelids fluttering. Swann crouched in front of him. "Don't worry, kid, it's not a bad one. Look at me."

Rowe looked at Swann, then away, glancing from face to face of the men who crowded around, settling on Charlie. "Just my luck," he muttered. "What a joke. Don't tell anyone how it happened. Tell them a guerrilla shot me."

Fifteen minutes later two medics roared up the hill in a jeep, with Frenchy and Woody in back, a stretcher across their knees. Swann grabbed the stretcher and set it down beside Rowe. The medics lifted Rowe onto it, then Frenchy and Charlie helped load him onto the jeep.

As the jeep started up, Muller leaned over and patted Rowe on the shoulder. "Look on the bright side, buddy. Maybe the Americans'll give you a purple heart."

Next morning Charlie and Powell shivered in the cold air as they started their assigned patrol in the back lanes surrounding the Miryang encampment. Their patrol, a routine feature of a unit's stay in a foreign country, was designed to keep the battalion safe against outside threats. Communist guerrillas were known to be active in the local hills.

At their briefing the night before a provost sergeant also told them to report and apprehend any soldiers skulking off on unauthorized leave. Plus, he said, grab any men trying to sneak back into camp after a nocturnal visit to the local population. Charlie was inclined to let the provosts worry about that. His and Powell's sympathies would be with their returning comrade, if they saw one. They could always look the other way.

Around them the local Koreans carried on with life, paying no obvious attention to the strangers in their midst. The temperature was a few degrees above freezing, the sky overcast. The spaced-out trees, bare of leaves, rattled their boughs in a light breeze.

"Hear anything about Rowe, Charlie?"

"No. Last word was he's been sent off to an American medical unit. I doubt we'll see him again, unless he heals real fast." Lieutenant Toogood had told them they'd be in Miryang for a maximum of six weeks of further training. After that they were committed to join the 27th British Commonwealth Brigade—Brits, Aussies, and Kiwis—who were already in action.

Charlie wondered if Sergeant Swann would suffer any consequences from Rowe's wounding. He suspected not. What the hell, there was a war on. Bound to be accidents. Even the most experienced soldier could run into trouble with the hazardous tools of their trade. Swann was lucky—there was a rumour that another sergeant had suffered serious injuries when an antipersonnel mine was triggered by mistake.

That night Sergeant Price mustered the platoon. "Here's what's happening," he said. "Over the next couple of weeks we're going to do a bunch of familiarization with some U.S. weapons, but we'll keep our Bren guns and .303s and Stens."

Was that a pause before he said "Stens?" Charlie waited for some sort of comment in light of the fact they were a man short after Rowe got himself shot.

Price carried right on. "U.S. mortars, bazookas, maybe flame-throwers. We'll be glad we have them, especially since the Americans have the supply lines to keep the guns and ammo coming. And we're also going to do a lot of patrolling, so take a good look at the hills out there, you're going to see a lot more of them." He gave a wolfish grin. "Reveille at 0430 hours, men, so get your beauty sleep."

Charlie still wanted out of 13 Platoon and back to his original platoon, although he was starting to wonder if the members of 13 were that much different than the rest of the Special Force. But in the meantime he'd train on some new weapons. Weapons he'd need to master for when he made it back to 7 Platoon.

"I'm tired of training," Muller said. "Time to shoot some gooks."

"You and me both." Powell had his .303 in hand. He slid open the bolt and blew away an invisible speck of dust from the chamber. "You fired any of those American weapons before, Frenchy?"

"Yup. Sure," Frenchy said. "Nothing tricky about them."

It sounded like BS to Charlie. "Sure you have," he said. "Where'd you use a flame-thrower? In Montreal, to light your mom's cigars?"

Powell laughed.

Frenchy grabbed Charlie's tunic with his left hand, pulling him close, and swung at his face. Charlie ducked, jerking back and popping a button on his tunic. "Darn you, Frenchy! Who the hell do you think you are?"

"I'm a goddamn lance corporal, and don't you forget it," Frenchy said, his eyes hard. "You piss me off, Black. You think you're too good for this platoon. You give me grief, and you'll find yourself in the hospital."

Muller jumped between them, holding his hands out, pressing Charlie back. "Break it up, boys."

Charlie's breath came in great heaves, but he calmed down in a hurry.

"That was kinda funny, Charlie," Muller said, the two of them off by themselves. "His mother smokes cigars?"

"Didn't get a laugh from Frenchy."

—

Frenchy had 2 Section up out of their tents and fed by 0500 hours. Charlie had to give him grudging credit—Frenchy might be a jerk, but he took his job seriously, and that might keep Charlie and the others safe if he did it well.

2 Section, 10 men, had one automatic weapon, their Bren Light Machine Gun. Frenchy assigned the kid, Powell, as number one, the man who carried and fired the Bren. Its extra weight wouldn't be a problem for him.

Muller, although only a private, would supervise and look over Powell's shoulder in any action.

"You, Black. You're number two on the Bren."

Charlie wasn't surprised, but a bit resentful. He'd performed well on the Bren in training, but of course Frenchy and Price wouldn't know that. He picked up and stowed in various pockets and his pack the extra loaded Bren magazines he'd provide to Powell when they got into action.

Sergeant Price gathered the platoon around him. "I've heard a lot of grumbling about not seeing action. Consider yourselves lucky because you're not ready to take on anybody yet. But you will be once I finish with you. In the meantime, pay attention and stay alert."

He led them out through the main gate and onto a dirt lane that meandered toward the hills east of Miryang. He assigned a scout, flankers, and rearguard, stationing himself at the head of the main body of men. Close behind him were Muller, Powell, and Charlie, with the Bren. The rest of 2 Section and Corporal Turner's 1 Section followed along.

The platoon moved to the base of the hill in single file, the men's mood buoyant. They were getting the kinks out, doing what they'd been trained to do, way back in Wainwright. They carried full packs under the grey sky, told this would be a three-day patrol. Charlie's pack felt heavy but comfortable, his rifle in one hand.

Their hill looked to Charlie like an easy climb until they spent a couple of hours on it. The path they started on petered out within minutes, leaving them to scramble over rocks and loose soil. The face of the hillside featured intermediate ridges and ravines, so that often he couldn't see the ground more than a few hundred feet in any given direction. Vegetation was low and leafless, with occasional stunted evergreens mixed with dead grass. Charlie's feet were getting acclimatized again to the rigours of cross-country marches up and down hills after the weeks aboard ship.

In front of Charlie, Powell cursed as he lost his footing when a rock gave way under him. He slid down onto his butt and scrambled back up, looking sheepish. Charlie was relieved to see he kept control of his weapon.

The slope eased and they came to a flatter area, perhaps a mile wide. Price directed them across a couple of rudimentary roads that had been chewed up by tanks and other vehicles, pressing on toward yet another, higher hill.

—

Charlie stayed behind Powell, ready to reload the Bren if they got into a fight, not that it seemed likely. He kept alert, watching for movement. Dunstan was out front at scout, rifle at the ready. Even the undermanned 13 Platoon—only two sections instead of the standard three— was an impressive sight to Charlie's eye, the column of men wending its way in arrowhead formation up the hill, ten-yard spacing between soldiers.

Price stopped and signalled with a downward motion of his arm. Charlie hit the ground, wondering if this was for real. He edged closer to Powell, who lay face down, the Bren aimed ahead and to the right, its butt against his shoulder.

"You see anything?" Powell asked out of the corner of his mouth.

Charlie shook his head and pulled a spare magazine out of his pocket, just in case. Sergeant Price crawled ahead to confer with Dunstan. After a moment he came back past Powell and Charlie to crouch beside Frenchy. He waved up Corporal Turner of 1 Section.

"There's something going on two hundred yards ahead at two o'clock. Frenchy, I want 2 Section with me. We'll move past whatever it is and circle around it, 1 Section to follow. Stay spread out." He scratched in the dirt with a stick. "Once we're in position we'll advance in open order, covered by the Brens. Clear?"

Charlie stayed focussed ahead and couldn't see what Price diagrammed in the earth, but pictured a semicircle around whatever it was he and Dunstan had seen.

Price signaled Dunstan to move ahead, and, crouching, led the platoon up the hill. Fifty yards further on Charlie saw the back end of a jeep sitting at a crazy angle, its front obscured in vegetation. Once again the men went to ground. Price posted sentries to watch behind them and ordered the Bren crews to position themselves well out to the right and line up their weapons on the vehicle. He sent two men to scout left and right of the jeep.

Charlie's heart hammered. Powell, face down beside him, sighted on the jeep, his right hand on the pistol grip, ready to shoot. Price ordered the riflemen ahead while the Bren crews stayed in position to provide covering fire.

The platoon closed around the jeep. After a few minutes Price waved the Bren gunners up. Getting closer, Charlie saw Dunstan standing with his back to the jeep, looking pale. Dunstan glanced at the sky and took a deep breath.

The jeep faced down at a steep angle, its front wheels hanging over the edge of a gully. Charlie smelled gasoline. He moved closer. In the driver's seat was a dead soldier, his sightless eyes turned to his left, his head resting on the steering wheel. The lower half of his tunic was black with blood.

"Powell, Black. Come with me." Price moved along a trail that led away from the grisly scene. Charlie and Powell followed him, copying his semi-crouched posture. He was examining the ground as he went.

"Cripes, Powell, that's blood," Charlie said, looking at dark, scattered stains on the ground. Powell had the Bren ready. They followed Price a hundred yards along the trail. He stopped. At his feet in a small depression was the crumpled body of a soldier lying on its right side, its face obscured by windblown leaves, its left arm behind it.

Price grabbed the dead man's tunic and pulled him into the open.

"Bastards," said Price. All three of them staggered back.

Like his comrade back in the jeep, the dead man wore the uniform of the 16th New Zealand Field Artillery. His elbows were tied behind his back. One wound was evident. Just the one—his right hand had been cut off.

Powell turned away and vomited.

Price sent Charlie to check out a sagging hut a few yards away. Through its half-open door he saw a single room with a sleeping rack in one corner. It didn't appear to have been lived in for some time, maybe months. Charlie reported back to Price, his hands shaking.

Cripes, he thought, looking at the dead New Zealander again, picturing his last moments, blood spurting. In a desperate run to hoped-for refuge, his captors laughing.

Bastards.

———

Charlie welcomed Sunday, marked as always by church services. But the best part of it was that after a decent noon meal the troops could draw a beer and have a few hours off. He and Powell opted to go for a hike toward the village of Miryang. It would have been like a Sunday stroll in a park at home except that they both had their rifles and kept a watchful eye on their surroundings, given the recent deaths of the New Zealand Gunners.

Republic of Korea troops, the ROKs, had ordered a no-go zone for all Koreans within a quarter-mile of the Patricias' camp. The result was a road that meandered along the sluggish Miryang River opposite the camp devoid of civilian traffic, and it was there that Charlie and Powell strolled in the unseasonal sunshine, their rifles slung. To their left was the river, separated from their path by thirty feet of tall dead grass and low leafless shrubs.

Powell stopped and swung his rifle to his shoulder.

"What is it?" Charlie grabbed his .303 in both hands.

"Hundred yards ahead, Charlie. Someone ducked off the road."

Charlie's senses tingled. He scanned left and right, took a quick look behind them, his weapon ready. The image of the mutilated Kiwi flashed across his mind. They moved ahead, each hugging a side of the road. "I don't see anything," he said.

"Fifty yards, maybe."

Charlie caught a glimpse of something moving close to the riverbank. "There!" He had his rifle at his shoulder, thumb on the safety, hands sweating, his vision focussed.

A sharp, high-pitched cry was followed by a splash.

Charlie crouched and charged, ready to shoot. He could see a figure on the riverbank, a wailing Korean woman. She clutched a toddler in one hand, the other extended toward the river, where another child flailed in the water. Charlie dropped his rifle and jumped, hitting the surface feet-first and going under. The dark, icy water closed over him. He struggled to the surface, his boots dragging at him. He could see Powell was yelling but he couldn't hear him. Powell pointed, and Charlie saw a small hand in front of him. He lunged and grasped it, choking. With his other hand he grabbed the root of a long-dead stump at the side of the brackish water.

Powell lay flat on his belly, reaching down. Charlie pushed the child's arm up and Powell grabbed it, hoisting him. Powell disappeared for a long moment while Charlie spat out Miryang River silt. Powell came back into sight, crouched, and gave Charlie a hand to climb out of the river. Shivering, Charlie looked around for his rifle while Powell attempted to calm the excited woman and her children.

A jeep roared down the road and screeched to a halt. In the front were two South Korean privates. A third man, an ROK officer, climbed down from the back and began berating the woman.

"Her kid fell in the river!" Powell shouted. "Leave her alone."

The officer, in an American-style uniform with a lieutenant's bar on the collar, continued to rant, but turned his attention to Powell, who shouted back.

Charlie put his hand on Powell's shoulder. "Slow down, buddy," he said, at the same time raising a hand, palm out, toward the lieutenant. "Speak English?"

Guess not, he thought, as the ROK officer continued shouting, this time at him, before turning back to the Korean woman.

Charlie guessed she was on some errand important enough to her to break the no-go rule, so when she saw the Canadians she tried to hide.

Powell frowned, his face red. He picked up Charlie's rifle and handed it to him. "That guy ought to lighten up."

The woman stood clutching her children, looking down. The Korean soldiers crammed the three of them into the back of the jeep with one of the privates. The officer, very satisfied with himself, climbed into the passenger seat and gave a curt nod. In the seconds before the jeep sped away the woman glanced at Charlie and pressed her hands together in front of her.

Charlie felt warm for a moment, but it was January on the Korean Peninsula, and he started shivering again. He and Powell hot-footed it back to camp, where he changed into dry clothing.

—

Charlie joined Muller, Powell, and Dunstan in the mess tent. The three of them were playing blackjack for pennies, of which Muller had a stack.

"Hit me," Dunstan said, and when Muller dealt him a ten of spades, threw his hand down in disgust. "Crap. That's enough for me."

"Anybody else want in?" Muller looked up as Frenchy joined them. "Charlie? How about you, corporal? Feeling lucky?"

Frenchy snorted. "Stakes are too high for me. Powell, you get into any trouble in the village?"

"We weren't in the village, but Charlie went for a swim."

"He what?"

"Jumped into the river," Powell said, and laughed. "Pulled a Korean kid out. Saved his life."

"What was it—knee-deep?" Frenchy asked with a wooden smile, showing his teeth.

"No, no. He went out of sight himself, it was way over his head. Right, Charlie?"

Charlie felt blood rush to his face. "Sure."

"Anyway," Powell continued, happy to have everyone's attention, "Sergeant Price and the lieutenant were impressed. I bumped into them while Charlie was getting cleaned up."

"You're a lucky man, Charlie," Muller said. "Do the Koreans give out lifesaving awards? Probably not. Let's try your luck at poker."

Charlie was relieved at the change in subject and joined in, as did Powell and Dunstan.

"C'mon, corporal," Muller said. "Sit in. Your credit's good with me."

"Got better things to do," Frenchy said.

Charlie looked up from the cards Muller was dealing. Frenchy had a closed look on his face. Charlie didn't know what that meant, if anything, but it was never good news when Frenchy was bothered by something.

Frenchy watched the play for a while. When Charlie looked a few minutes later, he was gone.

CHAPTER 8

Charlie made a habit of crawling out of his sleeping bag as soon as the call went out in the morning. The day after his rescue of the Korean child, he made his usual head start on breakfast and was walking back to his tent to pack up for another day of patrolling when Powell, looking worried, stopped him.

"Charlie, you seen Frenchy?"

"No, what's the matter?"

"Price was looking for him. Doesn't look like his cot was slept in."

Muller strode up from the direction of headquarters. "I just saw Frenchy," he said. "Over by the RSM's office."

Charlie wouldn't mind leaving Frenchy to his fate, but Frenchy was part of 13 Platoon and it seemed Charlie was too, like it or not. He walked to the regimental sergeant major's office—a tent, in fact—outside of which Frenchy stood at attention.

Charlie had no wish to meet the RSM, who everybody considered a prickly disciplinarian, no matter how casual the contact. Frenchy's uniform was rumpled and dirt-stained with bits of grass and debris stuck to it.

Charlie peered at him. "What's up with you? Been back on the assault course?"

"Bugger off," Frenchy said, out of the corner of his mouth. "I don't need you hanging around."

"You on charge? What did you do?"

Before Frenchy could answer Charlie heard voices coming from the other side of the tent, and around the corner strode the RSM and the regimental adjutant, Captain Parker.

"This man is on punishment," the RSM said, glowering at Charlie.

Charlie beat a hasty retreat.

While 13 Platoon was waiting for their instructions for the day, Powell filled them in on some details he'd heard. "Frenchy and a couple of pals of his in D Company got their hands on some booze, then left camp. When they came back they got into a real donnybrook with the sentries. The Provost Corps guys charged them all."

"Idiots," Charlie said. "Frenchy's over by the RSM's tent."

"The D Company guys are already in the slammer. It took them a while to find Frenchy. He was passed out in the bush near the main gate."

13 Platoon, less Frenchy, was assigned to a patrol with one of D Company's platoons. It bothered Charlie that Frenchy was missing. He didn't like the Montrealer, but he was their leader. The section felt rudderless without him. When they finished for the day, Charlie went looking for him.

The provost corporal on duty when Charlie approached the cells told him he was one of the policemen in the fight the night before. "But, yeah, your guy - Frenchy? He's a bloody wild man when he gets a skinful. He escaped from us last night, but he's ours now."

The provost corps were the policemen in the army, known to the troops as 'meatheads.' Not that Charlie would call the corporal that under the circumstances.

"So, can I talk to him?"

The corporal looked around. His sergeant was away on a break. "Make it quick. Two minutes."

Charlie trotted over to where the prisoners were dragging themselves through the obstacle course, a feature of the camp's jail. A meathead harassed them as they ran—doubled—from a sheer ten-foot-high wall they had to climb over to a muddy pit with barbed wire strung over it. The meathead nodded approval. Charlie grabbed Frenchy and drew him to one side. "What the hell got into you, Frenchy?"

"What's it to you?" Frenchy gasped between breaths.

"Plenty." He thought a moment. "They could send us all home."

"What are you talking about?"

"Well, maybe not that. But if we get any smaller—heck, we're under 20 men, with you in here—they might break up the platoon, use us as replacements when guys in other platoons get hurt or killed. Is that what you want?"

Frenchy scowled at him. "Fuck off."

"13 Platoon. That's us, Frenchy. But there *is* no 13 Platoon, officially. If we cause problems we'll be gone."

Listening to himself, Charlie wondered what had come over him. He *wanted* to be part of 13 Platoon?

The provost supervising the prisoners shouted from the far end of the obstacle course. "Long enough. Get out of here, Black, or you'll be joining your pal. Back here, Accardo, on the double!"

Frenchy, Accardo to the meatheads, trotted off. Charlie turned and hurried away, breathing easier once out through the stockade gate.

—

Lieutenant Toogood frowned. "You know Lance Corporal Accardo has been sentenced to a week in cells?"

"Yes, sir." Charlie had been summoned by Sergeant Price, and now he was standing at attention in front of 13 Platoon's only commissioned officer in one of the Headquarters Company tents. Price stood to one side.

"Did you know Colonel Stone stripped him of his rank?"

Charlie gulped. He wasn't surprised, now it was drawn to his attention. An army can't have a non-commissioned officer going AWOL and fighting with the provosts. He almost felt sorry for Frenchy, but he'd caused his own problems, getting drunk and up to heaven knew what.

"No, sir."

"1 Section needs an NCO, corporal. Congratulations."

Charlie's mind went blank, until he realized that Toogood had his hand extended. He shook it in a daze and felt like he'd been hit with a two-by-four as Price marched him out of the tent.

Dismissing him, Price looked Charlie in the eye and handed him a pair of used hooks. "Here," he said. "But I don't want to hear any more of this BS going around that you want out of 13, Black. Can I count on you?"

"Yes, sergeant."

The decision had been made for him; all he had to do now was learn to live with it.

He hunted up needle and thread and sewed his hooks onto the arms of his tunic. All the while, his thoughts raced. How would the men of 2 Section react to Charlie, at the tender age of 19, getting put in charge? What about Frenchy—when he finished his punishment, would he be back with 13?

Settling down a bit, he thought back to Lt Toogood calling him "corporal." Just a courtesy often extended to lance corporals. But he had to admit he liked the ring of it.

—

The battalion's training went on, with experienced officers and NCOs putting the men through their paces. When in Wainwright they'd taken part in exercises as sections and platoons, but now the emphasis was on company or even multi-company work. 13 Platoon was often paired with one or other of the 12 normal company platoons to take part in simulated attacks or defenses on the steep hills around Miryang.

Charlie led 2 Section and felt he was learning a lot. He was aided with his new responsibilities by the close supervision of Sergeant Price and Lieutenant Toogood and the more senior officers.

On a Sunday, Price appeared with a stranger in tow. "This is Private Orton," he said to Charlie who was talking to Muller and Woody at the time. "He's a replacement for Rowe, so he's in your 2 Section."

Private Joe Orton was on the short side, looking like he still carried some baby fat. As if he read Charlie's mind Price said, "Top of his training class back in Wainwright. Show him where to bunk."

"I'll do it," Muller said. Orton picked up his pack and rifle and followed Muller.

An hour later Muller and Woody sat with Charlie in the mess tent finishing dinner, when Muller glanced up. "Look who's back."

It was Frenchy with a loaded plate in hand. He sat a few places down from Charlie, on the same side of the table. He looked like he'd lost weight but was determined to gain it all back in one sitting.

"So you survived Big Jim's torture chamber?" Muller said to him. Colonel Stone was said to have designed the cells himself.

"Bloody glad to get out of there," Frenchy said between forkfuls of baked beans. "Everything normal around here?"

"New man," Woody said. "Joe Orton. Good guy."

Muller looked up. "Major excitement yesterday, Frenchy. B Company did a three-day patrol and was fired on by guerrillas."

"Anybody hurt?"

"Yeah, one guy wounded. Not too bad. He was patched up by the medics."

"I'm gonna see if I can get any more grub," Frenchy said, standing and taking his plate with him. "Any word on seeing action? Our six weeks of extra training Big Jim bought us must be almost up."

"Sergeant Price says we could move out any day," Charlie said. "We know the Americans want us in the line as soon as possible."

Frenchy turned toward Charlie, and his jaw dropped. He was seeing Charlie's new rank insignia for the first time, having been isolated in cells for two weeks.

Now what, Frenchy? Charlie thought, as Frenchy turned and walked away.

—

The sinuous parade of US Army 6x6 TCVs ground its way north along rutted Korean roads. It was their third day on the road, a road that twisted and bounced them around, testing the mettle of the drivers who kept them on it and the endurance of the soldiers in the boxes.

Dark clouds scudded overhead, with occasional flurries of snow or sleet blowing against the canvas-topped trucks.

The men on the two hard benches facing each other braced themselves in position and rocked in unison. Even so the background rumble and stutter of tires on rocks and gravel and the grind of the transmission lulled them into a semi-conscious state. Every two or three hours the vehicles stopped and the men climbed down, stretching their legs and stamping their feet to get their blood circulating.

After a long day on the road Charlie felt numb, muscles tired from constantly coping with the unforgiving seat. His thoughts strayed to a camping trip with his family while Jeff was still alive. They'd driven to the Okanagan. He and Jeff had canoed during the day, and the four of them roasted hotdogs and scorched marshmallows on the fire. The nights were cool and lit with a million stars. The family had slept in a tent not totally different from those the battalion had left behind in Miryang.

"What you grinning at, Charlie?" Powell reached across and nudged Charlie's knee with his rifle. "Thinking about someone you left at home?"

"No, just thinking about getting out of this truck for a change."

Frenchy stirred himself. "Beats walking."

When Frenchy had rejoined the platoon back in Miryang, Charlie was nervous about his reaction to his reduced rank and Charlie's simultaneous promotion. As a lance corporal, Frenchy had been arrogant and overbearing, but even so Charlie had to admit he was an effective leader. Now that Frenchy was once again a private, he was keen as mustard. His rifle was in pristine condition, his gear spotless, and he turned to with a will when given a task. Charlie fretted, not sure what Frenchy was up to—if anything.

Next to Powell and opposite Charlie slumped Muller, head lolling back against the canvas, dead to the world. Lucky beggar,

Charlie thought. Able to sleep through anything. A useful skill for a soldier.

In contrast to Muller Joe Orton, who had joined 13 Platoon in Miryang, was wide awake. He was a serious soldier and a likable character whom Muller and Woody had taken under their wings.

Charlie stayed alert as the light outside faded, another short February day coming to a close. The 6x6 gave a brutal lurch, crunching down hard, rattling Charlie's teeth.

"Whoa!" said Muller, blinking and looking around. Brakes squealed as their truck jerked to a stop.

"Dismount, end of the line," someone shouted outside. Muller stood, bent at the waist, and threw open the canvas flap at the back of the vehicle. Charlie kicked open the tailgate and jumped out, staggering when he hit the ground, muscles cramped. He stretched his legs and back, slung his rifle over his shoulder.

The line of trucks had stopped at the edge of a large open area surrounded by low hills. It was late afternoon, with the sun dipping below the ridge to the west. A rosy light permeated the scene. Charlie smelled wood smoke and something metallic. Blood? Flames flickered, with embers flaring and smoke rising from the charred remains of several buildings, maybe a small village.

Another scene flashed into Charlie's mind, a chaotic scene with the smell of wood smoke and burnt oil and blinding light and one locomotive piled upside down on top of a railcar where Canadian soldiers had died. That image, white-hot, was burned into his memory. It was not like this. This was dark, shadowed, eerie.

A group of soldiers already disembarked from their vehicles huddled nearby, looking at something on the ground. Charlie walked over and saw a body, dark in the low light, lying face down, its head twisted to one side at an impossible angle.

"Gooks," Frenchy said. "The Yanks must have wiped them out."

A few feet away lay another human shape. It was naked, lying on its right front, its left arm flung out as if reaching for help. Charlie could make out bullet wounds on the torso, beneath which was a pool of blood, black in the flickering light. He stared as he recognized remnants of khaki US Army clothing. "They're Americans."

Within a few yards were two more bodies, and further away were many more, some still half in sleeping bags. Many were stripped of their uniforms but there was no doubt they were black American soldiers, slaughtered where they lay.

Charlie's stomach heaved, driving the acid taste of bile into his throat. Fighting it, he walked a short way from the clearing, looking at the scrub bushes and rocks on the hillside. He got control of himself, thinking about how just hours before the enemy might have stormed along the path on which he stood, bayonets flashing and guns blazing. He'd not sleep easy that night.

Ordered to dig in, the troops flew at it with the added urgency of having seen the brutal end of their American comrades-in-arms.

"Make 'em deep," Sergeant Price said, and even in the cold February air they sweated as they made 'em deep. The semi-frozen earth flew off Charlie's shovel as he worked alongside Muller, the stink and horror of the dead Americans sticking in his nostrils and in his mind.

Price stalked among the men of the platoon as they laboured. "They didn't bloody well post sentries, either that or the sentries were asleep." A few minutes later: "They didn't dig in. They were machine gunned and hit with grenades, then the Chinese rushed in and finished them off with burp guns and bayonets."

"Burp guns," Muller said. "Always sounds funny. Guess it's not."

No, Charlie thought. Burp guns were a reliable, and deadly, Soviet submachine gun adapted by the Chinese. It had a much higher rate of fire than comparable UN weapons.

It was all too clear in Charlie's head. Dozens of men, either stripped naked after they were killed or naked and trapped in their sleeping bags, never able to escape them in the face of the attack. Two dead men slumped in a shot-up jeep, maybe trying to get to the machine gun mounted in its rear. And no sign of trenches or foxholes, the infantryman's best defence.

Powell took a break from where he and Frenchy were digging and wandered over. "They were all negroes."

"Price said he heard the Yanks are integrating soon, but not yet." Muller kept on digging. "I didn't see one white guy."

"Don't seem right." Powell shook his head and went back to his own trench.

Charlie had seen dead Koreans when they landed off the *Martinez* in Pusan, but the slaughtered Americans were more shocking and closer to home. Hard to look at. More than anything else he'd seen, it reminded him he was in a war zone, and they were all at risk. There'd be no turning back.

—

Sergeant Price had laid out the platoon's trench locations in such a way that the troops could cover each other in case of attack. Their slit trenches were six feet deep if the ground allowed, with a fire step on the bottom so that when the men stood on it they could see out to keep watch or fight. Charlie dug, keeping the trench narrow with room enough to turn around but still provide as much protection as possible from indirect fire from mortars or artillery. He'd be sharing this one with Muller, so it only had to be long enough for the two of them.

Charlie had no trouble keeping his eyes open during his watch, and in fact didn't sleep much at all, even though under cover in his trench with sentries posted. The dead US soldiers haunted him.

Charlie had hardly ever seen negroes in real life. He wondered if there were any in the Canadian army. There were non-whites. One in particular was prominent in the battalion. Sergeant Tommy Prince was an Ojibwa from Manitoba and a much-decorated World War II veteran.

Charlie's thoughts were jumbled, his brain trying to make sense of this new world. A world in which generals were killed in a casual road accident, black soldiers died in bed, and dead civilians lay unattended. Like fish that flew too high and died, out of reach of home.

He finally drifted off, until dawn brought a cloudy day close to freezing, threatening rain or snow. A 6x6 pulled up, stopping a few yards from where Charlie and Muller sat finishing their US army surplus C-rations, tin plates on their knees. The driver stayed behind the wheel but around the truck strode Sergeant Price, looking rested after spending the night in Powell and Frenchy's trench. "Let's go, corporal! Tell your boys I want their sleeping bags."

Charlie was on his feet. He picked up his vacated bag.

Muller was sitting up in the trench. "What's this about?"

"Sleeping bags. Toss them in the truck." Price's face was expressionless.

Charlie and Muller bundled up their bags and threw them on top of a heap of sleeping bags already in the truck box.

"We supposed to sleep on the bare ground?" Muller said.

"No, no," Price said. "The army'll look after you better than that. Go see the quartermaster, draw a blanket. Big Jim says no troops of his are going to be caught in sleeping bags, Chinamen tucking them in at night with a bayonet. Blankets only. One each," he added. "We're going to toughen up, boys."

———

Within an hour the battalion was ready to move. It was a small part of Operation Killer, a UN plan to push the North Koreans and Chinese formations north and destroy them if possible. Its immediate task was to take out Chinese occupiers atop a small mountain a dozen miles away. Like hundreds of other such features in Korea, it was designated on maps only by its height above sea-level in metres. Hill 404 was to be 2PPCLI's baptism of fire, and to get there they would proceed north along the valley floor. To left and right, making their respective way along the high ground to either side, were the 1st Middlesex Regiment and the 1st Argyll and Sutherland

Highlanders, sister units in the 27th British Commonwealth Infantry Brigade.

13 Platoon watched B Company lead the way and waited for orders to take up its position in the formation. It was an impressive sight, with all four rifle companies strung out on the snowy valley floor with the hills rising either side.

Charlie looked around at his section. They were fired up with their packs loaded, rifles slung on shoulders. They might be in 13 Platoon, but they'd volunteered to fight, and by God they were ready.

Sergeant Price appeared. "Stand down, 13 Platoon. Lieutenant Toogood has orders for us." He moved away, and Charlie saw him conferring with the lieutenant.

"What now?" Muller said. "How come we're not heading out with the rest of the battalion?"

Charlie shrugged. They'd find out soon enough.

"Let me guess," said Frenchy. "They need a special platoon to dig some new latrines, or maybe fill in some old ones."

"Shut up, Frenchy," Charlie said. Price and Toogood were coming toward them.

CHAPTER 9

"Listen up. We've been given a special task, but I know we're up to it." Lieutenant Toogood had Charlie's attention. A special task? He was hopeful but a little skeptical, given it was 13 they were talking about.

"The rest of the battalion are off to the north, but we've been given a job to do—we few, we happy few." Toogood glanced down at a map. "There's a village called Jujang li four miles west of here, and a few of the porters call it home. Their families are threatened by the guerrillas, hanging out in the hills and stealing from them. The guerrillas claim to know the men of the village are helping us. The result is that the men can't do their job, they need to stay home to protect their families. It's our task to protect the village and chase away the guerrillas."

Cripes, thought Charlie. The rifle companies, A to D, were away to engage the enemy. 13 Platoon—the rejects—would protect a local village. So much for getting a special job to do.

"Fuckin' riceburners," Frenchy said under his breath.

"You think the porters aren't important, Private?" Price said. "That pack on your back is seventy pounds plus. You want to carry food and ammo for a two-week patrol on top of that? The riceburners matter. The brigade needs them, and we're going to do whatever it takes. I don't want to hear any more bitching about it."

Riceburners. A new word to the Canadians. South Korean men and boys, hired as porters, risking their lives for meagre wages to keep vital supplies flowing to the frontline troops. Better than calling them gooks, he thought, a word the Canadians used for Koreans. Neither good nor bad, equally spent on North and South varieties.

A usable dirt road led to the village of Jujang li, but they weren't destined to set foot on it. One of the lessons passed on to the Patricias by Australians and Brits who had already been in the fight for months was that the Chinese loved swooping down from the hills onto troops and mechanized units on the roads below.

Lieutenant Toogood plotted a course half-way up the hill that loomed on the north side of the road. The men moved deliberately in loose file formation, Sergeant Price reminding them to keep a sharp eye out for guerrillas or Chinese who could be lying in ambush at any point. The hillside was mostly devoid of trees but featured countless hiding places with clumps of leaf-less brush, rocks, and hillocks. Charlie concentrated on sweeping the immediate horizon for the enemy, while also watching his footing on the steep terrain.

The weeks of extra training that Big Jim Stone finagled out of the then UN commander, General Walker, were paying off. Charlie worked up an easy sweat, even in the cold Korean air, as he kept up with Powell, the Bren gunner. They all carried extra gear: ammo for the Bren or an axe or pick or a Bazooka.

Four hours into their cross-country hike Toogood, at the head of the column, waved them to a halt. Charlie sank to the ground and retrieved his canteen. They were moving along a contour below the ridge above them on their right, with the road visible at times down the slope to the left. Ahead of them crossing their route was a sort of elevated ridge or spur that stretched from the high ground down to the road.

Toogood made his way up to Muller, who was scouting, and had stopped at the spur.

Sergeant Price joined them, and a few minutes later came back to the men. "Our village is just ahead," he said. "As of a week ago it was cleared by the Americans. But a week is a long time, and it may have been reoccupied by guerrillas or Chinese who hid in the hills when their army retreated. The lieutenant is going to go down and do a recce. Corporal, you're with him, along with Orton. Turn your extra Bren ammo over to Woody."

Keyed up, Charlie emptied his pockets of the Bren magazines, his hands shaking. *Calm down, calm down*, he thought. *This is for real, don't screw it up.*

Sergeant Price brought Muller, Powell, and Woody forward with the Bren to a position where they could provide covering fire to Lieutenant Toogood and his party. The platoon's second Bren in 1 Section was placed to cover the opposite hillside.

Orton and Charlie crouched close to the lieutenant. "Here's the drill," Toogood said. "One of you either side of me, keep up, ten yards out. One house in the village will show us a white flag. They're supposed to have an interpreter waiting for us. Once we're there, I might go in, but you stay out." He gave them each a look. "And keep your eyes open."

Lieutenant Toogood crawled over the crest of the spur, stayed crouched, and half slid, half walked down to where he'd no longer be silhouetted against the skyline. He straightened up, rifle in both hands. Charlie and Orton followed, taking up their positions on his flanks.

Charlie felt a heightened sense of awareness, vision crystal-clear, the sound of his footfalls magnified. A vague smell of woodsmoke reached him, along with a slight, familiar odour of human excrement that had been absent when they were up on the hill. Jujang li consisted of ten or twelve small houses showing some wood in their construction but with the appearance of having risen out of the ground itself, like they'd been there a thousand years. Off to the right were a series of rice paddies that stepped up the hill. Apart from the minimal sounds the soldiers made a hush had descended, no birdsong or even distant guns to disturb the foreboding air that permeated the scene.

Careful to keep up to the lieutenant, Charlie gripped his rifle in both hands, thumb close to the safety, the weapon cocked. Behind him, Powell would have the Bren trained in their direction, ready to provide covering fire. He trusted Powell, but all the same the back of his neck tingled.

He kept checking all around, his eyes returning again to the village ahead of them, his heart pounding. They reached level ground. Thirty yards ahead of them across a dry creek bed was the dirt road and the most central house in the village, its door open. Toogood held up a hand. Charlie stood still, nerves stretched taut. A diminutive figure appeared in the open doorway, waving a grey cloth.

"Keep those eyes peeled," Toogood said, and advanced on the house. Charlie and Orton hung back a little, so they could keep the buildings to left and right in their field of vision. Charlie took a quick glance back the way they'd come, catching a glint of light, maybe off the binoculars Toogood had left with Sergeant Price.

The figure in the doorway was a woman dressed in a one-piece drab-coloured dress that ended just above her ankles. Her jet-black hair was loose. She spoke in what sounded like broken English, waving her hands.

Toogood followed her inside.

Charlie gripped his rifle so hard his hands threatened to cramp. He relaxed each in turn, kept his thumb close to the safety. Low voices, so quiet he couldn't make out words that might be English, came from inside the house. Female and male voices. He scanned the brown hills, the dirt road, his half of the sombre village.

Toogood emerged. "There are eight porters inside here," he said. "Their wives and families are still in their houses. We need to check them all out, make sure it's only women and kids in them, no fighting-age men." He waved an arm at the platoon up on the hill, then held up two fingers. Charlie turned back to the village. All was quiet. He looked up and saw two men hurrying down to join them from the platoon's location on the hillside. Frenchy and Jackson from 1 Section.

Toogood sent Charlie and Orton one way, Frenchy and Jackson the other.

Charlie called out at the first building he reached. "Open up—coming in!" Not that he figured the occupants would know what he said, counting on the interpreter to have told the villagers what would happen. Orton looked ready and nodded at him. Charlie took a deep breath and pushed the door open. He was hit by the smell of woodsmoke and the unmistakable reek of small spaces with no ventilation and many bodies.

His eyes swept a central room containing a rudimentary kitchen, table, and three wooden chairs. Two small windows and an oil lamp cast a dim light. He entered a second, smaller room, apparently just for sleeping, where two women of indeterminate age and four wide-eyed kids huddled in a corner. Across the back wall stretched a piece of twine hung with clothing. Charlie kept the occupants in front of him where he could see them as he swung the clothing aside with his rifle barrel. Nothing. Charlie relaxed a little, nodded, and backed out.

Orton entered the next house, and so it went, with little variation house to house, until they finished their sweep of their half of the village. They returned to the central building where Lieutenant Toogood waited with Frenchy and Jackson, their sweep finished. Toogood waved Sergeant Price and the remaining members of the platoon down from the hill.

South of the village, on the opposite side from the road, an open meadow stretched perhaps five hundred yards up the hill. Sergeant Price directed 2 Section to dig in there, two hundred yards up from the village, their trenches strung out on a rough east-west line.

———

After two days watching over the village Charlie was getting edgy, the need to stay concealed meaning there was no physical activity. They were at fifty percent stand-to, with Muller on watch, his rifle at the ready. A frustrating time with a muted outlook: a brown hillside, a village that blended with its surroundings, and men in khakis. Their trenches were cold, and they were making do with a single blanket each. Charlie took off his boots and socks to check his feet weren't getting frost-bitten or suffering from the wet and lack of circulation. He found a pair of dry socks in his pack, which he put on in a hurry and jammed his feet back into his boots before they got even colder.

The sky was darkening when Sergeant Price came by the trench where Charlie and Muller were dug in above the village's western end.

"How long we going to stay here, sergeant?" Muller asked.

"As long as it takes. But the woman in the village thought the guerrillas would have dropped in before this," Price said. He glanced at his watch. "One hundred percent stand-to starts now."

For an hour every sunset and dawn, when most attacks took place, the men went to 100 percent stand-to. Every member of the platoon had to be alert and at their posts, ready for action. Charlie and Muller stood in their trench, rifles trained up the slope to the south, the village at their backs. Price told them Lieutenant Toogood, after consulting with the villagers, had come to the conclusion the guerrillas would approach from their end of the village. He moved on to the other trenches.

All was quiet but for a faint moaning of the wind in the dead grass and bushes on the hillside. The overcast sky darkened.

Charlie heard what he thought were Korean voices coming from the village but they were so faint he couldn't be sure. They grew louder, an aggressive male voice dominating.

"Muller," Charlie whispered, "I think they're here. Go tell the lieutenant."

Muller climbed from the trench and crept away in the direction of the lieutenant's trench. Hardly breathing, Charlie listened to the rising clamour of the ongoing conversation. After a moment or two it became quieter, but the male voice continued talking.

Lieutenant Toogood and Muller dropped into the trench. Toogood whispered. "Sergeant Price will lead 1 Section down into the village to drive the guerrillas out. With any luck they'll come this way."

Charlie double-checked his rifle. Bolt driven home, cocked, safety on. He rested the .303 on the parapet and tried to slow his breathing, thinking the enemy could hear his heart pounding.

There was still enough ambient light that Charlie could make out the outlines of the village huts at the bottom of the slope. A disturbance broke out at the eastern end of the village that Charlie assumed was Sergeant Price and the boys being deliberately noisy. The Korean voices stopped and even the wind died down. There were sounds of doors being shut and urgent, suppressed orders given.

Charlie heard faint, rapid footsteps, as if someone was running on the road. He made out one figure—no, two—coming up the slope from the village. They were 50 or 60 yards away and closing fast.

"Halt!" Toogood shouted.

The running figures broke stride as the flash of a gunshot flared from one of them. They kept coming.

"Fire," Toogood yelled, banging off a shot from Charlie's left.

Charlie flinched but fired, darkness making it almost impossible to see the sights on his rifle. Muller shot as well, adding to the din. One of the running figures collapsed out of sight. The second one swerved to the side and stumbled on. All three of the riflemen shot again and the figure went down.

Confused shouting erupted from the village. Charlie's ears were ringing from the gunfire but it seemed as if the noise from down the hill was moving through the village.

"You two stay here and make damn sure you know who you're shooting at." The lieutenant climbed out of the trench and angled down the hill toward the village.

Charlie wondered if he'd killed a man. It was impossible to tell, with everybody firing at once. His hands shook as he pulled out his canteen. Charlie didn't know what he thought about killing a man, if in fact he had done so. He didn't dwell on the issue.

"What if they're not dead?" Muller said.

"I don't know. If they're just wounded they'll probably try to crawl away."

"What if they're crawling toward us?"

"I'll tell you one thing for sure," Charlie said. "We're not leaving this trench to find out."

"It didn't bother Nogood."

"Nogood?" Charlie grinned to himself. "Part of his job, lucky guy," he said. "Guess he has to recce, keep track of what's going on."

Charlie thought about it. The troops were generally respect-
ful of their officers, some of whom were awarded nicknames.
Sometimes derisive, but often out of a sense of camaraderie,
almost affection. 'Nogood.' That was kind of funny.

An hour later, Muller said, "How long we gonna be at a
hundred percent stand-to, Charlie? All damn night?"

As if in answer, Sergeant Price loomed out of the darkness.
He dropped into the trench between them. "The lieutenant says
back to fifty percent stand-to, then one hundred percent at 0400
hours."

That made sense to Charlie. Let half the troops get some
sleep for two hours, then change around.

"But we're spread thin," Price continued. "We have you
two here, with Frenchy and Powell dug in next to you. The rest
of the platoon is scattered through the village, plus sentries posted
at each end and on the opposite hillside."

"Didn't hear any shooting from down below," said
Charlie.

"We think there were four guerrillas, but two of them made
it out the way they came in, from the east. The other two came
this way, the ones you and the lieutenant accounted for."

Price left again, off to check on the other sentries. They
reverted to fifty percent stand-to, Muller curled up in a corner of
the trench, wrapped in his blanket. At the other end, Charlie
made sure he didn't get too comfortable. Sentries who dozed off
could wake up with their throats slit, or, almost as bad, Sergeant
Price's size thirteen combat boot in their ribs.

—

Before dawn the platoon was back at morning stand-to,
everybody awake, watchful, rifles ready. An uneventful hour was
followed by a cold breakfast in their trenches. The village afford-
ed cold water for shaving.

Charlie watched as Lieutenant Toogood and Sergeant Price
examined the bodies of the dead guerrillas and walked over.

"North Koreans, sir?" Price asked the lieutenant.

"Villagers say so. But I don't know how they can tell. We're told there were lots of communist South Koreans who welcomed the North when they came."

One of the dead looked to Charlie to be middle aged, though he found it hard to judge. The other one, though, was young, younger than Charlie. Just a kid. Charlie didn't want to dwell on that. They're the enemy, and we're here to kill them. Before they kill us.

—

The platoon was on the move, back to where they'd last been with the rest of the battalion three days before, once again hiking along the hillsides, avoiding the road. The troops were in a jubilant mood. Half-way back, Toogood gathered them around him.

"Well done, 13 Platoon. A good three days' work. We've freed up the porters by driving off the guerrillas. That'll help the whole battalion in the long run. But now we're up against the clock, and our orders are to rejoin the battalion. Sergeant, anything to add?"

"Sir." Price eyed them. "Another reminder. The enemy can come from any direction, any time. They can be all around us." He nodded to the hillside above them where Muller stood, fifty yards away, his eyes on the horizon. "We're in their country, and they know it a hell of a lot better than we do."

"Question, sir," said Charlie. "What has the rest of the battalion been doing since we went off on our own?"

"You've heard about Operation Killer," Toogood said. "It's starting now. The rest of the Patricias have joined up with the Commonwealth Brigade, and they're pushing north. We'll catch up to them as soon as we can."

The weather was dry and cold but overcast, so they were able to make good time. As they rounded the last bend to get within sight of the trenches where they'd dug in three nights before, a light snow began to fall.

Back at their starting point, reminded by the locale of the fate of the black Americans killed in their sleeping bags, the men were hyper–alert. 13 Platoon dug in and placed sentries. They'd be on the march again with the dawn.

Chapter 10

Next morning at 0800 13 Platoon was on the move north through the wintry Korean landscape, trudging across open country and six inches of fresh snow. It was quiet, with no birds or other sign of life in the white expanse. Charlie was glad to be on the march and shaking off the chill of the frozen night they had spent fully-dressed and wrapped in a blanket, down in their trenches.

A broad, flat valley was punctuated in the distance by cone-shaped hills that rose hundreds of feet from the lowlands. Charlie's section led, with 1 Section close behind. Lieutenant Toogood posted a scout ahead and flankers either side. The usual jokes and banter that characterized 13 Platoon when they were under training were absent, the men more subdued as they moved into the active fighting zone.

In mid-morning Lieutenant Toogood ordered a halt and consulted a map, calling Price, Corporal Turner, and Charlie to look over his shoulder. He jabbed a finger at a spot on the map marked "404." "That's the hill's height in metres," he said. "And there," and he pointed at a peak in the distance, "is Hill 404. That's where the battalion, along with the rest of the 27th Commonwealth Brigade, is attacking. It's our job to catch up to them."

Charlie passed the information on to his section, and the platoon moved off.

After another two hours they intersected a set of rusty train tracks and followed them northeast as the valley narrowed. Forty yards ahead Frenchy, scouting, looked left and right and left again, back and forth, as they made steady progress.

They settled into the march, the column of laden men winding its way along the tracks. The heavy pack, rifle, and extra magazines for the Bren that Charlie carried had become second nature.

The hills closed in. Charlie felt a prickle of nervousness. Not fear, he told himself. Nerves. Extra vigilance. It was a cold and dry landscape, but there was enough brown, dead vegetation on the hills that a company of Chinese regulars could be hidden within a hundred yards of them.

Frenchy, up ahead, waved his arm.

"Hold up," said Toogood. He nodded at Price, who shed his pack and moved toward Frenchy, rifle at the ready. The men hunkered down, happy to sink to the ground. Charlie kept his pack on but leaned back against it. He watched as Toogood pulled out his map case again.

Sergeant Price reached Frenchy, who pointed at something ahead. Price started back toward the rest of the platoon. When he reached the lieutenant he squatted down beside him and muttered something, gesturing at the map.

Toogood nodded. "Mount up," he said, and grinned. "I have miles to go before I sleep."

Charlie noticed Nogood often said things like that, words that sounded familiar but darned if he knew where from.

He leaned forward, caught his balance with one hand on the ground and heaved himself up, bouncing his load to settle it. Nogood waved at Frenchy to carry on, and the platoon set off after him, with Price bringing up the rear.

Forty yards on Charlie saw that the railway tracks curved to the right around some leafless trees and scattered boulders and plunged into a black hole in the rock face, like a snake slithering into a rabbit burrow. Hill 404 could no longer be seen, the view blocked by the mountainous spur that had only one way through, and that was the tunnel.

Toogood left the flankers posted but waved the platoon off to the side into the cover of a house-sized boulder. They stood around him, adjusting their loads. Powell put the butt of the Bren down and leaned it against his hip.

"We know the rest of the battalion went through here three days ago," Toogood said. "It was safe then. They didn't encounter anything or we'd have heard. Doesn't mean it's safe now."

The men were quiet.

"Sergeant Price, I want a corporal and one other out front, fifty yards ahead of the platoon. Relieve Frenchy, give him a break. I want to get a couple of miles clear of this place as soon as possible."

Price gave Charlie the nod. "Take Muller with you, and move it. You heard the lieutenant. Keep your eyes open and keep moving. We have to get through the tunnel and dug in before the light fades."

Charlie and Muller exchanged a glance. "Okay, let's go," Charlie said. Muller nodded and stepped out. Charlie didn't know what Muller was thinking, but as they moved along the tracks toward the tunnel he felt a tingle of apprehension.

They came up to Frenchy. "The price of leadership, Charlie," he said, pokerfaced.

Charlie glanced back at the other members of 13 Platoon, strung out in single file on one side of the tracks. Lieutenant Toogood waved them on. Charlie turned back toward the looming maw of the tunnel and squared his shoulders. He shifted his .303 into a two-handed grip and resettled his pack.

"This is nothing for 13 Platoon," Muller said. He and Charlie picked up the pace and strode to the mouth of the tunnel.

It had not been a bright day but in spite of that it took a few minutes for Charlie's eyes to adjust to the reduced light. The tunnel grew darker and darker. A hundred yards in, Charlie glanced back and saw a glimmer of light that reflected off the raw rock walls. Ahead, there was nothing, just the feel of the rails against his feet as he blundered along them. He stepped to the right, feeling for the tunnel wall to give him a sense of direction. His foot struck something and he stumbled, cursing. His pack threw him off balance and he banged against the tunnel wall. He was down on his knees, feeling with one hand, rifle in the other, when he encountered a frozen cone a foot high.

"What the hell happened?" Muller whispered.

"Tripped on something. Ice by the feel of it."

Charlie stood and leaned briefly against the rock wall to catch his balance. He glanced back toward the vague sounds of the oncoming 13 Platoon but saw nothing. He stepped forward and bumped into an object that gave way and clattered onto the railbed.

Sergeant Price's low voice: "What's the holdup? Keep moving!"

"Ice," Muller responded. "Ice and... and..."

"Stalagmites?" said Charlie. His high school geography class, useful at last. "Watch your footing," he called back, then started ahead again, half crouching and feeling for safe footing as he and Muller made their way forward. The railbed was covered in ice.

It was hard to get a feel for progress with no visual marks to help.

"Did you guys stop for a lunch break?" Frenchy's voice, by the sound of it.

Charlie was glad to hear someone else tell him to shut up, as he imagined Chinese soldiers, alerted by the platoon's chatter, lying in ambush. Lying in wait the way the platoon had lain in wait and surprised the guerrillas back at Jujang li.

"The boys are keen to get out of this tunnel," Charlie said in an undertone, glad of Muller's steady presence beside him.

"No keener than I am."

Muller stumbled and muttered something under his breath.

"Just keep going," Charlie said. Just keep going. Christ. What if the tunnel was booby-trapped? He and Muller would never see a trip wire. Sergeant Swann, before Rowe was wounded in the Sten gun mishap, had shown the platoon how to make a booby-trap with a tin can, a string, and a grenade. He shook the thought from his head and kept moving.

"Light ahead," Muller said, his voice pinched.

There were fewer icy patches here, the footing more secure. Charlie and Muller edged close to the tunnel wall on the right, the outside of yet another curve, so they could see further ahead. Behind them the platoon was noisier now, encountering the icy patches.

"Speed it up, for Christ's sake. You guys taking a nap?" Frenchy again.

They pushed ahead, daylight beckoning. They must be almost out.

Muller stopped dead in his tracks, grabbing Charlie's arm. "What's that?"

Charlie peered ahead. The tunnel mouth was visible, the contrast bright against the interior. Something—a man? crouched, partially hidden behind a rock just outside the tunnel. Red Chinese? North Korean? His mind raced. If there was one, there could be a hundred. Sweat trickled down his spine.

Charlie glanced to the rear. He couldn't see the platoon, but he could hear them. Muffled voices, quiet clanking of equipment, the scrape of boots on rock. If this was a trap and the platoon kept coming they'd all be dead men. "Get back and warn the lieutenant," he said. "Tell him there's someone up there. I'll have a look."

Muller turned and disappeared back into the tunnel. Charlie kept his focus on the figure ahead. It hadn't stirred. Charlie's rifle was cocked. Behind him, the platoon went silent. He crouched, his rifle at his shoulder and aimed at the figure ahead. He took a deep breath and darted forward, moving fast.

A second figure came into sight, lying on its side. Charlie squinted against the daylight, his view of the world expanding the closer he approached the mouth of the tunnel. There was something odd about the reclining men. He blinked, not seeing weapons. The men didn't move.

They were dead. Long dead, maybe, given the freezing conditions. Three of them, stripped of weapons but still wearing padded Chinese winter uniforms and running shoes. There was no obvious sign of wounds, but black, frozen blood lay in a pool under one body.

Charlie released his a long-held breath. He scanned the surrounding hills, the bleak, snowy landscape, the clouds thickening overhead. The rusty tracks continued on in a widening valley. There was no movement. He turned and waved up Muller and the platoon. His platoon.

Three dead enemy didn't mean there weren't live ones around. While he waited for the platoon to emerge from the tunnel he moved forward fifty yards along the tracks. There was no sign of life ahead.

"Good job, corporal." Toogood gave him a curt nod as Charlie rejoined the platoon, Woody having replaced him as scout.

"Have to hand it to you, Charlie," Frenchy said. "Good to see you fight off those dead guys."

Chapter 11

Next day, they were two hours into their pursuit of the battalion. Orton scouted, with Lieutenant Toogood leading the rest of 13 Platoon along a shallow valley. They had left the tracks behind, striking off in a northwest direction. Charlie ran his thumbs under his shoulder straps, easing the weight of his pack. They had been on the move since clearing the tunnel, its dead Chinese soldiers left to guard the exit.

It was an area of low relief, surrounded by undulating hills that gained in height, each higher than the one before it. The hillsides were open and would provide little cover if they came under fire. Darkness wasn't far off.

There was no mistaking the fact that the countryside was in the grip of solid winter. Much of the ground was covered with dry, crusty snow, with deeper patches on north-facing slopes. Stunted trees rattled their thin branches in a cold wind. Charlie shivered in spite of the sweat that ran down his back. Here it was the third week of February, and back home on the west coast it wouldn't be unusual for daffodils to be poking out of the ground.

The platoon was headed north, aiming to join the rest of the Patricias. Radio contact was hit-and-miss, but they did pick up enough to know the battalion was in a battle. Lieutenant Toogood figured they had another eight miles to cover to get to the site, Hill 404.

"We gonna miss out?" Muller said.

Sergeant Price was close enough to hear. "Be careful what you wish for."

"Story of my life," Frenchy said. "Missed out on WW2, and here we go again."

Charlie had thought that many times, back in the safety of life in Canada. Here, marching toward battle in a foreign country, a nervousness about what was to come was offset by a determination to see action. Heck, they were trained and well led, Charlie told himself. Get on with it.

"Hold up." The lieutenant had his hand up at shoulder height. Orton had gone to ground, face down behind a patch of scrub brush.

Toogood waved the platoon down and crouched himself, shrugging out of his pack. He looked from side to side and reached for the binoculars hanging from his neck.

Charlie had Muller in front of him and Powell behind, not able to see much, between them and their packs. Sergeant Price scrambled past them to talk to Toogood. The lieutenant had his elbows propped on his pack, binoculars to his face, checking the horizon, as Orton squirmed back toward them.

Orton crawled back to Toogood and the two of them lay head-to-head, flat on the ground. Orton spoke in a low voice. "Something moved, sir, maybe a couple of hundred yards—"

A shot rang out and the lieutenant's rifle spun to the ground from where it had leaned against his pack. Toogood clapped his hands to his face and rolled onto his side.

There was shocked silence for an instant, then Sergeant Price had his weapon up, firing at a spot forward and to the right of their line of advance. "Beside that tree," he yelled.

Charlie saw a flash from the base of a tall tree silhouetted on the horizon. He scrambled to get his arms free of his pack, his rifle to his shoulder. He aimed and shot just as Sergeant Price bellowed, "Cease fire, cease fire."

"Black, over there. Look sharp." Price pointed to a slight rise in the ground, just a couple of feet high and twenty feet to the right. "Keep an all-round lookout. They could come from anywhere."

Charlie scrambled, keeping his head down but doing his best to scan the horizon, feeling exposed. His eyes came back to the skyline near the tree, where he could make out what could be the enemy, dark shapes hugging the ground. "Maybe six of them," he called out.

Price shouted. "Both Brens, wide right and move up fifty yards when I give the word. On my signal, the rest of you open up, aimed shots, make 'em keep their damn heads down."

"Now," Price said. Charlie aimed and fired. Scattered fire broke out, covering the Bren crews as they crawled off to the right.

"Cease fire. Fix bayonets."

Charlie's mouth was dry. He pulled his spike bayonet from its scabbard and snapped it onto his rifle barrel, his hands shaking, hoping he wouldn't get close enough to an enemy to use it.

His heart pounded, and his nose twitched as he breathed in the sharp odour of burnt powder. He had another round in the breech, rifle cocked, finger hovering over the trigger. The near ridgeline close to the tree from where the enemy had fired was still, nothing moving. He pulled the brim of his cap lower as if it would protect him as he scanned left and right.

Glancing over his shoulder he saw Toogood lying on his back in a slight hollow where he'd be out of the line of fire. Orton crouched beside him, a medical kit open and contents spread on the ground. Toogood was moving, gesturing with one arm, and Charlie breathed easier. Maybe it was nothing, a minor wound.

He squinted at the ridgeline with its lone tree two hundred yards away. Frenchy, Powell and Woody were much closer to the enemy and well off to the right, the Bren pressed against Powell's shoulder. 1 Section's Bren crew was just beyond them. The platoon's riflemen lay flat, weapons trained.

Something whipped past Charlie, like a minor disturbance in the air, as he heard a distant rifle shot. Christ! he thought and tried to flattened himself further.

"Stand by," Price said. "On my order, Brens provide covering fire. Two seconds later, we're all up."

"Now," Price's voice rang out, punctuated by the Brens as they let it rip.

"Up, up," he shouted. Charlie leapt to his feet, doing his best to keep up with the sergeant, rifle in both hands, bayonet extended, his heart thudding. Something zipped past his head. *Bastards*, he thought.

Almost like the drills back in Wainwright, the machine gun fire from the Brens raking the ground where the enemy waited, getting closer. Fifty yards. Twenty yards.

Price hit the deck. "Down, down!" He looked at Charlie. "Grenade."

Charlie jerked a grenade from his webbing and pulled the pin, waiting for Price's order, the firing lever firm in his grip. Price counted to three, and he and Charlie flung their grenades as the Brens continued controlled fire past the prone riflemen.

Charlie covered his ears, waiting. The grenades exploded. Price jumped to his feet and led the riflemen in a final charge. A Chinese soldier crouched behind the tree. He fired once but was cut down by a fusillade of bullets.

In front of them the north face of the hill fell away, a jumbled landscape of gullies, rocks, and scattered leafless brush.

The dead soldier's left foot wore a ragged bandage. He had been wounded before the attack, left behind in the rush to escape the Canadians. The only other traces of the enemy were a smoldering fire in a small pit and some scattered rice.

Charlie went back to help with Toogood. He picked up the lieutenant's pack and rifle, while Orton guided the lieutenant, both of whose eyes were obscured by his bandages. Toogood was silent. Price had ordered sentries already, two of whom watched the route back down the hill as the three of them made their way up.

Orton helped the lieutenant to sit and lean against his pack, down off the skyline.

"What's the situation, sergeant?" asked Toogood. "Anybody else hit?"

"No sir. We have good vis all round. No sign of the enemy."

"OK. Let's get dug in, pronto. And in the meantime, get me some help with this." Toogood put his hand on the bandage wrapped around his head. He looked like a mummy from the jaw line up.

Price assigned locations for the platoon's trenches. Charlie's was close to the tree, and when he attempted to dig he ran into its roots. He was relieved when Orton interrupted. "Give me a hand here, Charlie."

He unwrapped most of the outer bandage from Toogood's head, revealing a blood-soaked mass of gauze pads. "Hold this."

Charlie held the pads in place, while Orton produced a tube of ointment which he smeared on a new pad. Orton held the clean pad in one hand and he and Charlie gently eased off the old ones. Charlie had a quick view of Toogood's wound, a jagged rip in the skin and flesh that started on his right forehead and continued in a deep furrow, taking off most of the eyebrow and raking across the bridge of his nose. Blood welled up as Orton applied the new dressing. Charlie held it in place while Orton wound a long fresh bandage around Toogood's head, taking his time, getting it right. He angled the wraps so the lieutenant's left eye was uncovered, finishing off with adhesive tape.

"There you go, sir."

Toogood blinked his good eye. "That's better."

Sergeant Price had moved back to squat by Toogood and nodded his approval. "Good as gold, sir. Couldn't have done better myself. Corporal," he said to Charlie, "take Orton and get back to work on that trench. Make room for Lieutenant Toogood as well as yourselves."

The two of them dug, bashing through the tenacious tree roots and the rocky soil, working hard to get a trench big enough for three men. Light was fading before they finished, a cold breeze reminding them winter wasn't done with them.

Toogood and Sergeant Price had had a discussion a few feet away, just after the platoon had eaten their cold rations. Price was adamant that Nogood needed proper medical treatment as soon as possible, while the lieutenant put up a fight but had to admit he wasn't much use to the platoon in his present condition. Lieutenant Toogood walked unsteadily to where his radioman crouched and picked up the handset.

It froze hard in the night. Charlie had sentry duty from 0200 until 0400 hours, which was fine with him as he hadn't been able to sleep anyway.

Once he was relieved he tried to sleep, but his mind churned. Charlie wondered whether the lieutenant had been convinced that he needed to be evacuated. It made Charlie nervous, Nogood wounded and perhaps on his way out. It was one thing to lose any soldier, but Toogood was popular with the men and what was even more important, well respected for his leadership. He'd most likely be gone as soon as he could be transported out to get proper treatment.

Deciding it wasn't his job to solve that problem, Charlie tried to force misgivings about Nogood's wound and what his departure would mean to the troops from his mind. He dozed, and somehow his concern led him to memories of his brother. Jeff, his brother and hero, had always been larger than life to Charlie. Six years older, he was a star in high school when Charlie was still in grade school. He could swim faster, run farther, and play baseball better than anyone else Charlie knew. Bill wasn't the only member of the family who had a huge hole in his heart when Jeff died.

Thinking about Jeff led to thoughts of home and Wanda.

The Blacks had lived within a mile of Wanda's family, the Carters, for years, but it wasn't until two years before he enlisted that Charlie had become aware of her. One of Charlie's pals, Ken, had been a year behind him in high school and played on the basketball team. Attending one of Ken's games, Charlie noticed a trio of girls sitting down a row and a few places to the right on the gym's bleachers. No, it occurred to him later, he noticed one of the three. She had long blond hair and even from that distance he saw she had blue eyes that were at times directed over her shoulder in his general direction. Before the game was over he was startled to realize who she was. Somehow a few days later he happened to drive by her school bus stop and saved her from walking home in the rain.

Wanda, the only girlfriend he'd ever had, who wouldn't answer his letters. Wanda, the girl who took him into her bedroom when her parents were away for a weekend, hesitant but determined. With whom he had made love, the first time for both of them. But that happy memory was overlaid by that of the last time he saw her, when she'd pushed him out the door, furious at him for signing on with the Special Force.

Sleep was out of the question. Peering out over the dark hills with the sound of soughing wind in his ears, Charlie wondered what would next go wrong with 13 Platoon.

2 Section, Charlie's section, was in trenches to the west of the tree with 1 Section was dug in to the east, strung out just on the forward slope, the high ground behind them.

After morning stand-to Sergeant Price conferred with 1 Section, then came over to where 2 Section huddled together.

"Here's what's happening," Price said. "We've got to get the lieutenant's wound looked after properly, and it'll take a section to provide enough security to get him out. That'll leave me with the other section."

Not much of a unit, Charlie thought. Hope we don't get jumped when we're down to one section. "Which section will take him out?"

"Yours. Be ready for a slog of about eight hours round-trip," said Price. "You'll be met by a patrol from A Echelon, somewhere between here and the tunnel we went through yesterday. A replacement for Lieutenant Toogood will return with you." A Echelon, Charlie knew, was where supplies, extra equipment, and reinforcement personnel were stationed a few miles behind the front lines.

"Who's the new platoon officer?" Frenchy said.

"Lieutenant Strachan."

"Strachan!" said Muller. "He's a—"

"Can it, Muller. There'll be none of that bullshit in this platoon." Price looked at Charlie. "You and your boys take small packs with water and rations. We'll hold the fort here. You're out of here in ten minutes," he said, and stepped away to talk to Lieutenant Toogood.

———

The trip south was more down hill than up, but even so, Charlie's legs burned. He and Powell had split Lieutenant Toogood's gear between them. The lieutenant looked shaky. He was able to walk on his own, but his good eye was squinting in the day's cloud-obscured light, what could be seen of his face pinched with pain. Charlie wondered if Sergeant Price had been a little optimistic about an eight-hour round trip, and in fact six hours passed before Charlie spotted movement on a sidehill a half mile away. A few minutes later he made out their Canadian uniforms.

"Okay, that's them," he said. Toogood looked pale. "You okay, sir?"

"Right as rain, corporal."

Charlie led the way down to a low spot between hills where the two groups rendezvoused. The newcomers numbered six men, including a radioman. They were commanded by a sergeant Charlie didn't recognize, and with them was a tall, athletic-looking lieutenant.

Lieutenant Toogood shook hands with his replacement. "You have a couple of good sections here," he said.

"I look forward to meeting them all," the lieutenant said. "Sorry about your wound."

Powell reorganized Nogood's gear, transferring it from his and Charlie's packs to the lieutenant's new escort.

Toogood turned to Charlie. "Take care of yourselves," he said.

"You too, sir." Charlie wondered if he'd ever see him again.

CHAPTER 12

"What are we hanging around for?" Muller spoke quietly, but Charlie thought their new platoon officer heard him anyway.

"Right, Lance Corporal. Have the men fall in. I wish to inspect."

"Inspect, sir?" Charlie hesitated and turned to his section. "You heard the lieutenant," he said. "Fall in. Square yourselves off."

They shuffled into a line and stood at ease.

"Jesus Christ," Frenchy muttered under his breath. "What the hell are we doing?"

Charlie called them to attention. He wasn't going to salute in the field.

"My name is Strachan," the lieutenant said. "You'll find me tough but fair. Now, let's have a look at you."

Charlie was on the end of the line, and Strachan started with him, looking him up and down. "What are you doing with binoculars, lance corporal?"

"Lieutenant Toogood left them with me, sir." Charlie tried to keep his voice neutral. Strachan was one of those officers who rubbed his men the wrong way. Like calling Charlie 'Lance Corporal' instead of just 'Corporal'. No doubt Strachan wouldn't dream of referring to Big Jim Stone as anything other than 'Colonel Stone' although his official rank was 'Lieutenant-Colonel'.

Strachan's eyes narrowed. "Don't I know you from somewhere?"

"Maybe Wainwright, sir."

Strachan moved on, picking out some irregularity with everyone. He paid no attention whatsoever to their rifles, which Charlie thought odd, given that they were in a shooting war.

Nogood never inspected them in a formal way, but he sure as heck paid close attention to their weapons.

Charlie was wondering if he'd ever get back to the trench on the hilltop, a place where he could hunker down and catch some sleep. They set off with a scout out front. Strachan, carrying a Sten, stayed in the middle of the formation.

Strachan called a halt after a couple of hours. "Come, come, lance corporal. Surely we can pick it up a little."

"Yes, sir. The men have put in a long day on the march already. And the route doesn't get any easier."

"Very well."

Let him settle in, Charlie thought. He hasn't been where we have.

After another thirty minutes Strachan held up his hand. The men dropped to the ground, happy for the break. And Charlie was mindful that it also made him less of a target.

Strachan had a map in hand. "Are you sure we're headed in the right direction, Lance Corporal?"

"Yes, sir. This is the route we came down with Lieutenant Toogood."

"Not according to my map." Strachan pointed with his finger. "Look here. I've marked the coordinates 13 Platoon radioed to Tactical Headquarters." He waved at the topography ahead of them. He glanced again at his map and consulted his compass. Folding his map, he jammed it into a pocket and indicated a line of travel off to the right, waving his arm. "Right, then," he said. "That notch in the hills up there? That's your mark."

"Yes, sir." Charlie gestured. The men stood and followed him as he led the way. Their path was partially blocked by a very steep slope which they circled around before getting back on Strachan's chosen route.

An hour later Charlie had a quiet word with the lieutenant.

"Corporal," Strachan said, "you may have been here before, but I can assure you I can read a map."

Charlie forced himself to be patient, very aware of the hours slipping away. The time used up escorting Lieutenant Toogood out for medical attention plus the confusion on their proper route back to where Sergeant Price and 1 Section waited meant they were at least another day behind the rest of the battalion.

A half mile further on they stopped again. Strachan pored over his map. Red-faced, he folded the map and tucked it away. "Lead on, corporal," he said.

Which was fine with Charlie, because while scouting ahead he couldn't make out the expletive-loaded grumbling that arose from the men behind him.

For an hour-and-a-half they retraced their footsteps before altering course to the west. It was another three hours and dark was closing in before Charlie recognized the horizon with the lone tree on it.

Charlie was happy to have Sergeant Price greet their new platoon commander. Let him deal with Strachan. The lieutenant didn't have much to say when Price introduced him to the rest of the men.

Charlie breathed easier when he saw that in their absence the boys had deepened and enlarged all their trenches. After evening stand-to he slept like a dead man until he was called two hours later for sentry duty.

———

The next day was February 21, and the hills of Korea gave 13 Platoon another taste of Asian winter. When Charlie was roused by Muller he struggled to his feet and flung off snow that had accumulated on his poncho. A four-inch layer of snow greeted them, but that was just a curtain-raiser, as the falling snow gave way to freezing rain. 13 Platoon ate and marched early, catching up with the rest of the battalion by mid-morning.

The troops waited in the snow while Lieutenant Strachan attended a meeting for the officers where, among other things, he received orders from D Company's commander, Major Swinton. Strachan was in a snappish mood when he returned from the O-group.

"Thanks to the time we lost getting back here, we missed the action on Hill 404." He looked around at the twenty men of his platoon. "I don't intend to have that happen again. Sergeant Price, we're on the move in ten minutes. Our next objective is Hill 444. We'll be in support of 10 Platoon." He shouldered his Sten and walked back toward the radioman, who was crouched by Strachan's pack waiting for orders.

Charlie knew 10 Platoon was commanded by Lieutenant Mike Levy, one of the few officers around wearing parachute wings. Rumour had it Levy had been a POW of the Japanese in the Second War, escaped, and earned a medal while in command of a guerrilla force.

Strachan was tied up on the radio for a few minutes checking communications.

Price spoke in an undertone. "Yes, boys, we missed out on Hill 404. But don't worry. There are lots more in front of us."

Charlie looked over Price's shoulder, but visibility was reduced to a couple of miles in light rain and mist. The hills in their future were out there somewhere.

"I hear two of the officers took bad falls on 404 and they're out of action," Price continued. "So watch yourselves. Odds are 444 will be just as bad."

The platoon set off in support of Lieutenant Levy and his 10 Platoon, following two hundred yards behind them. It was hard going. Charlie marched along after Price but in front of Powell, who carried the Bren. Muller, his number two, carried extra magazines for the automatic weapon and stuck close. Frenchy was ahead as scout.

Their route followed a muddy path through rice paddies churned up by the passage of the thirty-five-odd men of 10 Platoon. Charlie tried to concentrate on the task at hand and not let his mind settle on the risks of attacking a hill occupied by Red Chinese. There were a lot more of them on earth than there were Canadians. Maybe it was just a question of who had the most at any one location, but he worried about the odds.

The clatter of medium machine gun fire from somewhere ahead brought him back to the reality of the battlefield. Strachan gestured and the platoon hit the dirt, crouching while the lieutenant figured out what to do. A minute later he signalled again, waving the platoon forward. Charlie lurched to his feet, shifted his pack on his back as he regained his balance, and followed.

They were low in a valley, crossing rice paddies that spread out ahead of them. Perhaps three hundred yards ahead the ground ascended steeply to what he guessed was Hill 444's summit.

A bullet whizzed by Charlie's head as he registered a new burst of automatic fire. He splashed face down in the paddy. The firing continued, coming in short bursts. Bullets were erratic, a few ricocheting off the water of the paddy or on the other side of a foot-high dyke, but most going high. Charlie kept his head down, figuring he could live with the stink of the rice paddy and water that seeped into his clothing a lot easier than he could live with taking a bullet.

"Where's that Bren?" Price shouted. "I want covering fire, and I want it now!"

Powell was face down, well out to Charlie's left, squirming to get the light machine gun up on its bipod and directed at the hill. Charlie was between Powell and Muller, number two on the Bren, so he pulled a magazine from his pocket and crawled to Powell's side.

The enemy gunfire stopped.

"Just to the right of that rock," Price shouted.

Powell adjusted his aim. "Ready."

Muller crawled around Charlie and came up between him and Powell, getting into position as number two on the Bren. That meant Charlie was free of supplying ammo to the Bren, he'd have to stand up in the face of the enemy fire, he'd—

"Covering fire," Price said, and on the left end of their line the Bren banged into action.

Price jumped to his feet and charged forward. "Up, up, let's see you up," he shouted. Charlie drove himself to his feet and veered right to stay out of the machine gun's line of fire. He followed Price, aware of others around him.

Powell fired steady bursts. Price reached the cover of a dyke at the edge of an elevated paddy and crouched behind it. Charlie splashed down beside him. Powell's Bren lay silent for the moment. 1 Section's Bren fired a couple more bursts.

Desultory fire came again from the base of the hill.

Sergeant Price glanced back over his shoulder and waved for the Bren gunners to recommence firing. Both let fly. Price, Charlie and the rest of the platoon were on their feet again. Charlie saw two or three figures on the hillside running to higher ground and disappearing into the scattered rocks and brush and folds of the hillside. He joined Price on the ground close to the base of Hill 444.

Price ordered suppressing fire, and the platoon responded with a staccato barrage of .303 rounds from their Lee-Enfields. Muller, Powell, and the 1 Section Bren gunners rejoined their comrades.

"Cease fire, cease fire."

The enemy fire also had stopped. There were no visible targets. Charlie jammed a five-round clip into his rifle, so he knew he had at least that many ready to go. His ears rang from the sharp crack of rifle fire either side of him. Still alive, still unhurt, after coming under fire. He felt his heartrate slow. He could do this—*they* could do this.

Somebody nudged him on the leg. It was Frenchy, who pointed back to the paddy they'd left behind. A solitary figure walked toward them, the mud and muck from the bottom of the paddy dripping off his face and his Sten gun. It almost obscured the lieutenant's pips on his shoulders.

To Charlie's relief the anticipated battle for the summit of Hill 444 never occurred, the Chinese withdrawing before the Canadians mounted their attack. The Patricias dug in on the summit that night, burrowing through the snow to chip away at the frozen ground.

"Like marmots on a Rocky Mountain meadow," said Alberta boy Orton.

Charlie shivered beside him. "Except they've got more fur than we have."

CHAPTER 13

There was no relief from the cold in the following days. On February 28 13 Platoon emerged from their trenches before first light and went to morning stand-to, everybody alert and watching. The day before they'd advanced part-way up massive Hill 419 in the face of long-range harassing rifle fire and dug in.

13 Platoon had supported D Company, following along behind. Their instructions had been to stay on D's left flank, but the topography of the hill made that problematic. Deep defiles and narrow ridges combined with heavy brush meant there were few possible paths to the summit. The enemy's defences held the advantage with mortars, machine guns and rifles zeroed in on the narrow approaches open to the attackers.

Charlie frowned as he looked long and hard at the snowy landscape. The sky was overcast and threatening, but there was a certain cold beauty to the slopes around them. Back in his school days, Charlie had often hoped for a good snowfall and the cancellation of classes. It wasn't so friendly on high ridges deep in the Korean Peninsula, where the higher they climbed the deeper the snow.

Off to one side of where the men gathered, Lieutenant Strachan studied the hillside above them through his binoculars.

Price went from man to man in the whole platoon, running his eyes over them, a casual but thorough inspection. Looking at both sections: their rifles, the two Brens, ammunition, grenades. Spare C-rations and all the other paraphernalia carried by the troops. He called them together and Lieutenant Strachan addressed them.

"We missed out on Hill 404," he said, looking like he was affected more than most of them by the cold, his movements jerky. Even his voice sounded stiff. "This is our day. We have a specific route to try, independent of D Company. The rest of the battalion is attacking along more obvious routes. The hope is they'll draw the enemy's fire, leaving us to come up on them unawares. Watch your footing. It's going to be steep, and the snow doesn't help."

Strachan paused to look around at the snow-covered ground they'd be attacking, but now he turned back to them. "Single file, five yard spacing. Don't bunch up. When—not if—we come under fire, hit the deck and get behind some cover." He looked around, focussed on Price. "Over to you, sergeant."

"Sir. 1 Section to lead. After me." He strode off, starting up a narrow path that could have been a game trail at one time but perhaps also frequented by villagers scavenging for fuel for cook-stoves.

Price moved with steady deliberation, watching all around but being very careful where he put his weight. Behind him came 1 Section with Lieutenant Strachan in their midst and Charlie leading 2 Section in their turn. By the time Charlie was on it the trail was well broken, but packed snow and ice under-foot made it slippery and dangerous.

The only available route was on the spine of a ridge that narrowed as they went along. Charlie tried not to think about what easy targets they'd make.

Making slow progress, the thin file of heavy-laden men snaked its way up the slope.

Coming to a fold in their ridge that dropped them out of sight of anybody watching from above, Strachan called a break. The troops flopped down, pulling out their canteens. Price had them up again in minutes. "Too cold to lie around, boys," he said. "On your feet!"

Ten minutes into the next steep pitch Charlie heard small-arms fire coming from somewhere above and to their right. Maybe that meant the plan was working and the Chinese, other-wise engaged, could be caught unawares by their miniscule force. Men gripped their rifles a little tighter, looked ready to return fire at a moment's notice. They pushed on. Charlie checked over his shoulder from time to time, making sure his section wasn't bunching up.

A whistling sound stopped them in their tracks, and a heartbeat later they had flattened themselves in the snow. A mortar bomb exploded near the front of the platoon.

"Everybody down," Charlie shouted, knowing his section wouldn't have waited for the order. He glanced back at his section, which was backstopped by Frenchy who brought up the rear. The men were sprawled at intervals on the trail or close to it, taking what cover they could in the brush and rocks. On both sides the ridge dropped away at a steep angle in narrow defiles, the bottoms anywhere from a few feet to ten yards or more below them.

Three more bombs fell close, marching down the trail toward them. Charlie covered his head, wondering if his time had come. A distant machine gun opened up. Someone cried out from up at the front of the formation.

Charlie looked back. Muller was the closest man to him, a good five yards away. "You okay, Muller?"

"Yeah, but I think I just pissed my pants."

Charlie doubted that but grinned.

"Warms you up, anyway," said Powell from down the slope.

All but the first mortar seemed to have been just off target, landing on downslopes to explode without hitting anyone. The automatic fire kept coming, clipping the brush inches above Charlie's head.

The screaming died away into an ongoing moan, punctuated by a cry for help. Charlie could see Sergeant Price and another soldier tending to someone up the slope, keeping their heads down.

"Anybody hit back there?" Charlie said, looking back at Powell, who had the Bren up on its bipod, poking its nose up the hill. Powell passed on his question, shaking his head after a few seconds. "All okay," he said.

"Can anybody see where that gun is?" Strachan called out.

Charlie couldn't, but he was pretty sure the machine gunner was at long range. He took a deep breath and knelt on one knee.

Bullets spattered around him as he dropped flat. "Just to the right of that rock face at two o'clock." He aimed and fired his own weapon where he had seen the enemy gun's flashes.

Powell let fly with the Bren, its stuttering fire mixing with the background of staccato .303 rounds. 1 Section's Bren was firing as well, adding to the bark of gunshots and melding in a curtain of sound.

"Cease fire, cease fire," Price shouted after only a few seconds.

Charlie stayed flat, his rifle cocked. H thumbed the safety on, his hands shaking, his heart pounding.

Complete and shocking silence ensued. No enemy machine gun, and no more incoming mortars. The man in 1 Section who had been hit by the first mortar bomb had also gone silent.

Price called back to Strachan, who was making his way forward. "McInnis, sir. He's gone." He lowered his voice. He and Strachan talked, then Strachan waved the radioman over and spoke a few words into the handset. Calling in the casualty so McInnis's body would be recovered later, Charlie assumed.

Price moved back to the head of 1 Section and got the men moving again. Charlie noticed that Lieutenant Strachan dropped back to the end of 1 Section, instead of being toward the front.

When Charlie came abreast of the dead private, Lieutenant Strachan was still there, looking down at the body, his face pinched and white. He glanced around, not looking at anybody, and hurried forward.

—

Price led them on an angle toward higher ground, picking a careful route out of sight of the Chinese on the summit. An hour into the renewed grind up the hill, the distant automatic fire and mortar activity started again. Strachan called a halt. The troops gathered around him. "We're about to come in view of the enemy," he said. "They may have thought they'd forced us to withdraw, but we're going to give them a surprise. We're Patricias, and our comrades are counting on us. We all know our jobs. Let's do them." He nodded at Sergeant Price.

"Our route is around that steep ground ahead of us," Price said, waving at a near-vertical rock face. "It looks like the slope flattens out to the left. When I get there, I want 1 Section on my left and 2 Section on my right, Bren guns at the extreme left and right. We'll drop down, and I want you Bren gunners to get ready. On my signal, suppressing fire from the Brens on the upper reaches of the hill. Riflemen to move up. Standard procedure. Questions?"

There were no questions. Lieutenant Strachan set off toward the left of the rock face, angling uphill. The troops followed, 1 Section then Sergeant Price then Charlie's 2 Section. The steep slope on their left flank confined them to a narrow path.

Charlie pictured the coming action. He anticipated a turn to the right as they cleared the granite face. Powell, behind him with the Bren, would move up and to the right, as planned. They'd execute a classic bounding attack on the Chinese. He was ready: magazine full, one up the spout, safety on. Charlie felt sweat trickle down his back, saying a silent prayer that they'd catch the Chinese off guard.

Strachan edged left and dropped back, clearing the way for the platoon to spread out as they advanced.

A machine gun blasted into action from their left front. Two men in 1 Section fell, the enfilade automatic fire raking them. Charlie felt like he was suspended in air, couldn't get down fast enough. Bullets ricocheted off rocks and tore up earth. The men were all on the ground, trying to take advantage of the minimal features on the bare slope.

All except Lieutenant Strachan, who turned back downslope, wide-eyed, running, somehow not hit. He disappeared from Charlie's sight.

Sergeant Price was between 2 Section and the enemy machine gun. Lying flat, he said, "Give me that," gesturing to Powell, who slid him his Bren. Price locked down the bipod, manoeuvred it into firing position, and let fly at the Chinese gun. 1 Section's Bren was already firing. Charlie had spare Bren magazines. He crawled up beside Price, ready to feed them in.

Price stopped his staccato bursts for a moment. "Everybody back," he yelled. "Everybody."

Charlie stayed with him as the other members of 13 Platoon squirmed backward. Heard above the rattle of the machine guns a mortar bomb exploded somewhere behind them.

Charlie, acting as number two, slapped a fresh magazine into the Bren. Price waved him down the hill, fired off the full magazine, and crawled back himself. Once they were back below the machine gunner's horizon, the survivors gathered in the shadow of the granite face. They had the bleak satisfaction of watching mortar rounds fly over their position to explode on the slope below.

Price posted two men as lookouts, watching for a possible Chinese counterattack. Two volunteers crept back up the slope and recovered the corpse of a member of 1 Section whose body had been pounded by the initial fusilade. A second man had also been hit, but he was able to make it back on his own. Orton volunteered and helped deal with his wound, a deep furrow on his rib cage where a round had plowed a painful path.

Charlie heard a shout from down the steep scree slope below them. He and Price looked over the edge to see Lieutenant Strachan, a hundred feet down, standing on one foot and leaning against a large boulder. Price's eyes widened and he glanced at Charlie.

Frenchy had come up beside them. "I'll get him," he said, and half jumped and half slid down the slope to where Strachan waited. Charlie saw them exchange a few words. Frenchy draped Strachan's arm over his shoulders, then supported him as they made their way back up the slope, picking a stable route to one side of the scree. The lieutenant couldn't put any weight on his left foot.

For the next three days the Patricias hung back on the lower slopes of Hill 419. The weather continued as cold, and the hill stayed as steep. The battalion sent probing patrols up toward the summit, only to be turned back by well-sited machine guns; the

Chinese seemed determined to hang on. Led by Sergeant Price, 13 Platoon made one such foray backing up D Company but were ordered to withdraw before contacting the enemy.

They made it back to their bivouac area in midafternoon, and settled in to fifty percent stand-to, their normal routine when in the battle zone. Sergeant Price went to receive further orders from Battalion Headquarters.

Muller dug, wanting his and Charlie's trench deeper and safer than they had managed earlier. Charlie was on stand-to, keeping an eye out. Frenchy walked over.

Muller straightened up and took a break from his labour down in the trench. "Too bad Strachan didn't break his leg yesterday," he said to Frenchy.

"No such luck. I couldn't see anything wrong with it, and Orton checked it out. Bruised, he thought."

Charlie didn't like Strachan, but as an NCO he knew nothing good could come from joining his men in a griping session about their platoon officer. "We'll know soon," he said. "Here comes Price."

Back from seeking fresh instructions, Sergeant Price called the platoon together.

"Been a change," he said.

Charlie tensed. Changes could mean bad news.

"Lieutenant Strachan's injury is worse than we thought," Price said.

"Good," Frenchy muttered. If Price heard him, he ignored it.

"I'll be acting platoon officer until we get a new one." Price looked them over. "Don't think that means discipline goes to hell. Anybody screws up, it'll embarrass me. You don't want to embarrass me." He stared. "Right, Frenchy?"

"Right, sergeant."

Price told the platoon that one of the factors that made the hill so hard to take was an adjoining higher hill, 614. It was also occupied by the Chinese, and from there they could look down on 419 and assist their comrades with machine guns and mortars. The Australians were assigned Hill 614, and like the Canadians, had been bloodied in several attempts to dislodge the Chinese. A last hard push by them had done the trick the previous day, which should make things easier for the Patricias on 419.

On the fourth day 13 Platoon was once again moving toward the summit. For hours they had listened and watched as distant artillery pounded the Chinese positions. A regiment of New Zealand artillery was part of the 27th Brigade, along with the Patricias, Australians, and two British regiments. The Kiwis were armed with 25-pounders, able to hit targets from five miles back.

Charlie had known nothing about the army, let alone the artillery, when he enlisted. One thing he knew now, for sure, was that he was damn glad to have artillery in support.

"Hard to believe anybody can live through that," Charlie said. "I almost feel sorry for them."

Muller was in line behind Charlie. "I don't feel sorry for anybody out to kill me. Let them bloody well go home, and we can finish this war pretty fast against the North Koreans."

Charlie wondered if the Chinese felt like strangers in a strange land, the way he did. He didn't bother saying that to Muller, who kept talking.

"I say, blow them all to bits. We didn't come here to back off."

"Nobody's backing off," Charlie said. They fell silent.

The Patricias knew they were there to make sure Korea didn't fall to Communism, and the North Koreans had attacked the South, setting off the whole war. Still, Charlie wondered if the UN had pushed it too far, chasing the North Koreans all the way to the Chinese border at the Yalu River. Maybe the Chinese soldiers didn't have a choice about being at war, any more than the American conscripts did.

Two US Thunder Jets closed fast from behind them. The platoon instinctively crouched, the aircraft coming straight in, only to swoop low over their heads and streak toward the summit. Objects tiny in the distance tumbled from the jets, and an instant later the top of the hill burst into flame.

"Napalm," Price said. "Cannisters of napalm."

"Holy shit," Muller said, eyes on the conflagration only a kilometre away. "Thank God for the US Air Force. Those guys should be finished. Nobody can survive that."

The jets circled and swooped in again and again, strafing the ground they had already napalmed. The furious noise of the machine guns and screaming jet engines rose to a crescendo that died as the aircraft rose high in the sky and turned away to disappear over the far side of the hill.

Charlie thought about it. Inhumane and ugly, but it was a shooting war, and he was glad to have all he help the Americans could provide.

—

Four hours later 13 Platoon moved in single file through a scorched landscape, remnants of foliage still smoking. An ugly stench battered their nostrils, a mix of residual gasoline fumes from the napalm and the repulsive reek from twisted, burnt bodies. The incinerated bodies were almost unrecognizable as human remains, scattered on the ground or in heaps in what had been defensive trenches.

Sergeant Price led them to one side, clear of the napalm's footprint. Charlie was exhausted by the days spent climbing up and down the slopes of Hill 419 and the ongoing cold.

Price marked out where he wanted their trenches and ordered them to dig in, telling them they'd be able to relax to twenty-five percent when they finished.

Charlie noticed a group of silent soldiers examining something fifty yards away, Curiosity piqued, he went to have a look. Stretched out on the snow were four bodies the men recognized as Canadians. Patricias. Dead and stripped naked.

Price and Muller had walked up beside him.

"Poor buggers," Muller said. "You don't want to get captured by the Chinks."

"At least now they'll get a proper burial." Price turned away. "And get those damn trenches dug."

—

"Look at this, Charlie," Powell said. He held the Bren cradled in his arms. It was cocked, ready to fire.

Charlie was beyond shivering, figuring it had to be twenty below zero. He stamped his feet and nodded at Powell. "That thing loaded?"

"Yup." Powell pointed the Bren at a spot above the horizon and pulled the trigger. Nothing happened. "It's so cold the oil in the mechanism has turned solid. This gun won't shoot!" He grinned. "Good thing we're home free for now."

Powell was happy, a weapon to service. He was already hunting for a clean rag to use to wipe off excess oil and get his Bren functional. Charlie left him to it.

"Struck it lucky for once," Woody said. His and Charlie's trench was located in a rare site with easy digging. He tossed his shovel to the ground. "So, what are we missing now? Oh yeah. An Oscar's Steakhouse. Man, am I—"

Charlie was thinking he'd settle for a White Spot burger, when Woody stopped talking, his mouth open. Charlie looked behind him. Making his way up the last steep pitch to the summit was a short Korean in tattered layers of clothing, a wooden A-frame on his back. Lashed to the A-frame was a large crate.

Another figure, equally loaded, heaved into sight. A sergeant hurried over to direct the newcomers toward the company headquarters. Charlie walked closer to the downslope, and saw a long file of Korean porters.

"I guess I'll settle for a C-ration," Woody said. "I don't see a T-bone in that mix."

This was the first time Charlie had seen the porters in action.

"Wonder if any of them come from that village we protected," Woody said.

Charlie wondered, too, but they'd seen a lot of abandoned or destroyed villages. He hoped the women and children there were still safe.

CHAPTER 14

I3 Platoon was dug in on a spur of Hill 419 that stretched to the west from the main summit occupied by the battalion.

Charlie was on watch during the two-hour stretch before morning stand-to. The night remained cold, the sky clear. High and bright, the moon washed out the earlier starlight. Charlie's trench gave him a sweeping view of the Korean landscape, a series of hills overlapping and succeeding one another stretching as far as he could see. Toward dawn the more distant peaks became gauzy with mist, the beauty of the scene contrasting with the ugliness of their war.

Not a sound reached him, the near-constant wind typical of their elevated hilltop absent. But here, high on the shoulder of 419, the reek of war assaulted him with the tang of burnt rubber and a smell of napalm-borne gasoline.

He had seen countless abandoned and flattened or burned villages that bore mute testimony to their former residents, now dead or homeless refugees. The roads were lined with evidence of the war's waste and destruction, the remnants of thousands of crippled military vehicles: tanks, trucks, jeeps, half-tracks.

Patricias he had come to know were wounded, killed, or missing. At times he'd witnessed the whole brigade, hundreds of men, under fire. He could only imagine the tens, even hundreds of thousands of men on both sides who had fought from one end of the Korean Peninsula to the other. Struggling and dying or surviving, depending on the luck of the draw.

He gave a thought to the US Marines, a proud force which had earlier reeled back under Chinese pressure, escaping from the Chosin Reservoir to the coast and evacuation. The 8th Army, caught off guard and sent packing from the banks of the Yalu to south of the 38th parallel.

Charlie looked around at 13 Platoon's trenches, where one man in four was on watch, his head sticking up from his trench. Their platoon was a tiny part of the battalion, and 2PPCLI itself a small cog in a huge UN army once again pursuing the Communist forces north. But Charlie's war was fought at an intimate level, rifle against machine gun, bayonet against grenade. His platoon had suffered multiple casualties and two men killed on 419, facts that preyed on his mind.

Peering at the near horizon, he saw no movement. All was quiet, the artillery silent, American aircraft still on their landing fields or offshore aircraft carriers until dawn, after which they'd prowl the skies. He checked his watch. Time for morning stand-to. He went to shake Sergeant Price, who was already awake, then called the rest of 2 Section. Their day was underway.

—

"Okay, here's the drill." Sergeant Price was back from O-group with the D Company officers. He held up a map, pointing to it as he talked. "Six miles from here is Hill 423. The Aussies cleared the Chinese off it ten days ago, but Colonel Stone has been ordered to make sure they haven't returned. He's given D Company plus 13 Platoon the job of checking it out. The last thing we need is the Reds regrouping behind us as we move forward."

"What's the rest of the battalion doing while we do that?" Frenchy said. "I heard we were due to get out of the line for a few days."

"Don't you worry, Frenchy, everybody's got a job to do. Nobody's getting a break."

"Wouldn't surprise me if they were. What's their task?"

"No need for you to know, Frenchy. Wouldn't want you getting captured and blabbing to the Chinese."

Frenchy rolled his eyes.

Price carried on. "First thing today the Americans will do a fly-over on 423, see if they can spot any Chinese. Unlikely to see them even if they are there, the buggers able to hide out all day.

That'll leave it up to us." He paused. "Thirty minutes, then we're on our way to have a look."

13 Platoon wasn't acting independently this time. D Company's 10 Platoon led the way, with Price and 13 Platoon close behind. After them came 11 and 12 Platoons, all in single file with five yards between men. An impressive sight, the sinuous formation wending its way along sidehills and up and down across low ridges, anywhere but along the road on the valley floor, making its way to Hill 423. A hundred or so men loaded down with the usual paraphernalia: rifles and light machine guns, anti-tank Bazookas, shovels, picks, spare magazines and bandoliers, and the dozens of items in their packs.

Charlie's confidence had been shaken by the tough, multiday battle on 419, but he breathed easier in the current formation, feeling a lot more confident with Sergeant Price in charge in place of Lieutenant Strachan. Price had an aura of invincibility about him, and it was obvious the battalion's leadership had confidence in him, leaving him to act as platoon officer.

D Company augmented with 13 Platoon reached the hill by 1600 hours. Deployed in sections, they were two-thirds of their way up 423 before encountering very steep grades with deep gullies carved in the side of the mountain. D Company's commander ordered an approach by 11, 12, and 13 Platoons, with 10 Platoon in reserve. Once again the shape of the ground meant the platoons were stuck with a single-file approach.

Clearing a last steep pitch, with the summit a couple of hundred yards straight ahead, Charlie steeled himself. To either side of him Frenchy and Woody looked tense, concentrating their attention on the ground ahead of them. They were out of sight of the other sections, bayonets fixed, waiting for a signal that could mean a charge into a hail of bullets.

A white flare popped. 11 and 12 Platoons had found the hill deserted of Chinese.

Charlie took a breath, and realized his teeth were clenched. Relaxing his grip on his rifle, he took a moment to let their reprieve from action sink in.

"Rats," said Muller, but Charlie could tell by the grin on his face he too was relieved.

"Come on, boys," Charlie said, standing. "Grab your packs and let's get up there."

They recovered their packs, left behind for the final assault. That accomplished, Charlie led them up the hill where they joined the other platoons of D Company, examining the many abandoned trenches. Scattered about were little heaps of spilled rice and broken cooking pots.

Muller poked in one of the trenches with his bayonet. "Look at this, corporal," he said, straightening. "Just caught a glimpse of it." Hooked on his bayonet was an Australian digger's hat, with its familiar shape, one brim fastened to the crown.

"Guess the Royal Aussies were here before us. But the Chinese came back again."

Price gathered the platoon. "Hang on here, men. I'll go talk to D Company, find out what's next. Odds are we're due for a break. Same as everybody else, Frenchy, you'll be glad to know."

Charlie felt relaxed, his nerves calmed down after their recent non-engagement. He noticed Frenchy and Muller examining something. Going closer, he saw Frenchy had a grenade in his hand. A quick check just to be sure—yes, the safety pin holding the firing lever down was still in place.

"What are you up to, boys?"

"Safety pin," Frenchy said.

"What about it?"

"It's too stiff. Hard to get out in a hurry."

Frenchy gripped the grenade in his right hand. He grasped the pin and gave it a tug.

"Whoa!" said Charlie.

"Just experimenting, don't worry. I didn't pull it out." He nodded at Muller. "Okay, gimme those pliers."

Frenchy took the pliers and squeezed the ends of the safety pin, almost straightening them.

"Okay, check it out," Frenchy said. He hooked the pin with his left forefinger and slid it out with a gentle pull. He held the live grenade up for Charlie to see. "Works like a damn!"

Charlie held his breath. "Are you nuts?"

"Relax, corporal." Frenchy worked the pin back into its hole. "See? Safe as the day it came out of the box."

Charlie breathed again. "Just make damn sure you don't make them too loose," he said, but borrowed the pliers to straighten his own grenades' safety pins a hair.

—

Charlie didn't know if they were just lucky, or if Price had pulled off some magic. 13 Platoon was picked up by two trucks and whisked off to a UN rest camp complete with showers, hot food, and cots. It was run by Americans, so there was no beer, but there were clean uniforms for them; just in time, Charlie thought, as he peeled off his stretched and torn underwear and tossed it onto a growing pile of castoffs.

One thing the Yanks did have, though, was ice cream that capped off a meal of steak and mashed potatoes. Charlie's mind told him to go for seconds, but he couldn't, his body adapted to spartan rations in the field.

He and the rest of the platoon were sleep-deprived and made good use of the cots, turning in early. They slept like hibernating bears—until a half hour before dawn, when they woke, ate one last cooked meal, and were on their way. Once again in the back of a rumbling truck, Charlie forgot all about the twenty-four hours they'd just had out of the line and chewed over Sergeant Price's words as they boarded the trucks.

"New assessment from the Intelligence Officer. The Chinese have stopped retreating. We're going to earn our pay, starting now."

PART THREE
THE IDES OF MARCH
MARCH 8, 1951

CHAPTER 15

The rifle companies led the way to the battalion's next objective, Hill 532. Behind them came their half-tracks carrying mortars and heavy machine guns, and a squadron of tanks attached for the current operation.

Charlie slogged along, scouting ahead, one step in his waterlogged boots after another. 13 Platoon followed, led by Sergeant Price, now officially Acting Platoon Officer. Lieutenant Strachan had been transferred to battalion headquarters. The troops were left to speculate why he was moved. "Who cares? We're better off with Price in charge," Frenchy had said, and for once Charlie had to agree with him.

The battle on Hill 419 had shaken him up, and the sight of the Canadian dead being hauled away gave him nightmares. Sergeant Price had carried on, outwardly unaffected by their casualties. Charlie took comfort in the sergeant's reputation and his confident leadership. He sure as heck never looked scared, although he might have been. But Charlie knew for sure that *he* was scared. The battalion had suffered a handful of men killed in action so far and any one of them—including him—could be next.

13 Platoon was on the right of D Company's 10 Platoon, led by Lieutenant Levy and his senior NCO, Sergeant Malloy.

The men advanced through a series of rice paddies that led to a village a quarter mile ahead. The hair on the back of Charlie's head tingled under his cap. He focused on the village, looking left and right, checking the ground, not wanting to trigger some sort of booby-trap or do a header into the human excrement mixed in with the ice, earth and mucky water of the paddies. The dykes between paddies wore a two-inch mantle of snow, making for a scene that, under different circumstances, might have been picturesque. Distant machine-gunfire far on his left reminded him—as if he needed one—that he was in a war zone. Reaching the outskirts of the village, he heard Sergeant Price from behind. "Hold it there, corporal. The rest of you close up and take cover."

Houses and other low buildings lined both sides of a central road that stretched in linear fashion across their path. Many of the buildings were damaged by shell fire or bombs and none showed signs of life.

Charlie dropped down, crouching behind a mound of village refuse. A runner appeared from the direction of 10 Platoon on their left, spoke to Sgt. Price, and hurried off again.

"Here's the story," Price said so they could all hear. "10 platoon is going to infiltrate and occupy the village, then we'll move through and carry on to the base of the hill."

The sun was well up over the horizon to the east. Pulling out his canteen, Charlie gulped some water while watching 10 Platoon, under the leadership of Lieutenant Levy, move in front of 13's position and spread out in the village. Two of the battalion mortar and machine gun crews in their half-tracks took up positions to provide extra firepower.

Levy came over and spoke to Price. "Okay, sergeant. We're in position to cover you. Move your platoon to the base of the hill. Once there, we'll follow after you while you cover for us. When we start up the hill keep your platoon on my right."

No birds sang, and the distant rattle of gunfire had stopped. The village was silent. Everybody in 13 Platoon was close enough to have heard Levy's instructions, so when Price stood and started forward the rest of them followed suit. They moved between the huts and through the derelict village, passing their comrades in 10 Platoon. Price was in the centre of the platoon, the men advancing with him, spread out either side with five-yard spacing.

Some three hundred yards across the open ground the hill rose, furrowed by deep gullies and low scattered vegetation. Halfway there something buzzed over Charlie's head at the same instant that he heard the clatter of a machine gun from somewhere ahead. He slammed to the ground, oblivious to the smell of the well-fertilized earth. Something heavy splashed into the muck to his right. He looked that way but couldn't make out who it was. Behind him he heard the distinct ping of a mortar bomb dropping into a tube and firing. The sound was repeated as the battalion's mortar crews tried to knock out the machine gun that had 13 Platoon pinned down. Charlie had never heard such a welcome sound. Peering ahead he could see the mortar bombs pounding the slope perhaps 200 metres up from the base of the hill. The machine gun stuttered again, but as near as Charlie could tell it was firing back toward the village, perhaps targeting the mortar crews.

Charlie saw Sergeant Price, off to his left, huddled with the radioman. "Roger," Charlie heard him say, and a burst of their own machine gun fire erupted from the village behind them.

"Everybody up, on your feet," Price yelled. Charlie scrambled up and ran beside his sergeant, aware of others to his left and right doing the same.

"Let's go, boys, let's go," Charlie yelled, driving forward.

The enemy machine gun burst into action again and Price shouted, "Down!"

13 Platoon again buried themselves behind the flimsy cover of a low dike separating rice paddies. Charlie caught a glimpse of half a dozen enemy soldiers part way up the hill ahead of them, running and disappearing from sight. The battalion's mortars fell silent.

The radio crackled and hummed, indistinct voices in the heat of battle.

"That's us, boys," Price shouted. "Up and at 'em!"

On their feet, dripping icy muck, 13 Platoon dashed for the base of the hill and took cover.

Two stretcher-bearers scuttled forward from the village to where a khaki shape lay. They rolled the body onto the stretcher and staggered back with it.

———

It was barely noon and Charlie lay on his side, rifle beside him, and sipped water from his canteen. 10 Platoon had bounded past 13, then for the rest of the morning 13 Platoon had followed 10. Lieutenant Levy initially led them up along a narrow spur of the hill but later decided he had taken a wrong turn, necessitating an hour's retracing of their path. The air was cold and the soldiers miserable. Snow on the ground was two inches deep in many areas and a foot deep in others, making the footing unreliable and dangerous, and Charlie had the aches and pain to show for it. He rubbed his left thigh and knee, counting himself lucky to have only bruises. The platoon had suffered another casualty when a sniper hit a 1 Section private in the arm. The man had been bandaged and assisted to the rear, but that made a second casualty for 1 Section after the man killed in the dash to the foot of the hill.

Barely into a five-minute break 13 Platoon's radio crackled. Sergeant Price put down the handset, clambered to his feet, and waved the men forward. He led them up yet another vague path trailing Lieutenant Levy and 10 Platoon. A couple of times Charlie caught sight of Levy checking his map. He hoped there weren't enemy snipers within range.

Muller edged up beside Charlie. "Crap, Charlie, can't the lieutenant read a map? He's led us all over hell's half acre. Where's Nogood when we need him?"

"Anybody could get lost in these hills," Charlie said. "Price told me Levy's been in lots worse situations than this. Heck, in WW II he escaped as a POW and then parachuted behind the Japanese lines with a guerrilla force."

"Yeah, Charlie, whatever you say. But I wish he'd just go in a straight line for a change."

Me too, Charlie thought, but Levy was one of those officers who was quiet but good at his job. That was enough for him.

An hour later 13 Platoon went to ground while Price was called away for new orders from D's company commander. Charlie was bagged, and knew he wasn't alone. Sergeant Price looked as unshakable as ever, but he seemed to have slowed down. He didn't show any signs of flagging, though, when he returned from the O-group. "We're to push on to the summit," he said. "10 Platoon will stay on our left."

Charlie took a deep breath and started up the slope. Rifle fire broke out ahead, accompanied by the thump, thump, thump of grenades.

13 Platoon clambered upward, slipping and dragging themselves toward the sound of battle. The snow was deeper here, the ground under it frozen but wet. Charlie stayed abreast of Sergeant Price, who maintained a steady pace. A Bren gun to the left of 13 platoon fired. Thirty yards ahead of them an unnatural horizontal scar lay across their path.

Price stopped and squinted. "Bunker," he said.

A head popped up behind the fresh earth, dropped out of sight for an instant and reappeared, hurling something.

Price fired at the figure. "Hit the deck!"

Charlie was down flat. Something landed five yards up the hill, and he tried to bury himself further into the earth. A grenade crashed, and he felt the shock wave and heard shrapnel whizz overhead. In the moment of silence that followed he peered up at what seemed to be a blizzard of grenades coming their way. Most fell short, but one bounced right over him to explode on the downslope.

A series of shock waves battered him, his ears ringing. He raised himself up on his elbows and for an instant saw a figure outlined against the sky beyond the bunker's parapet. He fired, his shot joining a fusillade of rifle and Bren fire. Sergeant Price crawled forward on his elbows, dragging his .30 carbine in his left hand, a grenade in his right. Charlie snatched one of his own grenades, eased out the pin, and squirmed forward, coming up even with Price, who glanced at him and nodded. They both flung their grenades. Explosions cracked and they leapt to their feet and dashed toward the bunker.

A Chinese soldier stood and fired a burp gun down the slope. Price shot from the hip and cut him down. A second man leapt from the bunker and ran up the hill. Charlie fired but the man kept running.

Frenchy, Muller and the rest of the platoon joined Price and Charlie where they had climbed intp the enemy bunker. Charlie's heart was pounding, every sense alert as he watched the slope above.

"Check your mags," Price said.

Charlie checked and saw only one round left in his magazine. He didn't remember firing more than a couple of times never mind nine. He jammed in a fresh clip.

To his right, Frenchy was leaning on the uphill side of the trench, rifle at the ready. He looked pale. He reached down, perhaps to pull ammunition out of his tunic pocket. Blood trickled from under his sleeve onto the back of his left hand.

"Let's see that arm, Frenchy," Orton said. He helped Frenchy pull his left arm out of his tunic and rolled up his shirt-sleeve. He had a gash, perhaps from a grenade or a bullet, in his left forearm. Orton took great care in wrapping it in a dressing. Price sent Frenchy down the hill with Dunstan as escort, in search of medical help.

Chapter 16

Price and the radioman crouched low in the Chinese bunker. Judging by the frown on Price's face, and seeing him slam the receiver into its cradle, Charlie figured they weren't connecting with 10 Platoon or anyone else.

He glanced over the parapet, looking back down the hill to the route along which they had approached the bunker, taking in the view the Chinese would have had. No wonder the battalion was getting shot up—he could see well down the slope, able to make out individual soldiers, stretcher-bearers, and sections of men advancing.

Meanwhile off to the left the sound of battle raged, with 10 Platoon engaged. 13 Platoon was alert, rifles and Bren guns pointed uphill at what might be another bunker. Intermittent firing from that direction ensured the men kept their heads down. Charlie couldn't see the enemy, but perhaps Powell could, because he let fly with short bursts form the Bren every few minutes.

There was a what looked like a communication trench that angled upward from their position. Price figured it joined with yet another enemy-occupied position above them.

Price asked for volunteers.

"Sergeant," said Humphrey, stepping forward.

Orton was right beside him. Charlie could see he was about to raise his hand. He was just a kid, new to the battalion. Charlie hesitated a heartbeat. What was the lance corporal hook on his arm all about, anyway? He caught Price's eye and nodded.

"Okay," said Price. "Take this." Price carried an American .30 calibre carbine he had picked up somewhere, which he thrust at Charlie. "You checked out with that?"

"Sure," said Charlie. "We fooled around with one back in Miryang." The carbine was shorter than his .303, so of more use in the cramped space of a narrow trench. He noticed it was an M2, which could fire as an automatic or semi-automatic. He left it in semi to conserve ammunition.

Price grabbed Humphrey's rifle. "Give me that, it won't do you any good in confined quarters. Take extra grenades.

"You both ready? Here's the drill. I'm guessing the next trench is only thirty yards up there. Stay low, keep as quiet as you can. If you can't go farther without being seen, stop. We'll give you time. Ten minutes from now we'll let fly with everything we've got, make sure the bastards keep their heads down. Soon as we stop, that's your chance. Charlie, you shoot anybody you see, your job is to protect Humphrey. Humphrey, yours is to grenade the hell out of them. Whatever you do, don't stand up, because we'll be lined up to fire over your heads. Hopefully they'll pop up when you lob in the grenades and we'll nail them. Any questions?"

The only question Charlie had was for himself, something along the lines of 'what the heck have I done?' He shook his head, checked his watch, dropped to his hands and knees and, carbine in hand, crawled into the connecting trench. It started out at the same depth as the bunker it took off from, but soon shallowed to perhaps three feet, and just wide enough for Charlie to crawl in. Humphrey stayed close behind.

The bottom of the trench was mostly rock, and Charlie's knees were bruised and scraped in short order. The trench grew even more shallow, almost nonexistent; as if the Chinese soldiers had quit digging or had been called off. Any further and they'd be in plain sight of the Chinese in the bunker above them. He thought they were getting close to Price's ten-minute limit.

He turned onto his left side, making as much room as he could, waving Humphrey forward. Humphrey was right-handed and turned his body so his throwing arm was up, resting his torso on his left forearm and squirming forward. He already had a grenade in his right fist, the pin pulled, only the pressure of his grip stopping it from exploding.

Charlie looked at his watch, the second hand coming up on the ten-minute mark. He was showing it to Humphrey when he heard a scrape, like metal against a rock. A voice whispered something unintelligible. Charlie thought his heart would stop. Moving with infinite caution he eased the carbine's safety off. The muzzle of a rifle poked over the lip of what must be the bunker ahead of them, a wicked-looking bayonet clipped under the barrel, pointing somewhere past Charlie. He held his breath.

A burst of rifle and automatic fire erupted from the Canadian trench. The rifle barrel ahead of him wavered, as if it was being picked up. "Back off, damn you," Charlie mouthed, but the soldier drove forward, his head and shoulders looming large, his rifle steadying on them. His eyes flared, and he was screaming, unfazed by the .303 bullets zipping around him. Charlie shot, and the soldier fell back out of sight.

The fire from the Canadian position still banged away. Humphrey released the firing lever on his grenade. He counted a couple of seconds out loud, and at 'three' he flung the grenade at the Chinese bunker. He grabbed another one and pulled the pin, counting again.

Charlie heard something on his left. He struggled to turn that way. Not ten yards away a Chinese soldier bore down on them, running in a crouch, rifle extended. Charlie swung the carbine and fired, missing. The Chinese soldier shot from the hip. Charlie clamped down on his nerves and squeezed the trigger twice. The soldier crashed to the ground.

The furious storm of .303 fire from below them hammered away. It was time to get the hell out. "Back up," he said, with Humphrey still jammed in beside him.

Humphrey groaned.

Charlie looked and saw to his horror that the front of Humphrey's tunic was bloody. Humphrey was trying to get his left arm free to reach forward. He had dropped a grenade and struggled to reach it. Its safety pin was gone, the arming lever flown away. It was about to blow.

Charlie couldn't stand up or he'd be shot by his own comrades or the enemy. They'd have to back out fast, in a split second, and still might be too late. He and Humphrey were jammed together in the narrow trench. Humphrey's eyes were the size of dinner plates, fixed on the grenade.

Charlie dropped the carbine, snatched up the grenade, and flipped it out of the trench. He covered his head with his hands, leaning across Humphrey to provide what protection he could. The blast came a millisecond after he tossed the grenade, the concussive force banging into him, fragments whizzing overhead.

His ears rang, muffling the din of the shooting by both sides. Humphrey's eyes were squeezed shut, his face crumpled in pain. Charlie squirmed backward, careful to keep his head down below the level of the shallow trench, until he was clear of Humphrey. Charlie hung onto the carbine with one hand, tucked Humphrey's feet under his other arm, and dragged him back down the sloping trench.

Once back in the original bunker willing hands took over and eased Humphrey out of the connecting trench. Orton ministered to him, cutting away clothing to reveal a jagged tear in his right upper arm. A tourniquet and initial bandaging stopped the blood flow, and an emergency injection eased his pain enough that he could sit up against the wall of the bunker.

Charlie caught his breath. Humphrey reached out with his good arm and grabbed Charlie. "Thanks."

"For getting you shot?"

"For getting me out." He grimaced. "For a second I thought you might leave me there."

"Thought about it for a second or two."

Humphrey managed a grin.

A machine gun started up from a new direction, off to the right.

Price bent over close to Powell, directing his fire with the Bren. He turned back to Charlie. "What happened up there?"

"The trench petered out. We were within a few yards of their bunker, and a couple of them rushed us. Humphrey heaved one grenade in on them, but he got shot before he could get the next one away."

Charlie heard shouts from above and saw a hail of grenades arc into the sky toward them. Most of them fell well short but the slope assisted the Chinese arms and a couple of grenades bounced to within a few yards of their trench before exploding.

I've seen this movie before, Charlie thought.

"Keep the buggers pinned down," Price said. "We can expect a counterattack any minute." He waved the radioman over, and this time connected with someone.

It seemed to Charlie that the noise of the fight to their left was dying down, but sporadic machine gun fire continued to rake the top of their bunker.

Grenades kept coming, just often enough to remind the Patricias the enemy was still there and was ready for them. Charlie had already passed his extra magazines for the Bren to Muller, and when he was handed back his .303 by Price he wasn't surprised its magazine was empty. He jammed in a clip, but realized he was low on ammunition.

Price straightened up from his crouch by the radio. "Orders to stand by to withdraw down the hill. 2 Section will lead. Black, you and Orton help Humphrey down, starting now. We'll hang on here for a few minutes until we get the go-ahead."

Charlie started out supporting Humphrey, with Orton carrying his rifle and gear. Twenty minutes later they changed around, Humphrey's good arm draped over Orton's shoulder.

A rifle cracked from long range. Charlie was a short distance ahead of the two men, but he heard the thwack of a bullet on flesh as they collapsed to the ground.

Charlie dashed back, looking around, not knowing where the shot had come from. He knelt beside them. "You hit?"

Humphrey, his arm with its bandages uncovered in the cold air, lay half across Orton, who struggled out from under him.

"He just went limp," Orton said.

"Cover us," Charlie said, and bent over Humphrey. He couldn't see any sign of a wound, but Humphrey was out cold.

A party of men approached from down the hill carrying extra stretchers, in search of D Company. Charlie talked them out of a stretcher.

Orton pulled up Humphrey's coat and tunic, searching for a wound. Charlie laid the stretcher out beside their motionless comrade. Orton caught Charlie's eye and pointed to a small entry hole in Humphrey's low back.

Humphrey was pale, his face smeared with dirt. His eyes were open; he moved his hands a little but didn't say anything as they transferred him to the stretcher.

Aw, Christ, Charlie thought. Let him be okay, God damn it.

They set off for the base of the hill, moving as fast as they could in the direction the stretcher party had told them an aid post was located. Twenty minutes later they stumbled to the bottom of the hill and the aid post. Charlie noted with alarm that Humphrey's arms dangled. They had been clasped across his midsection when they started out.

A harried medical officer took a quick look at Humphrey and applied his stethoscope, his eyes closed, concentrating. Straightening, he took the earpieces out of his ears and shook his head.

Charlie felt numb, his mind unwilling to deal with the death of Humphrey. Pressed into service by the medical officer, he and Orton made their way back up the hill with a stretcher, led by a guide to where another casualty lay on his back, arms crossed on his torso. What was left of his face was whiter than the patches of dirty snow around him. The dead soldier was unrecognizable, part of his face blown away by a grenade or machine gun fire.

Charlie found himself again on one end of a stretcher, the heavy end at that. He and Orton struggled down the hill, the dead man making no complaint when they slipped and he tumbled from the stretcher. The two men were close to exhaustion. They dragged the stretcher over beside the dead man where he lay face down in the snow. Propping the stretcher on its side beside him, they rolled him onto it. They sat a moment, breathing hard.

"Jesus, Charlie."

"What?"

"Who's next? Aren't you scared?" Orton said, his voice shaky. He looked drained, his face pinched. He and Humphrey had been close since Orton joined the platoon back a lifetime before in Miryang.

"Of course I am, but, you know, we came here to fight." Charlie had told himself that so many times, it came out automatically. "We're mostly okay."

Orton just looked at him. After a moment he heaved himself to his feet and reached for his end of the stretcher.

Why don't I feel more, thought Charlie. A month ago I was nauseated when I saw my first dead Americans. Humphrey's dead. Now this poor guy, who I might have played softball with or sat beside in a mess tent, all I can think about is how soon we can turn him over to someone else.

Back at the aid post they delivered their dead comrade to the battalion medical tent for a brief examination before he was laid out on the ground. He wasn't the only one. D company lost seven killed on hill 532, the battalion's costliest battle to date.

Charlie and Orton located the platoon hours after dark where they and the rest of the battalion had dug in halfway up the front of Hill 532. Charlie gulped down cold food and collapsed into a restless sleep, which was punctuated by a continuous barrage of tank cannons and artillery. The shells arced overhead toward the Chinese dug in on the upper reaches of the hill. The shelling continued when he stood sentry duty during the two hours before morning stand-to.

Dawn broke with the battalion at its routine one hour, one hundred percent morning stand-to, following which Charlie and Muller sat side-by-side, stuffing down a C-ration breakfast, their feet dangling in their trench.

Muller said, "Hear that?"

"No, what?" said Charlie, then realized that was Muller's point. The artillery had stopped.

Sergeant Price called the platoon together and briefed them on what was to follow. He led them on another attack up the hill, this time in support of B company. After a short but vicious exchange of gunfire the Canadians captured the hill, greeted by the doleful sight of close to fifty dead Chinese soldiers in the trenches and scattered about the hilltop. The storm of artillery and tank fire and the battalion's mortars had taken a toll on the enemy, giving Charlie a warm feeling about their Gunners.

Only a few days before, the Chinese had overrun a small American force on that same Hill 532. Charlie was shocked to see, once again, the bodies of black American GIs. Amongst them was the body of a lone Caucasian who had perhaps been their commander. He had been shot precisely between the eyes with a small-calibre weapon. Possibly taken prisoner, then executed by the Chinese.

Price stood off by himself looking at the gruesome scene, a grim expression on his face. He turned and walked over to Charlie and Frenchy, who had just returned from being patched up at the aid station.

"Got some news to pass on," Price said. "You remember Jujang li?"

Charlie had to think a second or two. "The village where we chased out the guerrillas?"

Price nodded. "We think the guerrillas came back. The intelligence officer got a report that it's totally destroyed, burned out."

"Aw, hell." Charlie felt like a dark shadow enveloped him. The death of Humphrey, all the other casualties. He remembered what the platoon was like when it defended the village. How deadly the firefight had been for a couple of the guerrillas; how triumphant and lighthearted the intact 13 Platoon had felt as they marched to rejoin the rest of the battalion.

In the short weeks since, Charlie had seen many destroyed villages. Korean, Chinese, and UN armies had fought and churned their way up and down the Korean Peninsula, razing any structure that could shelter an enemy. He wondered if the entire Korean population weren't refugees.

All around him, further than the eye could see and beyond, Korea was battered and bleeding. Surrounded by the battalion, Charlie was alone with his thoughts; alone with his doubts about keeping his men safe. About living up to his brother's standard. About surviving.

CHAPTER 17

Next morning 13 Platoon was on the far right flank of D Company as it moved northward, marching to yet another hill, 642. Charlie found himself in the middle of the pack, with Muller up ahead and Sergeant Price setting a good pace as 13 Platoon descended from the high ground to a valley floor covered with paddies. The smell no longer bothered Charlie as much, but the open ground did.

To their right a meandering stream flowed out of the highlands ahead of them. Past the creek was a road that ran roughly parallel to their route. The road would have made for a lot easier progress but that would make them an obvious target for skulking enemies. Instead, the road carried sparse local traffic. Interspersed among children and women Charlie saw some elderly men, but no able-bodied younger males, who would long since have been pressed into service by the armies of North or South. Or if they were lucky hiding in the hills.

With the Chinese troops falling back when the UN forces advanced, Charlie pictured a boxer who backpedals but gets in lethal punches while doing so. There was a constant fear that if the enemy troops took off their uniforms and dressed in civilian rags, they could pass for refugees and pop up behind the advancing Canadians.

It was freezing cold, with a skim of ice on the water in the smaller paddies. That didn't stop the muck in the paddies sucking at their boots, freezing water seeping in. Charlie could see Sergeant Price's breath as the big man puffed along, making heavy going of it. Charlie checked left and right, nervous, but his mind wandered. He didn't know when they'd get mail again, but he hoped next time there'd be something from Wanda. He told himself he wouldn't write again unless there was. At least his mother had kept him up to date with local gossip, including details about young Harry's exploits on a two-wheeler.

Clouds scudded overhead, the light muted, the drab hills in the distance with their shades of grey and brown reflecting Charlie's mood.

They made their way along the top of a dike that separated paddies, the water level a foot or so higher on one side than on the other. Stumbling, Charlie was jerked back to the present by Sergeant Price. "Christ, corporal, walk on your own goddamned feet."

Charlie winced and kept his mouth shut. Thirty-seven-year-old Sergeant Price had slowed, ground down by the physical demands of tramping up and down the hills of Korea with seventy pounds on his back. Not to mention dragging his boots out of the cloying ooze in the bottom of rice paddies.

Charlie slogged on, alternating his attention from keeping off Price's heels to keeping an eye on the paddies and hills either side of them.

As noon approached Charlie noted the land gradually rising. Ahead of them was yet another hill, on the slope of which were scattered large boulders and clumps of some sort of willow, now denuded of leaves but very dense.

The battalion spread out in companies across the bottom of the hill and awaited orders.

It was just a little knob of a hill to the west of the much larger 642. Sergeant Price's map showed it as nameless, like so many others, but it didn't even have a height printed on it. Somebody in the command structure thought Price and his 13 Platoon were just the ticket to check it out.

"Here's what's next, boys. Special assignment right here." The platoon was gathered around Price, who waved at his map, pointing at an ill-defined area with contour lines indicating a circular feature. He folded it and stuffed into a pocket. "Seems an American aircraft spotted movement on it a couple of days ago, nothing since." He rubbed his hands together.

"We'll go have a look, then we're out of the line for a few days."

"What's the occasion?" Charlie asked.

"Regimental Day, March seventeenth. Birthday of the PPCLI's first Colonel-in-Chief, Princess Patricia. Party time."

That got Charlie thinking about his dad, an earlier Patricia. Charlie knew almost nothing about the traditions of the regiment, but his dad would.

"How long will we be off?" Frenchy said.

"Don't know that yet," Price said. "We've got a job to do first. Pack up, and let's go."

He led the way westward along the base of Hill 642, filtering at right angles through the four rifle companies that would soon be attacking up the hill.

It took a couple of hours to get to where Price figured they should start their climb up the unnamed hill. The weather was cloudy and cold, with a breeze springing up behind them. The platoon advanced in arrowhead formation, 2 Section leading, with Woody as scout.

Scraggly bushes predominated, with dead grass and bare rocks and enough variation in the topography that they could stumble into danger in an instant. Still, they'd marched a long way already that day, and there was Price's promise of a break from the hard hills. Charlie felt good, one booted step after another, his pack heavy and the extra ammo and a pick he carried awkward but manageable.

Their objective was the top of the knob-shaped hill, and three hours later it was perhaps fifty vertical feet higher than they were, at the far end of a rare open meadow. To the left and right of the meadow were low trees. Price took 1 Section with him to the right, assigning Charlie and his 2 Section to the left.

He led his men up the hill, staying just inside the tree line. Sergeant Price and 1 section had the only radio, and they were no longer in sight. Snow covered most of the ground. At this level Charlie saw no evidence of human traffic, although the snow looked recent. Coming up over the last undulation to the top of the hill, he saw the remains of trenches and hundreds of footprints overlaid by a light skim of snow, some of which had melted. He signalled his section to stop and go to ground. Crouching, his nerves on edge, he concentrated on the land in front of him. Cloud cover rendered the scene a mixture of light and dark, varying from the snow cover to scattered small pine trees. He heard nothing. A vague scent of woodsmoke reached him. Seeing no movement, he stood and moved forward.

The trenches were damaged and half filled in, the ground under the snow chewed up, possibly due to strafing or rocket attack by American aircraft.

Price and 1 Section came into view forty yards away, breaking out of the trees on the far side of the hilltop. They met at the top, where the meadow reached their location. In the other direction the hill was covered in low vegetation with some hardy trees spotted here and there.

"Looks like they flew the coop," Price said.

"How long ago?" Charlie didn't like the feel of the place. It was one thing to chase the Chinese out of a location, but when they left without being pushed it worried him. He continued to look around but didn't see anything dangerous. Maybe the aircraft had forced them out.

Charlie waved up his section and detailed men to reconnoitre.

The previous occupiers' footprints had a light look to them, the Chinese running shoe prints not like the boot prints left by Canadians. Not for the first time Charlie wondered how they could stand the cold.

"How long are we…" Charlie's voice trailed off. Price was staring at something over Charlie's left shoulder.

Charlie turned and saw Frenchy and Muller peering at something on the ground, down in a little depression.

Price hurried toward them. "What have you—"

"Jesus, it's an American," Frenchy said, and took a quick couple of steps forward. He stumbled. "What the hell?"

Charlie gaped. A Chinese grenade rolled on the ground, tied to the end of a wire snagged by Frenchy's boot.

Price was there in an instant. He kicked at the grenade, a kick that could have won a Grey Cup game. The grenade flew three yards, bounced, and exploded.

Charlie was halfway to the ground as fragments ripped into nearby vegetation. Frenchy was down flat. Muller had turned away, crouching. Sergeant Price was on his back.

Charlie scrambled to his feet, ears ringing. Orton rushed to where Price lay. Powell, the Bren at his hip, watched the perimeter. Beside him Corporal Turner of 1 Section kept a lookout in the other direction. Charlie grabbed the nearest four men and sent them out to act as sentries, then joined Orton and Muller as they bent over Price. "What have you got?" he said, his voice catching. Price's face was bloody.

Orton had dressings and pads spread out on his pack. He wiped off Price's face, exposing a couple of deep gashes on the left side of his face. He patted the sergeant down, stopping at his left thigh, then coming back to it.

"Give me a hand," he said. "Roll him onto his right side."

Charlie, Muller and Orton shifted the big man. Price groaned, and Charlie breathed again.

Price's left trouser leg was blood-soaked and torn. Orton produced a knife and slit it open, exposing Price's pale left leg to the cold air. Fresh, bright red blood covered his upper thigh.

"He's gonna bleed to death," Muller said.

"No he's not. Shut up." Orton examined a wound in Price's thigh. He grabbed a couple of pads and pressed them in hard. "Hold these, corporal," he said to Charlie. He produced a long bandage. Muller helped lift Price's leg, so Orton could wrap it with the bandage. "Leave him on his side."

Price was starting to fidget, moving his head and arms. He let out a weak groan.

Charlie figured if he were a Catholic, he'd be crossing himself right now in gratitude. He picked up the sergeant's pack and laid it against his back to hold him in position. Orton again wiped the blood from Price's face. He covered his head wounds with small pads and adhesive tape.

Price blinked. "What happened?"

Frenchy was bending over them, hands on knees. "A grenade."

Price looked blank.

"A Chinese grenade. You kicked it away."

"Not the smartest thing I've ever done." Price turned his head a bit, looking around. "Oh yeah. A tripwire. What the hell were you looking at, anyway?"

"A GI."

Charlie went over to see what had attracted Frenchy and Muller's curiosity. An American corporal. He peered closer. "A dead Chinese soldier, in an American uniform," he said.

"Sneaky bastards." Price sounded almost admiring. He made a small movement with his left arm and groaned, his face white.

"Don't move, sergeant," Orton said. "I think I've stopped the bleeding for now. I'll keep an eye on it." He grabbed the axe which he kept strapped to his pack and hacked off a couple of tree branches.

"What are those for?" Charlie asked.

"His leg might be broken. Even if it's not, we want to immobilize it."

"I was going to ask if he'll be able to walk."

"Not a chance."

Charlie talked to the radio operator in 1 Section. They called Tactical Headquarters where Big Jim would be calling the shots but couldn't make contact. They did reach D Company's radioman, who relayed their message to HQ. Sergeant Price injured; helicopter evacuation requested.

"Stand by." The Headquarters response came through via D Company amid a burst of static.

Leaving the radio operator to it, Charlie went back to where Orton had Price propped up in a sitting position, leaning against his pack. Price took a swig of water and wiped the back of his hand across his mouth.

Frenchy came over and squatted beside him. "Sorry about that, sergeant. I should have seen that wire."

Price gritted his teeth and used his arms to shift his position, his face drained of colour. He caught his breath. "We all know grenade booby traps are a good defence. Guess I should have given you lesson two," he said. "Don't trip on the damn wire when the enemy uses them." Orton gave him a painkiller, and the sergeant lapsed into a semi-comatose state.

Their reclaimed hilltop was some 75 yards long east to west, and half that wide. 1 Section took the eastern end, where they cautiously cleared out and enlarged old trenches, while Charlie's section took over the western end.

Charlie called Frenchy over. The lance corporal looked unlike his normal self, his posture sagging. "Get a couple of men onto the perimeter, Frenchy. Have them double check for anything suspicious. Maybe more booby—"

"Okay, okay, got it!" Frenchy straightened up and muttered, "Jesus Christ." He turned to Powell. "Come on, kid." The two of them started a careful reconnoitre.

Charlie fell back on instinct and training, checking things over in his mind, avoiding thinking about the loss of Sergeant Price's leadership. Let me get us through the night, he thought. One hour at a time. Maybe we'll get a replacement for Price.

Before stand-to at dusk, the radio came alive. They could expect a helicopter an hour after dawn, when US aircraft would be in the air to protect it against ground fire.

It was mid-morning before the chopper hovered over their hilltop. Orton and Muller stood Price up on his good leg. Watching the helicopter as it descended, Charlie said, "Good luck, sergeant."

Price took his left arm off Orton's shoulders and reached forward, grabbing Charlie's .303. "Gimme that," he said, and thrust his own .30 calibre carbine at Charlie, the same one he had used in the Chinese connecting trench. "I left my ammo for you."

The bird hit the ground, bounced, and settled. Muller and Orton supported the sergeant, who hopped on one leg, all three of them crouching, to the helicopter. Charlie could see the two helmeted pilots, who didn't return his wave, focussed on their job. Price never looked back as he was laid out in the pod, along with Charlie's .303.

Charlie ducked and shielded his face as the helicopter lifted off, blasting snow, gravel, and bits of debris at the men on the ground. He blinked, his eyes watering, and went in search of the radioman to see if any orders for 13 Platoon had come in.

An hour later Tactical HQ ordered the platoon back the way they had come, down their hill. Coordinates directed them to where the rest of the battalion would be gathering to await the arrival of transport.

Price had been right. Days off. Days needed.

Chapter 18

March 17, near Chipyong Ni. Regimental Day for all Patricias. They had come off the hills, out of the deadly valleys and gullies the day before. It was their turn for a break, with other members of the Commonwealth Brigade taking up the slack.

Charlie strolled from the mess tent, a beer in hand. He had checked for mail and come away empty-handed; but it was hard not to feel good about the world. It was relaxed routine all-round, hot water for shaves and showers, no morning stand-to. Gone at least for today was the underlying fear of a bullet or a grenade or a bayonet.

Sports were the order of the day, with baseball and tugs-of-war attracting crowds of fans, including visitors from other battalions. Charlie watched a boxing match that featured Lieutenant Levy of 10 Platoon. Brigadier Code, who commanded the Brigade, joined in the applause for the fighters.

Charlie wandered toward the platoon's tents, where he saw a familiar figure slumped on an ammunition box. "What's the story, Powell?"

Powell had a letter in his hand; mail had caught up to them. He gave it a feeble wave.

"Bad news?"

Powell took off his cap and rubbed his bristly hair with his other hand. "Shirley, my girlfriend. At least she thinks she is. Says she's pregnant."

"She thinks she's pregnant?"

"No, I'm pretty sure she knows she's pregnant. But she *thinks* she's my girlfriend."

"But she isn't?"

"Jesus, corporal. I hardly know her. She just moved into our neighbourhood a few months before I enlisted."

"What are you going to do?"

"Well, nothing. I'm stuck here. I don't care what she does."

"Hah!" said Charlie, thinking Powell looked like a worried man, and did care. "Here's to Baby Powell." He raised his bottle.

"Whatever you say, corporal." Powell got to his feet. "Last thing I need, you know?"

"Maybe it's a mistake, maybe she's not really pregnant," Charlie said, realizing as he said it that he knew nothing about pregnant women.

"I guess we'll find out." Powell crumpled the letter in his hand and stuffed it into a pocket. "See you later," he said, as he walked away.

Powell was young, very young. He still should have known what he was up to, and in any case, there was nothing Charlie could do to help the situation.

He went back to the mail clerk's tent, and this time they found letters for him. A small handful addressed with the formal copperplate his mother used, two with Harry's halting print, one from Jackie, and—he did a double-take—a slim missive with Wanda's decorative handwriting.

He stopped where he was and ripped it open to unfold the single sheet.

"Dear Charlie," he read, holding his breath. "It seems like you've been gone a long time. I saw your mother yesterday, and she says you're fine and not in much danger, but I can see she's anxious. Also, Mr. Roberts at the bank asked about you, so I thought I'd better find out from the horse's mouth. (Joke!)" She recounted how her semester at Normal School was going, and that the student teachers had had two fun dances with live bands.

Charlie tensed, not wanting to hear about fun school dances. But what could he expect? Here he was, committed to the army, and here he'd stay. He had more or less another year to show his father what he could do, finish up with the Patricias, go home and...thirty feet away Powell frowned at a letter, maybe the offending letter from Shirley. Well, Charlie thought grimly, Powell has certainly proved himself in one way.

What an ass I've been. The thought came to him unannounced, fully formed. He had come to think how precious Wanda was to him, and how he had botched things with her, joining the army out of the blue, never discussing it with her. He went back to Wanda's letter and read, "There's never much on the news about Korea. Nobody talks about it at all. Daddy says it's not really a war, everybody calls it a police action." Tell that to Humphrey's family, he thought. Tell it to Sergeant Price and Lieutenant Toogood.

He shook his head, and looked ahead to Wanda's closing. "Love, Wanda." That was something, but what did it mean? Did she *have* to go to those dances?

He walked to his tent, but even there he heard Powell mumbling to himself.

Charlie ignored him, concentrating on a new letter to Wanda. He was frustrated at not being able to just talk to her, but she had written him at last. He told her about the injury to Sergeant Price, without any details. But it was hard to explain what the war was like. He stuck to the weather and the scenery. 'I really miss you,' he added, and closed it, 'All my love, Charlie.' Was that too much? Should he say more? He folded and sealed his letter and turned it over to the post office before he could back out.

Powell had disappeared, and Charlie went in search of more relaxed company.

Later in the afternoon Charlie joined Woody and Muller, who were outside their tent sitting on a groundsheet.

"How long we here for?" Woody asked.

"Couple more days, at least that's what one of the D Company sergeants told me," Charlie said. With no platoon officer, not even an acting one as Price had been, 13 Platoon felt adrift. Charlie was the senior Other Rank in 2 Section, but also senior to everybody in 1 Section. Their corporal had been grabbed to replace a casualty in one of the other platoons.

"Seems kinda weird, it's so quiet here," Muller said.

Charlie wouldn't call it quiet, what with hundreds of men milling around, drinking beer and eating the cake the Quartermaster had supplied for their birthday celebration. But he knew what Muller meant. No tanks rumbling, no artillery banging, no aircraft buzzing them.

"Well, well. Look at this." Woody was looking past Charlie, who turned and saw Powell making his way toward them. He had an empty beer bottle in one hand, which he tossed to the ground. "Got any more of those?"

"Cripes sake, Powell, you've gone through your ration and then some," Charlie said. There were teetotallers in the battalion who would trade their beer ration for war souvenirs or anything else judged attractive. Powell looked glum, his mood not improved from when Charlie had seen him last. "Take the weight off," he said, making room on the groundsheet.

"Nah." Powell shook his head.

"Do yourself a favour, Powell," Muller said. "Get your head down. You'll thank me tomorrow."

Powell frowned. "Don't fuckin' think so. I know some guys who'll share a drink when they have it." He shambled away.

Charlie started to get up, not sure what he was going to do. But something.

"Aw, let him go," Woody said. "He'll pass out soon, and we can find him, bring him back. Wouldn't be the first time."

Powell was a good guy and a good soldier, but he had a weakness for booze. Charlie sat back, watching Powell disappear between some tents.

Charlie wasn't surprised when he woke before dawn, their usual time to be at stand-to. He grumbled a mild curse, then dozed, happy to take advantage of the battalion's down-time. Waking a short time later, Charlie luxuriated in the comfort of having taken his boots off before turning in. He clasped his hands behind his head.

Hearing a distant shout, indistinct and muffled, Charlie raised his head.

"Medic. Medic!"

Someone ran past the tent, then someone else. The shouts degenerated into quieter, urgent conversation, several people talking at once.

He rolled out and jammed on his boots. Outside, he heard a hubbub from his right. He headed that way, drawing close to an area past the communal showers. A floodlight snapped on, revealing men stumbling from a large tent, dragging a body. They deposited it beside another one already lying face-up on the muddy ground. A figure Charlie recognized as a medical assistant pounced on the latest arrival and pressed a stethoscope to the man's chest. "Stretcher!"

Charlie started to run to the medical unit when a man almost knocked him over, a stretcher cradled in his arms. Charlie grabbed one end and the two of them laid it out beside the comatose figure where the medic crouched. Willing hands picked up the unmoving man and deposited him on the stretcher, which was quickly lifted and rushed away by others, the medical assistant trotting alongside. They disappeared into the labyrinth of tents.

Charlie pointed at the figure still on the ground. "What about him?" he asked a medic.

"No rush for him. He's dead."

Stumbling back out of the way, Charlie made room for two more men who pulled another body from inside the dark tent. The medic got down on his knees in the mud, stethoscope in hand.

Muller came up beside Charlie. "What's going on?"

"Not sure. They—"

"Shit," Muller said. "It's Powell."

Powell was as pale as the summer clouds in Charlie's dreams of home, his eyes closed. Charlie started forward but was fended off by the medic. He and Muller followed stretcher-bearers carrying Powell's body into the medical tent, where it was surrounded by a half-dozen men who bent over him, busy with stethoscopes and some sort of tubing. Charlie and Muller were ordered out of the tent by a tall medical assistant.

"What can you tell us?" Charlie said.

"We've got two of them in here now," the medic said. "Looks like alcohol poisoning."

"The last one, Powell, he's in our platoon. Will he make it? What are you doing?"

"Pumping their stomachs. Might be lucky and get them in time. We should know soon."

Charlie sent Muller off to find the rest of 13 Platoon to make sure they, at least, were accounted for. He waited outside the medical tent, determined to go nowhere without some answers.

Four more soldiers arrived on stretchers. One of them showed signs of life, moving his arms.

An hour later Charlie talked to the same tall medic, who went off to see what he could find out about Powell.

Charlie paced until he returned. "What's the latest?"

"He's okay at the moment. He's one of the lucky ones, but your friend Powell's not going anywhere for a while."

Charlie felt like Powell's considerable bulk had itself come off his shoulders. The kid was going to live. His sense of relief was shortlived. What had he said to Powell the day before? Nothing. Powell was upset about the news he'd received when his girlfriend told him she was pregnant. Charlie had no way to know if Powell was justified in not wanting to be involved with the girl; that was a separate matter. What he had done was leave Powell to solve his own problems, which he had tried to do with booze. Powell was just a kid, in over his head. Sergeant Price would have looked after him.

"One less man in the glorious 13th," Frenchy said, talking to Charlie and Muller later.

"It's not just us," said Muller. "Other platoons are missing guys too."

But we're in 13 Platoon, we're the ones who have to keep proving ourselves, Charlie thought. And there are fewer and fewer of us.

Frenchy turned and walked away.

"What's his problem?" Charlie said.

"He's been a little touchy ever since he stumbled on a rock, and I told him to watch where he steps, especially around trip wires."

Charlie just looked at him.

"I was joking. And what was Powell's big problem?" Muller said. "Before this he didn't hit the booze any harder than the rest of us. Did he say anything to you, Charlie?"

"When?"

"When you talked to him yesterday."

"Girlfriend trouble," Charlie said.

Muller didn't respond. Maybe Charlie wasn't the only one who felt guilty.

When Big Jim Stone was on the warpath, even the Regimental Sergeant Major looked like he'd rather be somewhere else. 13 Platoon was on parade with the rest of the battalion, right behind D Company as usual. Charlie's section was down to eight men, now that Powell was unfit for duty following his encounter with wood alcohol. Common scuttlebutt was that the drinking party had made use of canned heat that came with C-rations. Soldiers desperate for a drink, any drink, heated the material to its liquid form, added water and juice powder which was also in the rations, and tossed it back. Four couldn't be revived by the medics. Two were blind. The rest of them, including Powell, had been saved by having their stomachs pumped before their bodies shut down.

The battalion had suffered dozens of casualties, men killed in action. Big Jim Stone could live with that; they were in the business of killing or being killed. But self-inflicted injuries of any sort, even if not intended, would not be tolerated.

The bodies of the dead men were stretched out on the ground and their surviving comrades—the whole battalion—were made to march past and take in the wretched sight. Powell, still under medical care, was spared the gruesome spectacle. But once the doctors finished with him he'd face the wrath of Big Jim.

Charlie was still thinking about Powell when word reached him that two replacements, Ridley and Trent, had been assigned to 2 Section. Nobody much wanted to talk to them. The veterans would wait to see if the newcomers survived for a couple of weeks, grinding up and down the Korean hills. Not to mention coming under fire.

Charlie hoped the assignment of replacements meant 13 Platoon was still alive, if not well.

CHAPTER 19

Stone didn't give the Patricias a chance to feel sorry for themselves; they were on the march again, off to another nameless Korean hill. Heading north, they were told, in pursuit of the Red Chinese. Charlie, his lance corporal's single hook on his arms, shared the familiar but uncomfortable confines of an American 6x6 with the rest of his section. The men slipped into their somnambulant state, semi-dozing, barely conscious of their surroundings, just awake enough to stay seated on the hard wooden benches.

He still smarted from the tongue-lashing delivered to the assembled battalion by Lieutenant-Colonel Stone. Big Jim had ranted for an hour, slamming the men foolish enough to drink wood alcohol, then parading the battalion past the dead bodies of the four dead men. Charlie hadn't had any direct part in the debacle, but Powell, one of his men, sure had. Charlie felt responsible. Powell was gone, either still in medical care or Big Jim's cells.

It turned out that the shuffle of personnel during their rest period was more extensive than Charlie had realized. 13 Platoon's 1 Section ceased to exist, its members used to shore up other platoons which had lost men due to sickness, injury, or death. The rapid change felt dizzying. Only 2 Section remained and it constituted the sum total of 13 Platoon.

Contrary to the disappearance of 1 Section, 2 Section gained numbers. Their two replacements, Ridley and Trent, were a study in contrast. Ridley was tall, slim, and quiet, with red hair. He was in awe of the veterans he was joining. Trent compensated, a soldier of medium height, muscled like a rhino. He wasn't with them ten minutes before they knew he'd tried out for the Winnipeg Blue Bombers, the best team in Canadian football in his opinion, where he'd been the final cut before the season started.

The two of them were ignored for the most part, except when a veteran figured they needed to be smartened up so they wouldn't put the whole platoon at risk.

The ride north lasted two days this time. After a chilly night bivouacked along with the rest of the battalion, 13 Platoon gathered around Lieutenant Brian Munro. Munro was known as a competent officer and commanded 2 Platoon. With him were his three sections plus, for now, Charlie's section, all that was left of 13 Platoon.

"Our job is to push the enemy off the hill ahead of us." Munro had a map in his hand and gestured at a snow-covered, massive mountain to the north. "That's Hill 1250, our highest so far, so get ready for ice and more snow. 2 Platoon, with 13 in support, will be on the right flank of the battalion. The map shows all kinds of spurs and steep slopes, so watch your footing. Intelligence says the Chinese are up there, waiting." He folded his map but pulled several more out of his pocket, handing them out to section leaders. "Platoons will act independently. A mile up is a sort of plateau where it gets steeper; I'll have more to say when we get there. That's it for now."

A three-hour slog in winter clothing with parkas featuring a fur-lined hood had them sweating. Their ascent under an overcast sky gradually revealed what in different circumstances would be breathtaking scenery. All around, near or far depending on which way he looked, Charlie saw snow-covered hills and peaks that paraded away to the horizon. Late March in Korea looked a lot like late March in the Canadian Rockies. On these lower slopes of Hill 1250 the fresh snow was melting, but a chilly headwind made it clear a formidable challenge lay ahead.

As promised, Lieutenant Munro called a halt and walked back to speak to Charlie, who pulled out the map Munro had given him earlier.

"Here's where we want you, Lance Corporal Black," Munro said, pointing with a gloved hand to a spur that started a few hundred yards from where they stood and rose in a northwesterly direction toward the summit.

Charlie oriented himself, following the direction Munro indicated on the landscape, then looked down at the map, making sure he had it straight.

"Some reminders," Munro said. "Your job if you encounter the enemy is to chase them if they retreat, but not get into any pitched battles. We don't have the manpower for that, the idea is to make firm contact and report back.

"We're on our own up here. Given the size of the mountain and the need to make progress, we've outrun our artillery. There'll be no help from them. And even if they could catch up, the upper reaches of this hill are so steep the twenty-five pounders are useless."

"What else, sir?"

"Porters. They're not available. The food on your back is what you get. Make it last." He looked at Charlie. "Any questions? No? Alright, off you go. Oh, and these hills make for terrible radio communications. I'll send runners if anything changes, but in any event your orders are to be off the mountain and rendezvous with me right here three days from now, same time."

"Sir." Charlie noted the time, pocketed his map and picked up his rifle and pack. The platoon wordlessly followed suit, and they set off toward the heights of Hill 1250.

On the lower hills they'd climbed since starting their pursuit of the Chinese there had often been paths to follow, game trails or routes used by Koreans in their daily lives before they were interrupted by the war. The use of wood-burning stoves left many of the hills denuded of significant forests or other natural cover, but at least the trails meant a path forward was available. Here on the upper reaches of 1250 where the paths did exist they were exposed, narrow, and open for all to see, perfect spots for ambush.

The steep sides of the ridge that 2 section was climbing made Charlie's heart pound.

At times he felt unworthy, not deserving of the right to lead. He was too young, too inexperienced, not able to cope with guys like Frenchy, who could be counted on to push his boundaries. He didn't doubt his men were watching him, thinking they were a lot safer when Sergeant Price was in charge. Added to that, he was very aware that every step they took away from 2 Platoon and Lieutenant Munro meant a greater distance from any help he could call on.

The afternoon wore on. Muller was out ahead with Woody bringing up the rear. After climbing up a steep section, Muller dropped out of sight over the lip of a wide declivity. When Charlie had a look at it he saw there was room for defensive trenches and called a halt for the night.

"Sentries ahead and to the south on our backtrail," Charlie said. He placed them, going with Muller in one direction and then Dunstan in the other, locating them so they also had eyes on either side of their location, which featured dangerous drop-offs. It was unlikely they'd be attacked from those directions.

They dug in. Under the inches-deep snow cover was a thin layer of frozen earth and gravel. Charlie and Ridley tried a likely spot, but had to move a few feet when they ran into solid rock. They managed a two-foot-deep shell scrape before hitting bedrock again. It would have to do.

Charlie took a regular turn on sentry duty, after which he slept as best he could, wrapped in his blanket and poncho. At times he'd wake, shivering, wondering what he was doing, thousands of miles from home, his clothing frozen from the sweat soaked up during the daylight climb. In those half-awake moments he knew he didn't belong here, he didn't belong leading men who relied on him, he didn't belong... He nodded off, feeling like he was in over his head.

Something hit his shoulder. Charlie woke at once, sitting upright in his trench. Ridley flinched back. "Hey, corporal," he hissed. "Someone's out there."

Charlie rested his elbows on the edges of the trench and levered himself up, grabbing his carbine. Ridley pointed north to where he had been on watch.

"Wake the others. One hundred percent stand-to." Charlie checked his .30 was loaded, safety off. He cocked it and switched the safety on again. It was still dark, any possible moonlight obscured by clouds. He stared north, making out the vague shape of the land but little else. An all-round look revealed nothing. The only sound was a slight rustle of frozen branches and Ridley, moving from man to man.

Everybody was awake now, crouched in their minimal trenches, rifles ready. Charlie nodded at Ridley, and together they moved out toward where Ridley had heard something. They reached the spot he had been posted on sentry duty. Charlie stopped and listened, holding his breath. Nothing. He glanced at Ridley, who shrugged.

Charlie gestured with his head for Ridley to come with him. The two of them moved ahead, slow step by slow step. Charlie's heart was in his mouth, watching where he put his feet, fearing a bullet at any moment. Visibility improved with the faint light of coming dawn, and the air was very still. Sixty yards past where Ridley had stood his lonely watch something caught Charlie's eye. Indentations in the snow showed where two men had lain face down, with clear marks left by the toes of their shoes. It was easy to picture Chinese soldiers with rifles trained on 13 Platoon. They knew the Canadians were close but were unwilling to take them on. Tracks in the snow led away toward the north. The two men followed the tracks for another hundred yards before turning back.

"Stay here," Charlie said as they retraced their steps back to where Ridley had earlier stood sentry-duty. "I'll send someone to relieve you."

Ridley's hands were shaking as he blew on them, his brow furrowed under his toque.

"You did good," Charlie said. "They've gone, and they seldom attack during the day. We'll be moving on as soon as it's daylight."

Charlie was careful to make noisy progress on his way back to their trenches, but even with that there were several rifles on him until he was recognized. Ridley isn't the only one on edge, he thought. "One hundred percent stand-to for another hour. Eat after that, and we'll push on."

He sent Dunstan to relieve Ridley, thinking the kid could stand to be back with the other troops, give his nerves a rest.

He'd like to have a rest for his nerves, too. He could use some reassurance that they knew what they were doing. Reassurance their sergeant could have given, and Charlie tried to.

CHAPTER 20

Shortly after morning stand-to a runner arrived from Lieutenant Munro, confirming Charlie's previous orders: get to the top of Hill 1250 if unopposed, but if opposed make firm contact with the enemy and in any event be back at the rendezvous forty-eight hours hence. The man had a copy of Charlie's map, and the rendezvous position was marked, back where 13 Platoon had departed from 2 Platoon on the lower plateau. Charlie sent the runner back the way he had come with a message to Lieutenant Munro that they had found traces of the enemy in the snow but were not in firm contact.

"No surprise," Charlie said to the platoon. "We push on." He brought in the sentries and checked they weren't leaving anything behind except their shell scrapes. The platoon moved off in single file, Woody leading.

Were the marks in the snow that Ridley had found those of Chinese troops? Of course they were, and the more he thought about it the more it worried him. How far ahead of the platoon were the Chinese? The enemy scouts would have seen the miniscule force pursuing them. What if they decided to swipe 13 Platoon off the side of the mountain? Charlie licked his chapped lips and looked around for the hundredth time that day.

The spur climbed ever upward, the soldiers sweating despite the freezing air. To either side the land fell away, at spots verging on vertical, at others more gradual, but always enough of a slope that Charlie found himself tending to edge away from the periphery. At one point the only way forward was to follow along a ledge on the left of the razor-sharp ridge, a natural path a yard-and-a-half wide. It sloped away to the left with a flat ten-foot-wide plate on a sickening slope outside the path, beyond which was a drop of a hundred feet or more to another rocky ledge.

The men strung out with ten yards between them, fighting the tendency to bunch up, making it hard for an ambush to target more than one man at a time. Charlie breathed easier when they cleared the ledge and were back on a wider section of the ridge. For a quarter of a mile a rocky cliff rose above them on their right, shielding them from the icy breeze, and their breath rose in clouds. The air was cold, visibility unlimited under a leaden sky, with snow-covered crags and hills clear in the distance.

The vague trail meandered higher. Charlie's fingers ached as flurries of small, dry snowflakes swirled around him. When he stopped for a minute to blow on his fingers his breath was whipped away.

It was nearly noon when they approached a large rock formation on the left and a small hillock covered in stunted evergreen trees to the right. The way forward lay between the two features where they'd cross a low ridge, a raised notch like a rifle's rear sight. Woody, scouting, scuttled across the exposed high point. Next came replacement Trent, upright, legs pumping on the challenging slope, looking like a fullback carrying would-be tacklers with him.

Trent was flung back, both his arms flying wide, his body thumping hard onto his pack as a machine gun rattled. Bullets ricocheted off the rock and kicked up snow and dirt where Trent had walked an instant before. Charlie hit the ground as another burst of automatic fire clipped small branches and pine needles from the trees to the right. They rained down on Charlie and the rest of the platoon, who had made themselves as small as they could. The gun stopped.

In the awful silence that followed Charlie tried to come to grips with what had just happened. He raised his head. Trent lay motionless on his side, his rifle a yard behind him, his pack slewed beside him on the ground.

Charlie shed his pack and scrambled over to where the fallen man lay, unmoving. He was facing Charlie, who could see one eye was gone, the other one wide open. Charlie, staying low, shifted his position. A gaping hole in the back of Trent's skull leaked smeared grey-matter.

Muller had opened his own pack and pulled out a package of first aid materials, but when he crawled up alongside Charlie and took a look at Trent he dropped it. "Shit," he said.

The enemy machine gun started again, but the bullets weren't directed at them or the spot where Trent had been hit. It sounded to Charlie as if they were targeting someone farther away. Woody, who was cut off from the rest of them.

For an instant Charlie's only thought was to get the hell out, to flee back the way they had come. Get hold of yourself, Charlie, he thought. His training, his weeks of fighting under the direction of Sergeant Price, kicked in.

The platoon was protected by being beyond the machine gunner's horizon. Except for Woody. Where was he, had he been hit too?

Squirming forward and to the right, Charlie worked his way through the stunted trees on the hillock, trying to see what lay ahead. He must have shaken a branch, because the gun burst into action again, bullets zipping into the trees. Twigs and snow off the tree showered him. Charlie backed up and flattened himself face down until the shooting stopped.

"Woody!" he called. "Where are you? Are you hit?"

"I'm okay," Woody said, sounding calm. "But I'm pinned down."

Charlie eased forward again and caught sight of Woody who was lying prone, down and to the left, forty yards past the high ground where Trent had been hit.

"Can you see where the gun is?"

"'Fraid not."

Charlie didn't know what to do. He didn't know if this counted as 'firm contact,' but he sure as heck didn't want it any firmer. He wiped sweat, pine needles, and grit off his face. "Stay down," he said. Now what?

He wriggled back from the front edge of the hillock. Looking back, he beckoned Muller, who had the Bren now that

Powell was gone. Muller and Dunstan, his number two, edged forward into the clump of trees where Charlie waited.

"Can you see anything, Muller? That damn gun?"

"Nope. But if he shows himself, I'm ready."

Frenchy eased up beside Charlie. "What are you going to do about Woody?"

"Woody's safe for now." But Charlie knew time was short. The Chinese could be stalking Woody, alone on the forward side of the notch.

"You stay with the Bren, keep them on target. When I give you the nod, I want continuous fire on the Chinese. Keep their heads down. Got it?"

"No problem," Frenchy said.

Charlie slid back, staying low. He beckoned to Orton and Ridley, who crawled up next to him. "Right. After me," he said, then called out, "Now, Frenchy!"

The Bren let fly. Charlie gave it a three count, gathered his legs under him, and sprinted forward. For an instant he held his breath, waiting for the slam of a bullet, then he was over the high point, diving forward to the cover of a slight fold of dirt and rock.

Orton and Ridley had followed and were down on their bellies off to the right of him, taking advantage of minimal cover behind scattered boulders and clumps of vegetation. Woody, ten feet to his left, nodded at him.

"Cease fire," Charlie yelled.

13 Platoon had crossed the gap and was under cover except for the Bren crew. From his new angle Charlie was pretty sure he could see where the enemy fire had come from. A couple of hundred yards ahead, in an elevated position surrounded by jumbled rocks and stunted trees, he saw faint movement as the gun rattled into action again. It raked the high ground and the clump of trees where Frenchy and the Bren crew sheltered.

He and the other riflemen laid down supressing fire while Muller, Dunstan and Frenchy sprinted through the notch.

Charlie took stock. The whole platoon was committed; it would be suicide to retreat with the enemy gun in action.

The machine gun was the only evidence they'd seen of their enemy. What if there were snipers lying in wait while the platoon concentrated on the gun? What if…*What if any number of things. Make a decision, Charlie.*

"Frenchy, you and the Bren, suppressing fire on my order," he yelled. "The rest of us, on the count of three. Fire!"

The Bren chattered. Charlie counted aloud, and on 'three' he moved, crouching, running hard for fifty yards and flinging himself flat again, sensing the other riflemen around him.

"Cease fire!"

The Bren fell silent. Charlie thought he saw movement where he had placed the enemy gun, and it fired, rounds spraying the ground around him. He made himself as small and low as he could behind minimal cover, catching a glimpse of Ridley, fifteen feet away, doing the same.

For the next twenty minutes they repeated the manoeuvre, the riflemen advancing, alternating with the Bren crew. Sporadic fire came their way, stopping when the Bren answered.

They settled in thirty yards short of the machine gun nest.

"Fix bayonets." Charlie kept his eyes on the rocks in front of the gun location but heard the chorus of clicks as the men obeyed. His mouth was dry.

"Grenades. Me, Frenchy, Orton. Then we go." He set down his carbine, unclipped a grenade with his right hand, and held it up so the others could see and follow suit. Pulling the safety pin, he cocked his arm and counted aloud. On "three" the three of them flung their grenades and hit the dirt, waiting for the explosions. Charlie held his breath, praying none of the grenades hit something and bounced or were thrown back. There was a muffled roar. Charlie leapt to his feet and charged, the rest of his section with him, scrambling up, safeties off and bayonets fixed, up the slope and over the top.

The enemy position was empty but for hundreds of spent machine gun shells and a smear of blood on a rock.

"Nobody move," Charlie said, breathing hard. "Check for booby traps."

They froze, looking around, checking everywhere. No wires or strings, no armed grenade under a loose rock waiting for a careless boot to trigger it. Charlie sent two men further along the trail, making sure they hadn't walked into an ambush.

Frenchy and Orton reported back. "Just some footprints in the snow, going away, two hundred yards out," Frenchy said.

Charlie posted sentries and had half the men dig out C-rations while the others stood-to.

Woody slapped Muller on the back. "Man, was I glad to hear you pinning those bastards down," he said. "Kinda nice to be back with the rest of you, much as I hate to admit it."

"That'll teach you to get out in front," Muller said, and gave Woody an elbow in the ribs. Charlie too felt exhilarated, like they'd swung the hammer at a carnival and rung the gong. He noticed that Ridley didn't eat. He'd started out as one of the first sentries Charlie posted, then when he was relieved sat by himself, staring in the direction the retreating enemy had taken. Charlie was happy to see Orton go over and talk to him.

Pulling out his map, Charlie located their position as best he could. They were still at least a half a mile from the summit, and if anything, the route ahead looked steeper than what they had already traversed. What did Munro say? Get to the summit or make firm contact.

The Chinese were masters at delaying actions. A typical battle would see firm resistance to the UN forces, who would bring artillery and air support. But the low overcast meant no aircraft, and artillery was not within range. That left the final option, an infantry attack, which the book said was not to be undertaken except with superior numbers. Their seven-man section didn't translate as 'superior numbers.'

Charlie checked his watch. 1600 hours. Given what was thickening cloud cover, they'd start to lose daylight soon. Not enough time to get to the summit, even if it wasn't defended.

In the quiet after their firefight, Charlie started to second-guess himself. He'd lost a man, one out of only eight. Trent, a stranger to the fight and to the platoon, alive one minute and dead the next. What could Charlie have done differently? Would

Sergeant Price have seen the enemy trap before it closed? Should he be leading the way and following the withdrawing Chinese, even in the face of his small numbers and darkness coming on?

Fifteen feet away Frenchy made some sort of comment to Muller and Dunstan, both of whom glanced his way.

Charlie went back to his map, trying to concentrate. Was that bastard Frenchy undermining him? What could he do about it if he was?

He took a deep breath. He wished he could go back, wished someone else was in charge, that someone else had the damn lance corporal's hook on his sleeves. Even Frenchy. But Frenchy was up and down, drunk when he should have shown leadership.

Charlie felt alone, like a lame animal cut out of the herd. He knew there was worse to come.

Chapter 21

"Pack up," Charlie said. "We've got two days to get back to the rendezvous with Lieutenant Munro. Orton, lead off." In all likelihood the only enemies within miles were now behind them, higher on 1250. "Muller, you're backstop."

Frenchy looked at him, the hint of a smile on his face. What the hell was there to smile about?

Charlie felt like running, but there was nowhere safe to run. And if he wasn't here, who would look after the boys?

They set off on the backtrail, passing the notch in the topography where Woody had dodged a bullet but Trent caught his. They went through Trent's pack, distributing his unused C-rations amongst them. They took his rifle and ammunition and a couple of personal items. Family photos, letters. What was left behind they hid under some rocks and debris, unwilling to leave it in the open for the enemy. Frenchy and Woody took a shoulder of Trent's coat each, cradling his torso, and Ridley his feet. The air was icy, the wind picking up. Visibility was closing in, with dry, hard snowflakes swirling around them.

"Slow down, Orton," Charlie said. The kid was forty yards ahead, but behind Charlie the men carrying Trent struggled to keep up on the narrow, steep trail.

He could hear Frenchy, going on about something. What was it now? Why the hell couldn't Frenchy let things be? Ridley kept silent, with Woody making the odd comment.

"…chickenshit…" Frenchy's voice, sounding querulous.

Charlie clamped his jaw, gritting his teeth.

The trail looked familiar. They were within a hundred yards of the narrow section that had slowed them on the way up. He called a halt, dropped his pack, and strode back to where Ridley, Frenchy and Woody eased Trent's body to the ground.

"Come with me," he said to Frenchy, who fell in behind him. When they reached Muller, Charlie gave him a nod. "Okay, we've got it."

Muller went forward.

Charlie watched him go, and turned to Frenchy, who looked confused. "What—"

Charlie hit him as hard as he could, and Frenchy went down like a poleaxed steer. He got to his hands and knees, shaking his head. He charged, the momentum as he caught Charlie with his shoulder carrying them both to the ground, their fists flailing. Charlie was rocked by a blow to his temple, but Frenchy was slower than usual. Charlie hung on as they rolled on the ground, neither of them gaining an advantage.

Charlie scrambled to his feet, his chest heaving. "Stop the whining, Frenchy. I'm sick of it."

Frenchy's eyes blazed and he let out a wordless growl. He feinted with a fist and lashed out with a kick to the crotch but Charlie dodged it and punched Frenchy again while he was off balance. This time Frenchy stayed down.

Charlie caught his breath, gasping and shaking his right hand, his knuckles already swollen.

"Don't you say a goddamn word, Frenchy, or I'll fucking shoot you." He picked up his carbine from where he'd dropped it. "Keep your mouth shut from now on. When we get out of here, you can try to go somewhere else, some other platoon. This is *my* platoon."

He shook with rage, taking no notice of Muller and Woody who stood a few feet away. Charlie stalked past them to where Trent lay abandoned in the snow.

He called Orton back from his scout position. "Give Ridley and Woody a hand with Trent. Dunstan, at the rear. Muller, you're scout."

Muller moved forward. Frenchy, his face swollen and one eye partially shut, followed him, not meeting Charlie's eyes as he passed. Muller scouted ten yards ahead, negotiating the narrow ledge that Charlie had been nervous about on their outward trek. He moved at a slow but confident pace, planting each foot.

"Carry your packs across," Charlie said. "Come back for Trent." The icy ledge looked shiny even in the reduced daylight. Muller was half-way along the feature when Orton started out.

"Stay well apart," Charlie said, calmer now, thinking defence. When he was ready to take his turn he stepped out, trying not to think about the narrow trail and the rocks below. The snow above must have thawed a little, snowmelt flowing down and across the ledge to freeze again, where it lay under a thin skim of snow. He caught a glimpse of Orton, who slipped, but recovered, stood still a moment, and carried on.

—

Charlie stayed focussed on the narrow trail. His pack was nothing out of the ordinary, but it made him feel top-heavy. His rifle over his left shoulder, he planted one foot after another. He'd be extra careful, his hands still shaking but his feet firm.

He felt good, like he was in charge. That bastard Frenchy. Maybe he didn't deserve to get sucker-punched, but he asked for it. Frenchy was tough, he had to allow him that. At least he was when it came to using his fists. Now he'd see if Frenchy could take a punch and live with it. Charlie shook his head, just as his right foot shot out from under him.

He tried to roll to his right to stay on the flat part of the ledge but couldn't do it. His pack weighed him down. There was nothing to hang onto on the slippery surface and he slid slowly downward, like a snail oozing down a window pane. His left hand was useless, trapped against the ice-covered rock under him, unable to gain a grip. Grasping at any handhold, anything, the fingers of his right hand fumbled at the icy ledge. He yelled, an incoherent bellow.

He squirmed and tried to dig his toes into the face of the ledge, deperate for any purchase. An instant later there was nothing solid under his feet. He was going over.

Something jerked his left shoulder. His rifle had been slung over his shoulder when he fell, and now it lay partly under his upper arm, pressed against the slope, its sling tight in his armpit. His terrifying slide stopped.

Afraid to make the slightest move, Charlie stared at the ice-encased surface of the rock. His rifle had caught on something. He shifted his focus to the trigger guard in front of his face and rolled his eyes upward.

Someone's fingers were wrapped around the barrel, covering the front sight.

"I hope your safety's on."

Christ, it was Frenchy. Charlie tilted his head a fraction. Straight above the muzzle of his rifle was Frenchy's outstretched arm and face. He lay spread-eagled on the slope. If he let go of Charlie's rifle…

"Me too," Charlie said.

Frenchy spoke again. "Don't anybody move."

"I don't know how long I can hold on." Charlie recognized Woody's voice. "I feel like I'm gonna slip."

Christ. Frenchy had hold of him, but he in turn was held in place by Woody.

"You might have to let us go," Frenchy said. "If you start to slide."

Charlie could only stare. He saw Muller, who had been across the dangerous portion of the trail, edging back toward them. Someone else was with Woody. Orton?

Charlie almost laughed. The whole damn section, trapped on the ledge. If any of them slipped, they'd all go. Or at least he and Frenchy would. Here he was, his life in the hands of the man who, moments earlier, he had hated.

"Grab this," Muller said.

The corner of a grubby blanket slid down the slope, stopping short of where Charlie's right hand lay, fingers splayed on the ice, maintaining an illusory grip. Someone flipped the blanket. The end of it brushed the back of his hand. He held his breath and eased the pressure on his fingers. Nothing happened. He turned his hand over and grasped the corner of the blanket.

Letting out a cautious breath, Charlie watched as the slack in the blanket was reeled in. After a moment it was taut and exerting an upward pull.

Don't let go, don't slip, don't let go, he felt like shouting. He took shallow breaths as the blanket and his right hand's death-grip took more weight. His body turned a little, and inch by inch he was drawn up the slope. The pull on his shoulder where his rifle was still slung eased. His feet no longer hung over the abyss.

Muller had somehow anchored himself onto the ledge, and he helped Charlie to get on all fours and tenuous safety.

Charlie stared down at the ledge, unwilling to look sideways to where his life had hung in the balance. Muller steadied him so he could stand, still with his pack on his back. He picked up his rifle and followed Muller forward and off the ledge, where they shed their packs.

The path off the ledge widened to ten feet or so. Charlie and Muller hadn't been there for two minutes when they were joined by Orton, Frenchy, Woody, and Ridley. Frenchy produced cigarettes and passed them around, Charlie waving him off, but glad for the moment of calm.

Charlie stood, as an unaccustomed feeling of belonging swept over him. A laugh welled up before he could clamp it down. His knees felt weak, and he bent at the waist, hands on knees. "Holy crap, I thought we were all going over." He looked at them, Frenchy with his cut lip, but all of them looking like a weight had come off their shoulders. "Thanks, Frenchy," he said. "Thanks. Good going, all of you."

"Ha ha, I never was very good at heights," Woody said. "Damn glad you're not heavier."

Charlie listened while they bantered, letting off steam. The talk died and they finished their cigarettes. "Let's get Trent," Charlie said. He picked up his carbine and started back the way they'd come, edging out on the ledge once again. He sensed someone behind him but stayed focussed on where he placed his feet. Reaching solid ground at the other end, he turned.

Frenchy stepped up beside him. "Figured someone had to keep an eye out for you," he deadpanned. They were joined by Muller and Dunstan. Dunstan kept watch, while Charlie and Frenchy picked up Trent. It was heavy going, there not being room on the narrow path for two men on Trent's upper body.

Light faded as they loaded up again with packs, rifles, spare gear, and their dead comrade, and continued their march.

—

On their second night a thousand metres above sea level Charlie shivered, huddled in his blanket. His mind played tricks on him, reliving the shock of Trent's death and the firefight with the retreating Chinese, their bullets zipping overhead. But fear of dying by enemy fire was nothing compared to a clear nightmare of sliding off a trail and plunging headlong over a cliff. Or in another version of the nightmare, reliving the abject terror of backing along the trail, losing control, and going over the edge entangled with Trent's body.

Giving up hope of sleep, he set aside his blanket and poncho and crawled out of his trench. Making as little noise as possible he made the rounds of the sentries. All seemed quiet, but Woody told him Ridley had stumbled off to the crude latrine fifteen minutes before and hadn't returned. Charlie went to check on him but found no trace of the man.

He hurried back to the trenches. "Everybody up," he hissed. "Stand-to. Ridley's missing."

Muller said, his voice groggy, "Enemy pick him off?"

"We'd have heard something."

Dawn was creeping in, the light increasing to where they could track Ridley in the layer of fresh snow. Charlie and Woody crept out to the latrine, where they saw tracks heading down the mountain, the reverse of their route up two days before. They followed them, senses tingling. Had Ridley been captured? Killed?

Three hundred yards on Charlie caught sight of him, sitting hunched under his poncho. Puffs of breath rose from the bent form. Charlie touched Woody's shoulder and put his other fore-finger across his lips. "Get back to the section. I'll be along soon."

Charlie stepped toward Ridley, who had to know he was there but gave no sign. His rifle was muzzle down. He had both hands folded over its butt, his forehead resting on his hands. For a moment Charlie doubted his first impression. Ridley was green, and he'd already gone through tough ordeals. He saw his co-replacement Trent shot dead, he'd fought a brief battle, he'd seen the violent enemy. Maybe Ridley just needed to assess things on his own?

Ridley's right hand dropped, grazing the trigger guard. The muzzle of his .303 was pressed against the toe of his left boot.

"Don't," Charlie said.

"Think about it, Ridley. It's not worth it." Charlie concentrated on Ridley's right hand where it hung adjacent the trigger guard.

He moved so he was in front of Ridley, who looked up at him. His eyes were swollen and red, leaking tears that trickled through his stubbled red whiskers. "You saw that," he said. "You saw what happened to Trent. He never had a chance."

Ridley's shoulders heaved. "He wasn't scared, corporal, and look what happened to him. I seen you—you're scared too." Ridley's finger moved into the trigger guard. "Maybe you can take it, but I can't."

Charlie squatted. "Ridley, you pull that trigger and you'll regret it the rest of your life. Guaranteed."

"You think I care about that?" He sobbed once, his shoulders heaving.

"We're all in a strange place out here, it could happen to anybody. You're part of 13 Platoon, Ridley."

Ridley shook his head.

"There are only seven of us, Ridley. 13 Platoon is just hanging on, we hardly exist. We can't lose you too." Charlie reached out. Just as his hand touched the rifle, Ridley's finger twitched. Charlie froze.

"Woody risked his life, coming out here, looking for you, going back to the platoon on his own. I need you to come back with me. Now."

Nothing moved, the men and the mountain around them silent. Charlie held his breath.

Ridley raised his eyes and gave a slight nod. Charlie wasn't sure what that meant, but he gripped the stock of the rifle just inches above Ridley's foot, holding his breath. Ridley's hand fell away from the trigger guard, and Charlie lifted the .303 and put the safety on. He stood, and dragged a forearm across his brow.

"Come on." He turned up the mountain.

After a moment's hesitation Ridley fell in behind him. Charlie double-checked the safety was on and the weapon not cocked before handing him his .303. "Your weapon is a disgrace," he said. "I want it to see it gleam an hour from now."

A runner appeared with a message from Lieutenant Munro telling Charlie that his section should maintain their present position and stand by for further orders. Charlie sent the man back with news of their casualty. Two hours later four figures climbed up from the valley below. He recognized one as 2 Platoon's lean commander, Lieutenant Munro; his companion was also lean but half a head taller and with a start Charlie saw three pips and a crown on his shoulders. He was Brigadier John Rockingham, commanding officer of the entire Canadian Brigade: Patricias, Vandoos, Royal Canadian Regiment, and all their related services and firepower. Even if the 2nd Princess Patricia's was the only Canadian battalion in Korea, with the rest of Rocky's command back in Washington State sharpening their skills before shipping west.

With the officers were two stretcher-bearers, who took charge of Trent's body.

Rockingham had distinguished himself in World War II, with a very successful time in command of a battalion in France. He looked at home in a coat and battledress with mud ground into the fabric, appearing like a man who had just scrambled up the side of a daunting peak—which of course he had.

"At ease, men," he said. "This is my first taste of the conditions you Patricias have been dealing with for the past weeks. I can tell you that it's as tough as anything we faced in Europe seven years ago. The good news is that the rest of the Canadian brigade has finished training at Fort Lewis and will join you shortly."

The brigadier mentioned the good relationship between the Patricias and the US and other UN forces, and how well the Pats were performing as part of the 27th British Commonwealth Infantry Brigade.

"I've heard nothing but positive things about you. I hope to meet with many if not all of the Patricias before flying back to Canada." He took a keen look at the battered and somewhat bedraggled group of riflemen, and nodded.

Rockingham made a point of speaking to individual soldiers, asking about their families, if they had concerns. While he did that, Lieutenant Munro took Charlie aside. Charlie gave him a brief summary of the previous day's action including the loss of Private Trent, and the elusive enemy they fought.

"How's morale?" Munro asked.

Charlie didn't miss a beat. "Top notch, sir. The men were strong through it all. We're ready for anything."

"Well done. Sorry about your reinforcement. The other fellow okay?"

Ridley. "So far so good," Charlie said. He had weighed up the risk of Ridley arcing out or holding it together. "He had his moments, but he settled down."

Munro raised his eyebrows but didn't pursue it. "Hold your present position pending further orders. Make your supplies last."

Charlie watched as the two officers left to proceed back to platoon and company headquarters. Not that there were much by way of amenities there; the Patricias were running a lean and efficient operation. Even the brigadier had to climb the mountain on foot, on his own until he reached the fighting troops in their frigid locations.

13 Platoon hunkered down for another day, then received orders to return to the lowlands. They were to rejoin the rest of the battalion for another push northward.

CHAPTER 22

Charlie watched as Lieutenant Mike Levy jabbed his finger at a number on a map: 795. All three 10 Platoon section leaders and Charlie, representing 13 Platoon, were gathered around Levy and Donald Malloy, his platoon sergeant.

It was April 14, almost a month after the disastrous Regimental Day, followed by the protracted stay on Hill 1250 when they lost Trent. The hills of Korea over which the Patricias had trudged and fought since were starting to run together in Charlie's mind. It had taken a long day's march to reach the base of 795, a rugged feature, followed by another night in a trench. At these altitudes and the advancing season it was still chilly but at least snow hadn't built up overnight.

Levy led his platoon up a gully that looked as if it could be a route to the top of 795. Charlie and 13 were a hundred yards to the right of Levy's platoon and flanked on their right by 11 Platoon, making their way up yet another fold in the rugged landscape.

Charlie felt wrung out. They'd been climbing hills and fighting for nearly a month since their Regimental Day break when they lost Powell to his taste for alcohol. It was hard going, the footing treacherous with loose rocks that could give way under a man's weight.

Machine gun fire opened up from above. The bullets seemed to be directed off to the left, perhaps at 10 Platoon. A moment later a rifle fired, the bullet whining off a stunted tree on Charlie's right. The section went to ground on the steep hillside, with Charlie waving up Muller and Dunstan with the Bren. A burst from a machine gun ricocheted bullets off a nearby boulder. Charlie nodded at Muller who opened fire with the Bren, placing a series of short bursts against the ridgeline in the approximate area from which the enemy had fired. While Muller and Dunstan kept the Bren in action Charlie and the other riflemen made their careful way forward and upward.

The whistle of incoming mortar fire forced the platoon to hunker down, but instead of the crash of high explosive mortar bombs smoke canisters popped, emitting a yellow cloud that enveloped the platoon.

"Where the fuck did that come from?" said Frenchy.

Charlie didn't care whether it was smoke from friend or foe but the Chinese machine gunners had gone silent, unable to see their targets. To his left he heard Levy urging his troops on. "Up and at 'em, boys," Charlie said, standing up and pushing up the hill.

It was difficult to see more than a few yards. Progress was slow, as they picked their way between large boulders that festooned the hillside.

The mustard-coloured fog lightened. Charlie found himself in the open, the hill as steep as ever, but enemy gunfire flashing from the ridgeline. Somebody on his left grunted as Charlie heard the thwack of a bullet's impact. "Down, down," he shouted, and an instant later a flurry of grenades arced down the hill toward them. Most of them fell short and exploded further up the slope, shrapnel whipping overhead. A wounded man crawled toward Charlie, groaning; Charlie recognized one of Lt Levy's men. The shower of grenades stopped. Frenchy and Woody helped the stricken man, half dragging him down the steep hill. The enemy was too far away, and uphill at that, to attempt a grenade response. Charlie fired a couple of rounds where he thought he saw movement.

Any activity by the platoon brought a fusillade from two machine guns. Pinned down by the now ferocious fire and unable to advance, Charlie ordered the section back down the hill using the cover of some remaining wisps of smoke. They joined the survivors of 10 Platoon, who had suffered one killed and six other casualties.

Next morning they were back on the hill under desultory long-range rifle fire, keeping low, staying out of a direct line of sight from the crest. As he turned to wave up the Bren gunners, Charlie heard the distant whine of jet aircraft. With his binoculars he picked out two jets, circling miles away. As he watched they broke off and turned toward him.

Side-by-side, their profiles reduced to the dark circles of their fuselage with slender wings either side, the jets came straight at him. He shouted a warning and dove for cover, images of napalm flames flitting across his mind. The aircraft flashed overhead, swooping mere feet above them, the noise shattering. They dropped their deadly canisters of jellied gasoline and the near side of the Chinese-occupied hilltop burst into ugly yellow and orange flames. Black oily smoke flared over the funereal pyre.

—

They were close now, within three hundred yards of the top of 795, hunkered in a low spot out of the line of fire. It was time to see if any resistance remained. Charlie thought that, like many air strikes, this one may have hit the Chinese hard but it never stopped them for long. It was up to the ground troops to get to the top of the hill and engage their stubborn enemy face-to-face. He was distracted, thinking about how vulnerable they were, flesh and blood about to advance on a hilltop infested with enemies who could be crouched over machine guns and rifles, ready to rip them to shreds.

Charlie dropped his pack to the ground. The others followed suit, not wanting to be encumbered with all their trappings for the final assault.

Large packs, ponchos, smaller packs with extraneous ammunition and grenades landed in a heap; they'd stick with spare .303 clips, loaded mags for the Bren, and the grenades hung on their shoulder straps. Woody was last to get all his paraphernalia off, and flung his poncho onto the pile.

Charlie hefted his carbine and looked at the slope ahead of them. He'd order the men to move out on a broad front, ten yards—

An explosion boomed. Woody's poncho bucked up into the air, the men diving for cover in all directions.

"What the hell was that?" Charlie said. Not a mortar round, nothing incoming—maybe a booby trap? But he hadn't noticed anything out of the ordinary when he dropped his pack.

"Jesus Christ," Frenchy said, getting to his feet, eyeing the pile of gear and looking embarrassed. "Straightening the pins on our grenades." He glanced at Muller and chuckled. "Somebody overdid it."

"Don't look at me," Muller said.

Woody retrieved his poncho and held it up.

Charlie could see daylight through holes in the garment. "Not gonna help much when the rain starts," he said.

Checking around, Charlie was relieved there were no other troops in the immediate vicinity, especially no officers. And thank God nobody was hit. Might be tough explaining to Big Jim back in Battalion HQ, standing at attention and charged with heaven knows what military crime.

"Lighten up, corporal," Frenchy said, still laughing. "It wasn't your poncho."

It took them a couple of minutes but they collected themselves. Muller with the Bren, the others grasping rifles, bayonets fixed, ready to move forward and upward at Charlie's nod.

In spite of the napalm and strafing attacks by the jets the Patricias faced token resistance as they climbed toward the crest. They returned scattered rifle and light machine gun fire, but the enemy was ephemeral, withdrawing yet again. The Chinese left behind those incinerated by the USAF Thunder Jets, their blackened and misshapen bodies still at their posts.

CHAPTER 23

The Republic of Korea troops that were promised by the UN commander to relieve the Patricias were late. 13 Platoon had been told they'd be out of there and off Hill 795 by early morning, then mid-morning, then noon, but it was 1600 hours before they were cleared to march down off the hill. The sun broke through and lit up the near hills, promising a break from the bleak winter weather that had been their lot for weeks. They were to be met at a nearby crossroads by troop carriers.

A two-hour hike brought them to the map reference. Lieutenant Levy's 10 Platoon was there ahead of them and had sentries posted. The men of 13 Platoon were happy to find a spot where they could shed their packs and light up.

Lieutenant Levy squatted with a group of his men. Charlie wondered if Levy had somehow heard about their accidental grenade discharge, which could have thrown his attack off course with disastrous results.

Muller was sitting on the ground close to Charlie. "I hope I don't stink as bad as you do, Charlie."

"Not to worry, showers coming up. Maybe even clean socks."

"Gonna feel good," Muller said, and added, "Here comes Lieutenant Levy."

Charlie stood.

"Your boys did a good job up on 795, corporal," Levy said.

Charlie blinked. "Thank you, sir."

Frenchy had sidled up. "How long have we got in the rest area, sir?"

"We should be good for a few days at least."

Levy was a quiet-spoken man who commanded respect. The members of 13 Platoon leaned in and listened. "Right here is where this war started last June. The North Koreans came down this valley." He swept his arm north to south. "At the moment we're just north of the 38th Parallel. Once transport is here it'll take us south, past the former border, for a few days off."

Levy went back to his own platoon just as Charlie heard the rumble of vehicles approaching from the south. It turned out to be the anticipated TCVs, the ubiquitous canvas-covered trucks. The men climbed aboard and settled in for however long it would take them to get to a quiet location out of the shooting zone. A Echelon, Charlie thought. A source of reinforcements, showers, laundry, mail. And beer. Canadian beer.

The convoy stopped just past a hand-lettered sign proclaiming the spot 'Happy Valley,' a couple of miles north of a village called Kapyong.

Charlie shed the clothing he hadn't taken off for a month and tossed it onto a growing pile. Peeling off what was left of his socks and throwing them into a garbage can, he joined the rest of 13 platoon who were cavorting in the shower lineup. The large tent was humid and steaming, an amazing contrast to the last few weeks on the cold Korean hills.

Luxuriating in the hot water, Charlie soaked himself a second time, rinsed off, and went on to the next station where he picked up fresh clothing, feeling like he'd won the Irish Sweepstakes.

10 Platoon and their 13 Platoon hangers-on had been the last of the Patricias to find their way to Happy Valley. Once showered and in clean clothing they made their way to their tents and collapsed.

A cooked breakfast—not just C-rations out of a can— had Charlie feeling like a king, or at least a minor prince. He took a stroll, coffee in hand. There was a tug-of-war going on between the troopers of an American tank squadron and the 2PPCLI Headquarters Group. Big Jim Stone was himself leading the cheers for the Patricias. He scowled mightily until his boys prevailed and then for a few seconds almost looked relaxed. He had just returned to the battalion, recovered from a bout of smallpox. It would take more than that to keep him out of action.

Charlie lolled on the ground, supported by one elbow and leaning against a crate of supplies. He had coffee in his free hand and watched a softball game umpired by Lieutenant Levy.

Muller appeared. "Charlie! Adjutant wants you, on the double."

"What for?" Not that it mattered. When the adjutant summoned you, you went. He gulped the dregs of his coffee and patted down his trousers, knocking off bits of debris. At battalion headquarters, the captain sat behind a folding table covered with papers. "At ease," he said, and pawed through the documents.

"Ah, here we are." He looked up. "Congratulations, Black."

"Sir?"

"You're promoted. Take charge of your section, corporal. With Sergeant Price out of action, and nobody around to replace him, you're on your own for now. Your section is all that's left of 13 Platoon. Orton is yours, right?"

"Yes sir."

"Did you know he applied for a change of trade, to go on a course for medics? In any event, he's lined up for it. Tell him to report to the RSM to get the paperwork sorted out. And while you're at it, send Accardo in to see me."

"Acc—" Charlie had almost forgotten Frenchy's actual name.

The captain sent him on his way with a wave of his hand. Charlie felt a surge of pride, and for a moment at least stopped doubting himself.

What was up with Frenchy? The adjutant was hard to read. Was Frenchy to be promoted? It could cause problems if he also made corporal. His mind turned to Orton's transfer out of the platoon. Orton had proved himself many times. They'd miss his enthusiasm and medical expertise.

"Black!"

It was Sergeant Smith, his platoon sergeant from way back in Wainwright, when Charlie'd been a gung-ho member of 7 Platoon.

"I see you've been promoted. Good going, Black."

"Thanks, sergeant."

"We've all earned a break. A couple more days here'll help morale. Think you can keep 13 Platoon out of trouble?"

"Probably depends on how many beer Big Jim lets us have."

Smith laughed but had other things on his mind and went on his way. "Keep your head up, Black, look all 'round" he said. "Noncoms tend to get picked off, eh?"

Charlie found Frenchy trying to talk Muller out of one his beers and told him the adjutant wanted him.

"What for?"

Charlie shrugged. He wasn't surprised when Frenchy reappeared a few minutes later to root through his pack for a needle and thread and sewed his lance corporal hooks back on.

Charlie took advantage of the downtime to search out a set of corporal's insignia and sew them onto his own sleeves. He was glad to see Frenchy's promotion was to lance corporal; that would make him an easy choice to supervise the Bren crew.

He returned to the ball diamond and sat on the ground next to Muller, overtaken by a feeling of wellness and even satisfaction when Muller gave him a slap on the back at the sight of his new rank insignia.

Orton looked him up. He'd heard about his transfer for medical training from the RSM. "Sorry to leave you in the lurch."

"Don't worry about us, Orton," Charlie said. "Anybody can throw on a band-aid, right?"

Later that day more men from other platoons returned from five days of R and R in Japan. They looked exhausted. And no wonder, if their feats of drinking and laying waste to Japanese women were even half true. Nobody from Charlie's section had yet to experience the Japanese interlude, but they were all hopeful.

"Makes you want to get back there, right, Charlie?" Muller said, giving Charlie a dig in the ribs. "Give you a second shot at the US Navy Shore Patrol."

"Very funny. They're the last people I want to meet in Japan."

Dropping off to sleep that night, Charlie fingered the shallow scar on his forehead, a reminder of the only time he had visited a Japanese bar. He hoped he get the chance to write a new chapter of that story soon.

Included in a truckload of supplies that arrived next day was three weeks' worth of mail. Men claimed their envelopes and letter forms and packages and hived themselves off into what privacy they could manage. Charlie lined up to retrieve his.

"Charlie!" Somebody slammed into him from behind and grabbed him around the shoulders. Powell, clean-shaven and in an impeccable uniform, grinning from ear to ear. "Did you miss me?"

"Sure did. I had to carry all that extra ammo we usually loaded you down with."

"Believe me, I'll carry more than that if I have to. Heaven save me from ever having to do time in Big Jim's cells again."

Charlie looked at him. "Something's changed."

"Yeah. In between doubling up and down hills with my rifle at the high port and scrubbing out cells on my hands and knees, I did a lot of thinking. Plus—know what?" He waved a letter. "I've got a baby girl waiting for me back home."

Powell went off to look for other members of the section to share the good news. He didn't have a beer in hand. Maybe he'd sworn off alcohol after his near-death experience.

It was late in the day when the postal corps had Charlie's backlog of mail ready for him. Finding a quiet spot in an army camp crowded with young men who had just had the pressure of combat removed wasn't easy, but Charlie retreated behind a line of trucks and sat on a running board. He sorted the envelopes, savouring the pleasure to come.

His family numbered their letters on the outside so he could read them in order and tell if anything was missing. This batch had editions 33 to 42. He was amazed to see a letter addressed in his father's handwriting. What would his dad say, after his long silence? That would be the icing on the cake. He saved it for last and tucked it on the bottom of the pile.

That was the end of his self-discipline. He tore open Wanda's letter.

Dear Charlie

I received all your letters—I think. You should number yours, too! It's nice to be able to keep track of what you're up to. Things have been very quiet around here, you'd never think there is a war on, the way people act. The papers do talk about the war, but that's about it.

School is going fine, since I have lots of time to study, no boyfriend around! Hint, hint!

Holy smoke! Wanda wanted him home, things were okay, she was thinking about him. Saying he was part of her life even though far away. He couldn't stop grinning. He stood up and took a couple of deep breaths before reading the rest of her letter. She recounted her family's doings, comments about her instructors at Normal School, her classmates. Her letter closed:

So don't poke around there any longer than you have to, Charlie. Because when you get home we're all going to be very happy.

All my love
Wanda

He shook his head and looked around, making sure he wasn't dreaming. He did a quick reckoning. He'd signed on for eighteen months, eight of which were history. Less than a year to go. Maybe he'd be home even before his time was up. Rumour had it that no more than twelve months need be served in Korea. A hint of what the future might hold flashed across his mind. A future for himself, Wanda, and his family.

Folding Wanda's letter, he tucked it into his breast pocket, sat again, and opened the first of his family's letters. There was a short update from Jackie and several from his mother, passing on bits of gossip about mutual acquaintances and what Harry was up to.

He opened the latest from his mother.

Dear Charlie

The mailman just delivered your letter telling us about the time you're having with your friends, and having received the socks we sent.

It struck him how quirky the mail was. He was pretty sure he'd written about the socks way back when they had the break from action for Regimental Day. Seemed like a lifetime ago.

I'm very sorry to have to tell you, but your dad had a stroke. We got help as soon as we could. Doctor Brown came within an hour, but it was too late. Jackie has been a big help, I don't know how I'd get by without her. The service will be on this coming Saturday. I know you can't be here. We'll be thinking about...

Charlie rocked back and banged his head against the truck's door. His eyes were open but unfocussed, the tents, trucks, jeeps, and forbidding Korean landscape blurred, his mind blank. He stood, blinking. His dad, dead? Looking down, seeing the letter in his hand, he read it through to the end, the brief plans for a funeral. Bill would be buried by now. What would life be like? He shook his head, waiting for answers, finding none.

He had last seen his dad in hospital in Edmonton, when he'd taken a couple of days leave and the battalion went on without him to the west coast. He inquired at the front desk and was directed to a surgical award.

"How are you, Dad?"

Bill's eyes widened. "What a surprise!" He had been flexing his left shoulder, his lower arm encased in plaster and supported by his right hand.

"I guess you're not going to be laid up for very long," Charlie said. Bill looked determined, working to get over his injury.

"No longer than I have to be."

Bill was happy to see him for a moment, then his face fell as he took in Charlie's uniform. "So the misadventure continues."

"No, no, Dad, it's going fine," Charlie stammered.

"You know what I mean. I don't care that it's going fine." Bill's face was set as Charlie remembered it, his mouth a firm line across his strong face. "I don't want to see you in that uniform again."

They hadn't exchanged a dozen words after that. Charlie left the hospital, feeling numb.

Now, holding his mother's letter, Charlie's mind reeled. He felt like he'd been skinned, dragged naked across bare rock. Thrilled about Wanda one minute, the next beating himself up for dooming his father to dying an angry, withdrawn man.

Putting his mother's letter aside, he saw Bill's letter, forgotten in the rush of emotion. He steeled himself. Would his father berate him from the grave, doom him to a lifetime of guilt?

Dear Charlie

This is hard for me to write. I think your mother told you I'm back home after I made it out of the hospital in Edmonton. It wasn't until weeks later that I started to feel better. Your mother was very worried when she heard about the train crash. Thank God you weren't aboard.

I never hid from you and Jeffrey the fact that I had what some fools called a Good War in 1914-18. As sure as night follows day, when World War II came along I gave Jeffrey my blessing and even encouraged him to join up. Once he was overseas, though, I hardly dared take a breath, I was so worried about him. Then the hammer fell, and he was killed, gone forever.

And now I worry about you.

You are the only son we have.

I still think you made a mistake by volunteering, but it was your choice to make.

Come home safe.

Your father

Charlie stood up, still gripping his dad's letter, and walked. He walked past the tents, the long lines and clumps of parked vehicles, the men playing softball, the staked-out tents occupied by relaxing soldiers and their gear. He was oblivious to the tears that streamed down his face.

Not trusting himself, he stayed away from 13 Platoon's area until long after lights out. Bill had turned a corner and perhaps had been ready to look straight at Charlie, to talk to him. To share Charlie's fears, and to talk about his own. But he never would. Bill was gone, and Charlie felt a huge rip in his heart. He already missed his dad, his old dad, the happy warrior before Jeffrey was killed. And he would never prove anything to him, because he was no more. Charlie crept into his shared tent and lay down in the unaccustomed comfort of a cot and clean bedding, only to lie awake for hours.

PART FOUR

HILL 677

APRIL 23, 1951

CHAPTER 24

On April 23rd, 1951, four months since the Patricias marched ashore off the *Private Joe*, Charlie woke at 0400 hours, his mind calm. He dressed in a clean uniform and pulled on his boots. He left the platoon tents and their snoring occupants and walked in the general direction of headquarters.

The heavy generators were silent, the camp still. He shivered; he could see his own breath as he made his way past the rows of tents, trucks, and half-tracks, feeling at ease in the midst of the familiar equipment. What would be going on back in Cloverdale? It would still be the previous day, with Wanda attending classes.

And what about his family? His mother's days would be long without Bill's presence, however quiet he had been since Jeff's death. Young Harry, whom Bill had always paid attention to in spite of his grief, would miss his grandfather. Jackie, Charlie's sister-in-law, would be busy with her job and her own life.

And what of him? What was he doing in Korea, thousands of miles from home, when the goal that had urged him on—the need to please Bill—was no longer there?

There were scattered lights on, the brightest ones located at the manned gate to the camp, where a small generator hammered away. He became aware of the increased scent of night soil, the villagers adding fertilizer to their paddies now that spring was arriving. Heading toward the gate he saw a sentry with a slung rifle over his shoulder, lounging against a jeep parked at the side of the road. Through the open gate he could see the Happy Valley sign. Happy were the troops, with nothing ahead of them but a few days of fun and games, maybe even a trip for R and R to Japan. Mail, showers, and clean socks, a near-perfect break from trudging up and down hills in search of a retreating enemy. Happy he had been, until he opened his mother's letter.

When he thought about his dad his heart ached. He wished he could have spoken to his father, spoken to him about Jeffrey, about Bill's own time in World War I.

He could picture the old soldier, his proud bearing before Jeffrey was killed. What he, Charlie, wouldn't have given to have Bill proud of him too. And now at the end of his life his father had come to accept Charlie's presence in the army. Had Bill come to terms at last with Jeffrey's death? Or did he carry feelings of guilt to his deathbed, unable to forgive himself for encouraging Jeffrey to do what so many young Canadian men were doing in World War II, joining the armed forces to rid the world of the Nazi tyranny?

Charlie hoped his dad had found peace before passing on, or at least acceptance.

But life continued. He was a corporal in the Special Force, responsible for a section of men; men that he knew would stand behind him, men he could lead. He felt the stirrings of a new motivation, a sense of belonging.

He was short of the gate by fifty yards when he saw a vehicle charging toward the camp, its headlights undulating on the rough road. A sentry stood in the middle of the drive and held up his arm. A mud-covered Jeep skidded to a stop. The officer in the passenger seat gestured and said something to the sentry. The vehicle jerked ahead. Charlie jumped aside as it shot past him toward the headquarters area. In the darkness he couldn't make out who was in it. Charlie walked on to where two provosts, a corporal and a private, manned the gate.

Charlie nodded at them. "Who was that?"

"Lieutenant Islington."

"What did he have to say? What's his rush?"

"You think he'd tell us? He just ordered us to get the hell out of his way."

Something was up. Charlie knew it, 13 Platoon knew it, the whole battalion knew it. At 0800 hours Frenchy looked him up.

"Where are all the officers?"

"Darned if I know." The officers had been front-and-centre the last couple of days, taking part in sports and relaxing with their men. Now they had disappeared.

Eight hours later, Malloy, the 10 Platoon sergeant, hurried over to where Charlie and Frenchy stood in front of their tents. "Get your platoon organized, Corporal. Pack up your gear, we're moving out in an hour."

"Moving out? What's up?"

"You have your orders. Move it!"

"Where are all the officers?"

"That's not your concern," Malloy said, turning his back.

Charlie knew when to shut up.

"Damn!" Frenchy said. "It's all happening. Whatever it is."

The senior NCOs were everywhere, organizing extra ammunition, water, and food for the troops to jam into their packs. Giving his cot and sleeping bag a farewell glance, Charlie wondered if he'd be back here again. He triple-checked his carbine and slung a bag of .30 calibre magazines and ammo around his neck. The men of 13 Platoon were keyed-up but quiet, talking in low tones as they went about their business, packing up and assembling in a group.

A convoy of jeeps and trucks streamed into camp and came to a stop. The missing officers disembarked and fanned out. Forty yards away Sergeant Malloy gathered 10 Platoon, and Lieutenant Levy joined them. Levy spoke intently to his men for some minutes, then turned and hurried toward Charlie.

"13 Platoon all present and accounted for, corporal?" Levy said.

"Yes, sir. But we're down to seven men."

Levy shook his head. "Not even a real section. That'll have to do. You're now attached to 10 Platoon. You'll take orders from me, and from Sergeant Malloy here in my absence." He paused, looking at Charlie. "Any questions?"

Charlie squared his shoulders. He'd only been a lance corporal for a matter of weeks, and a corporal for twenty-four hours.

He liked Levy, who already had his hands full. They would have their own platoon officer if Lieutenant Toogood hadn't been wounded. "Yes, sir. Where are we going?"

"Just found out myself. South Korean troops were holding the line a few miles north of here. They've been overrun by God knows how many Red Chinese." Levy stopped to look at his watch. "We and the Australians are moving out to put a stop to them. We'll be the only thing standing between them and Seoul, so make damn sure you and your section are ready." Levy turned on his heel and headed back to his own platoon.

"This is it! Yahoo!" Charlie flinched. He hadn't noticed Muller standing right behind him.

The rumble of truck and half-track engines rose in the background. Noncoms shouted orders and officers rushed around, looking determined.

The battalion hadn't scrambled like this since they'd landed at Pusan. Whatever was about to happen, it would be big. Big, and frightening. Charlie kept busy, organizing his own gear and checking the platoon's progress.

He called them together. Dunstan was already geared up and ready to go, waiting for whatever Charlie had to say. Woody joined them and thumped his pack down on the ground, his rifle slung on his shoulder. Red-headed Ridley arrived with no fuss, looking competent. Wearing a happy grin, Muller came over and stood with the Bren propped on the ground, his hand loose on the barrel. Frenchy, looking detached, stood off to one side as Powell, his pockets bulging with Bren magazines, rushed up to stand beside Muller, looking excited at being back with his mates.

Charlie looked them over. But for Ridley, they'd been together since their time on board the *Private Joe*, as the Patricias marched and fought their way north after the retreating Chinese. Their identity was that of 13 Platoon, and it didn't matter that it was a platoon in name only, a bare section. They'd fight for each other.

"We're attached to 10 Platoon," he said. "Lieutenant Levy says we're in for a battle." Charlie looked at each of them in turn.

"We've been in fights, and this will be one more. We stick together, we'll be fine."

He left it at that. They were as ready as they could be, but he wondered if it would be enough. All around them the battalion erupted into action, readying itself to fight.

CHAPTER 25

Along column of 6x6 trucks lined the Happy Valley sideroad, their engines running, khaki-clad drivers behind the wheels or standing outside on the ground smoking. The weather was improving every day; it was warm and dry. Beyond the trucks on the main north-south route Charlie could see a ragged column of humanity, flooding south toward the village of Kapyong, some two miles further down the valley. Parallel to the unpaved road was the sinuous Kapyong River, a modest waterway that emerged from somewhere beyond the hills to the north to end up in the Han River, completing its journey to the sea once past Seoul. South Korea's much-battered capital city lay a little over twenty miles to the southwest.

Charlie stood at the side of 13 Platoon's designated truck in the line, doing a visual check on each of the soldiers as they climbed in. He nodded to Woody, the last man to climb up, and was about to swing aboard himself, when Lieutenant Levy came by.

"See that hill, corporal?"

Charlie looked where Levy pointed. A massive hill perhaps two miles away that loomed over the Kapyong valley and its neighbouring hills.

"That's where we're going. It's a hard climb, but nothing we're not used to. Hill 677."

The truck bounced and jerked its way north. Inside, 13 Platoon did the familiar dance, shifting back and forth under their canvas cover. It put Charlie in mind of the agonizing trip across the Pacific in the *Private Joe*, where they swayed to the motions of the hull. There had been a lot more to 13 Platoon then.

Charlie thought about his section, and how best to use them. He could leave Frenchy in charge of the Bren crew, with Muller on it and Powell his number two. Woody and Dunstan in a second trench, himself and Ridley in another. It would have to do.

Muller reached across and whacked Charlie on the knee. "We're gonna do it, Charlie. We'll stop those bastards in their tracks."

"Sure." Charlie tried to grin. "If anybody can do it, it's us."

"Watch out, you Chinks," said Dunstan. "The bums from the slums are coming for you."

Pushing the braggadocio into the background, Charlie checked things off. Extra .30 ammo slung around his neck. Spare mags for Muller's Bren parcelled out to Frenchy and Powell. Bayonets on their belts. C-rations, water and a blanket in every pack. Grenades clipped on. The infantryman's best friends, shovels and a pick.

This was a short trip. The troops climbed down, rifles in hand, and stood by their packs, waiting for orders. To the south was the valley they'd just ridden through, flat and brown in the late winter-early spring. In front of them was 677, a daunting hill a couple of miles across, rearing up from the plain.

The leading rifle companies were already on their way up a dirt track that appeared to lead toward the heights. 13 Platoon waited its turn, falling in behind D Company. Once onto the slope Charlie settled into a patient march, the men around him silent.

Frenchy couldn't help himself. "Tail end Charlie, as usual!"

Nobody laughed.

The afternoon light was giving way to early twilight as they climbed. Their route narrowed in spots, circling around boulders and outcrops of granite bedrock. Small, local landslides were negotiated well enough by the single file of soldiers. But the steep slope, a constant challenge, seemed to go on forever. When Charlie took a moment to look back, he could see out over the valley of the Kapyong River, as far south as their recent Happy

Valley location and, in the distance, the battered village of Kapyong.

"Kind of strange," Woody said. "Usually the bastards are shooting at us when we climb these damn mountains."

"Big Jim must be sure there aren't any Chinese up there," Charlie said.

The gradient eased off. They were perhaps halfway to the highest point of land, on a kind of steep-sided plateau, having climbed the south-facing slope. To the east the plateau dropped away to the valley of the Kapyong River, across which there was another, somewhat lower hill, 504. It would be defended by the 3ʳᵈ Royal Australian Regiment. But to the north and west Hill 677 sloped sharply upward, toward knife-edged ridges and fingers of land.

The companies separated. A, B and C fanned out to locations north and east of the central plateau. D Company's 10, 11 and 12 Platoons set off to the north-west and the height of land, with 13 Platoon trailing them.

Lieutenant Levy stood to one side of the trail and waited until Charlie and the rest of 13 Platoon came up to him. "Here's the plan," he said. "Battalion tactical headquarters will set up somewhere near here. But see that highest peak?" He jabbed a thumb over his shoulder. "That's where D Company will dig in and defend. We'll figure out where to place the individual platoons when we get there, and you're with us. Any questions, corporal?"

Tactical headquarters meant small numbers of personnel and their assorted radio trucks, jeeps, and half-tracks. Charlie wondered if the vehicles would be able to negotiate the steep, narrow climb, but that wasn't his problem. "No, sir."

"Okay. We're off." Levy adjusted his shoulder straps and strode away to catch up with 10 Platoon. Besides his pack, he carried a Thompson submachine gun Charlie had heard he'd picked up from a dead Chinese soldier, along with a box of loaded magazines. Pretty ironic—the Chinese would have taken it off an American. Neither the Lee-Enfield .303, an accurate rifle but with a bolt action, nor the Canadian-made but temperamental Sten were for Levy. He was ready for a close-quarters battle.

CHAPTER 26

It had been a long grind up the south face of the hill, a hike that although difficult wasn't anything the soldiers of 2PPCLI weren't used to. But now D Company's 10, 11, and 12 Platoons, augmented by 13, were up against steeper terrain by far, crawling up the ridges that they hoped would give them commanding, defensible positions.

At the head of 10 Platoon scrambled Lieutenant Levy, with Charlie and 13 following. Frenchy brought up the rear, keeping the men closed up. The minimal banter that had accompanied their transport by truck and the climb to the plateau had died away.

At times Charlie found himself gripping clumps of grass with a free hand or on all fours to get up the more extreme pitches. With the increased altitude came a reduction in vegetation, consisting now of coarse dead grass a foot or eighteen inches high, occasional low shrubs, and scattered small conifers. Thank God we're not attacking up this open slope, Charlie thought.

2200 hours. A half-moon bathed Hill 677 in monochrome light. As they climbed their line of sight to the east cleared, with Hill 504, where the Aussies were digging in, visible.

Looking up the path ahead of them, Charlie saw Captain Mills, his binoculars focussed on the valley to the left of 504. Wally Mills was second in command of D Company but, with the company commander on leave, was in charge.

Pulling out Toogood's glasses, Charlie focussed and saw the valley floor virtually alive, swarming with men tiny in the distance. Chinese troops, their determined advance carrying them toward the base of the Australian hill across the Kapyong River. The platoon was silent, taking a breather, and in that silence he heard the distant crackle of small-arms fire.

D Company pressed on; but every man paused at times to look over to where their Commonwealth compatriots were engaged in a fierce fight. Explosions and gunfire engulfed the northern base of Hill 504.

677 was in sharp relief in the moonlight, its stunted vegetation and rocky surface crystal-clear. Charlie was in the lead now, and behind him clambered Muller and the rest of 13 Platoon, strung out down the steep face. Charlie could hear the scrape of boots on rock, the clank of equipment slung over shoulders. In his mind's eye he saw the long file of a hundred burdened men working their way ever upward, their fate at the top of the hill awaiting them. The corporal's stripes on his arms felt heavy, weighty but bearable. This was what he was meant for.

"Dammit!" Muller's voice.

"You okay?"

"Banged my knee. Fuck!" He sucked in a breath. "It's fine."

Charlie turned back up the slope. At the periphery of his vision a strange fog crept in on them, propelled by a mild breeze. It grew thicker, smelling of burnt grass or brush. Ahead of them, 10 Platoon went to ground. Charlie held up a hand, and 13 Platoon stopped. "What's up?" he called out.

A 10 Platoon lance corporal looked down the slope at him. "We might be lost. Captain Mills is up there somewhere. The lieutenant's checking the map."

Charlie felt for Lieutenant Levy. They were part way up a steep hill, surrounded by fog, with no landmarks visible. The muted sounds of small-arms, artillery and grenades emanating from the Australians' battle added to a feeling of disorientation.

Ten minutes later they were on the move again, climbing ever higher. Charlie's legs burned, the vegetation changing as he climbed. The rare trees were stunted, their bare branches shivering in a light wind. Dead grass covered the ground. Steeper pitches featured an obstacle course of large boulders, over which the long line of soldiers clambered, their packs dragging at them.

They left the fog behind, and Charlie paused and looked around. Through the valley to the north of them he could see the Kapyong River, which meandered east past their hill and then turned south. East of them and to their right, across the river, lay the Australian position, Hill 504, almost 200 metres lower than their hill. From that direction came the constant, subdued roar of the ongoing battle, an inexorable slow-motion wave of gunfire, tracers, and artillery flashes. Chinese tracer rounds arced from the valley floor upward toward the beleaguered Aussies. The intermittent rattle of the defenders' light and medium machine guns was punctuated by the sharp hammer of American Sherman tank cannons. Underlying it all was the muted un–musical background noise of bugles, whistles, and screams of the Chinese and their small arms fire that rose and fell but never went away.

—

Charlie drove his shovel down hard. It hit a rock, the vibration rippling up the handle. "You'd think I'd be used to this," he muttered to himself. He had just taken over from Ridley, who stood close, his rifle cradled in his arms. They were at fifty percent stand-to, half the men digging. They had only just arrived at their destination high on a ridge in an area designated by Captain Mills and Lieutenant Levy.

It was hard going, scraping through the shallow overlay of hardpacked soil and into the rock and gravel beneath. Their slit trench wasn't even a foot deep when Charlie checked his watch. 0300 hours, April 24. They were at fifty percent stand-to until 0500 hours when they'd go to a hundred percent.

A narrow ridge ran from the high ground to the south of them descending in a northward direction. 13 Platoon was assigned to the west-facing side of the ridge, their three trenches laid out in a V-shape toward the west. Ten Platoon was on the east side of the divide, a hundred yards away. Charlie could see the 10 Platoon slit trenches if he stood up, but he had no idea where 11 and 12 were located, except that they were further away to the east past 10's location. South of them, out of sight behind a high point, was Captain Mills and D Company head-quarters.

Lieutenant Levy had instructed Charlie that he wanted 13 Platoon able to protect 10 Platoon's left flank. Levy anticipated a main line of attack from the north, his defensive slit trenches oriented in that direction.

13 Platoon dug in on a ledge, the upper part of a gentle slope that faced west. On Charlie's right front Woody and Dunstan scraped in turns at the rocky soil. To his left the Bren gun trench benefitted by having two men digging at a time, Frenchy manning the Bren and looking out while Powell and Muller ripped and gouged at the earth.

A terrifying crack and blinding flash of light threw the slope ahead of them into stark illumination, followed a split-second later by another. Charlie threw himself as low as he could into his half-dug trench.

He raised his head and looked around. All was quiet, his vision dazzled. "Everybody okay?"

"Good here," Frenchy said, and Woody chimed in as well.

"What the hell was that?" Frenchy said.

"Artillery for sure," Charlie said. "Let's hope it's ours, some sort of ranging shots, and not Chinese."

"Those Kiwis better know what they're doing," Frenchy said. "That was too close."

The 16th Field Regiment, Royal New Zealand Artillery was part of the 27th British Commonwealth Brigade commanded by Brigadier Burke, as was 2PPCLI. At any given time the 16th Field could be given artillery assignments to protect the Patricias or others, or to conduct offensive shoots against the Chinese.

Charlie's ears rang. *Too damn close,* he thought. At least the flashes of light hadn't revealed any enemy troops.

Two minutes later, every sense and nerve on edge, Charlie heard someone approaching from behind. He turned and made out Sergeant Malloy scrambling across the high ground that separated them from 10 Platoon.

"Those damn trenches aren't going to do you any good," Malloy said. "Get them deeper if you want to survive. Four feet."

Charlie knew four feet was the aim, but he also knew how unyielding the Hill 677 ground was. Not that he was about to quibble with Sergeant Malloy. They were already putting their backs into it, spurred on by the artillery rounds. Malloy went back to his own platoon. Charlie kept watch while Ridley scraped away at what was so far a minor gouge on a lonely hilltop. But for their trenches, they were as visible as earwigs on a china platter.

Charlie found himself harkening back to when 13 Platoon boasted of more then one section, had a platoon sergeant and a radioman. The latter's equipment might often be unreliable, but provided at least a hope of effective communications. He took another turn on the trench, hacking at the stubborn ground, down to eighteen inches, while Ridley kept watch.

"Someone coming."

Charlie put down his shovel and looked where Ridley pointed. A runner from company headquarters trotted up. Message delivered, he took a deep breath and headed off the way he'd come.

Charlie squatted at a point between the three trenches. "Listen up. Big Jim and the rest of HQ made it up the hill. So here's the situation." He paused, getting it straight in his own head. "We're at the extreme left of our troops, along with 10 Platoon. Somewhere out past 10 are 11 and 12 Platoons, maybe up to 500 yards away to the east. Strung out past them are C, B and A Companies, spread across the north and east faces of the hill."

"Last I looked we're all alone up here," Frenchy said, glancing at the ridge between them and 10 Platoon. "What stops the buggers from coming up in between the companies?"

"If headquarters made it up the hill the mortars and heavy machine guns will be up too. They'll help fill in the gaps between platoons and companies."

"Don't see how that can help us up here."

Charlie didn't either but didn't say so. D Company was on its own.

"That was a hell of a pile of Chinese we saw down in the valley going after the Aussies," Muller said, his voice unaccountably constricted.

"Should be a lot fewer by the time they get to us," Frenchy said.

The trenches were down to solid rock, a couple of feet wide, maybe eight or ten long, only two feet deep. The rocks and gravel they had dug out was shovelled onto the forward sides, forming a bit of a parapet. They stayed at fifty-percent stand-to, half the troops dozing and the other half watching outward, rifles ready. Defending for once, rather than attacking a dug-in enemy. They were on the high ground with Charlie's carbine, rifles, grenades and one automatic weapon between them. It would have to do.

Morning twilight, one hundred percent stand-to, and seven men squatting in their trenches, watching. Charlie checked his carbine, counted the hand grenades in the trench beside him.

"Charlie!" Frenchy hissed.

Their narrow ledge, perhaps thirty yards in width total, tilted away from them to the west. Beyond the ledge was a much steeper slope, with some narrow gullies that ran down the hillside. Two hundred yards down one of them, something moved.

"Stand by," Charlie said, and brought the stock of his carbine to his shoulder, thumb on the safety. In the silence he heard a metallic click as Muller cocked the Bren.

Laying down his carbine, Charlie grabbed his binoculars and peered down at a file of men advancing toward them. He couldn't see any weapons.

"Hold your fire." His voice sounded shaky.

Chinese troops were everywhere in the river valley, and they were beating the hell out of the Australians, but there was something odd about these figures.

"Who are they, Charlie?" Frenchy said, his voice low.

Charlie continued to watch through the binoculars. "I don't see any guns. Not sure how many there are."

The lead man in the group crested the steep slope and turned right, moving across the front of 13 Platoon's position. They were in remnants of Republic of Korea uniforms, bedraggled and stumbling, seeming to Charlie to be aware of the Patricias and their weapons, but paying no attention. They shuffled out of sight to the south and had no sooner disappeared than more came in sight.

Charlie climbed out of his trench and jogged over to jump down into the Bren trench, where Muller had the gun's butt against his shoulder, peering down the barrel at the fleeing men.

"Christ, Charlie, what do you reckon?"

"Lieutenant Levy said the South Koreans were supposed to be blocking the Chinese to the north, but they bugged out. Looks like these guys are survivors, still running."

"What if they're Chinese?" Frenchy said. "They're gonna be all around us and we won't even know it."

"All we can do is stay on our toes. Keep a sharp eye all around." He checked on Woody and Dunstan before going back to his own trench where Ridley had his head on a swivel.

It got quiet.

"Know who scares me, Charlie?"

"Who?"

"Whoever's chasing the ROKs."

Chapter 27

Lieutenant Levy jumped into the trench beside Charlie. "You have to move, corporal," he said. "Company commander's new orders. Come with me."

Charley grabbed his carbine and followed Levy, who walked at a vigorous pace north, along the ledge and away from where 13 was dug in. Levy stopped, moved again, stopped. "Here," he said. "I want you here. We've reorganized our machine gun coverage and firing arcs, and you have to move. Company commander agrees. I want you where you can see my 10 Platoon trenches, and we can see you. Mutual support."

Turning away, he added, "Make it fast, corporal. Things are going to pop."

From this forward position Charlie could see for himself that things were, in fact, heating up. Chinese troops trotted along the base of 677; if they kept on, they'd be in a position to surround the battalion. To the east and across the Kapyong River the Aussies were still holding out. When he turned back, Lieutenant Levy was gone, back to 10 Platoon. Charlie shivered, exposed— if he could see the enemy, they could see him, although they were down in the river valley and maybe a mile away. For the moment they were concentrating on the Australians on 504, but that could change any minute. He hurried back to the 13 Platoon trenches and gave them the good news.

Greeted with a chorus of curses, Charlie said, "Shut up and get at it." He threw his personal gear into his pack and stacked miscellaneous weapons and ammunition on the parapet. "We'll be up where 10 Platoon can cover us when we need help."

Levy had pointed down the slope at the gullies. "They'll come up there, corporal." Using that as an axis, Charlie assigned the Bren group to dig in on the front left, with Woody and

Dunstan front right. The Bren gunners would be able to give supporting enfilade fire across the front of 10 Platoon's sections as well as to Woody and Dunstan. He and Ridley were back at the base of the "V", where he could see the other trenches and lend support where needed.

The platoon didn't give up on the soldier's God-given right to gripe and mutter, but they moved fast, grabbing their gear, jogging up to the positions Charlie indicated, and flying at the hard earth once more. Charlie checked their now-abandoned scrapes, picking up spare gear and ammo left behind.

They stayed at fifty percent stand-to, half of them digging at any one time. It wasn't quick, but the slit trenches took shape, the men redoubling their efforts after glancing down at the relentless movement of Chinese troops in the valley. The scene was punctuated by battered oncoming ROK troops, who continued to straggle up the steep trails and disappear to the south.

Charlie changed around with Ridley every fifteen minutes or so, one of them on watch and the other digging. He kept an eye on Ridley, making sure the kid was alert and concentrating on the ground in front of them, as well as peering around himself, double-checking. It wasn't any easier when Ridley was on the shovel, the constant movement of the Chinese troops in the valley of the Kapyong keeping his nerves on edge. He fought against the feeling of being alone and vulnerable. A whole ROK division, maybe 10,000 men, had bugged out in the face of the Chinese onslaught. The Patricias—down to a few hundred troops—were awfully thin on the ground.

The drone of heavy aircraft engines insinuated itself into Charlie's consciousness, fading out, coming back, fading again.

"Hold the fort," he said to Ridley. He walked then crawled to the steep height of land thirty yards back from his trench, to where he had a clear view of the landscape. To the south of him was Captain Mills' D Company HQ, and in front was Lieutenant Levy's 10 Platoon, with the miniscule 13 Platoon just off the left and facing west. 11 and 12 Platoons were spread out east of 10 Platoon, out of sight because of the rugged landforms of the hill.

An American DC3 circled low over their hill, looking gigantic at short range. "PATRICIAS, THIS IS BRIGADIER BURKE," bellowed an amplified voice that overrode the noise of the radial engines. "I KNOW WILL DO YOUR DUTY. I HAVE EVERY CONFIDENCE YOU WILL BE A CREDIT TO YOURSELVES AND YOUR REGIMENT."

Brigadier Burke, the officer commanding the 27th British Commonwealth Brigade, had at his disposal the Patricias, the 3rd Royal Australian Regiment currently in a fierce fight on Hill 504, the Middlesex Regiment, in reserve, and the New Zealand artillery.

Cripes, Charlie thought. First time we've had a brigadier fly over to buck us up. He knows, and we know—we're alone out here, and we're in for a fight.

CHAPTER 28

It was mid-afternoon on April 24, and visibility was good under a cloudy sky. Charlie could see Powell's head sticking up out of his trench and, off to the right, Woody in his. The serried Korean hills marched one behind the other into the distance, the calm vista belying the brutal reality. In the valley below his perch on the brow of Hill 677 Chinese troops moved sporadically, taking cover when threatened by American aircraft but never stopping. Long-range artillery took bites out of their formations, but still they came.

Sharing Charlie's trench was Ridley, who didn't talk much. He'd come close to losing his nerve back on frozen, remote Hill 1250, but had held it together since. He hadn't grumbled when Charlie ordered him to dig a new trench and had continued to work at a steady pace.

"Try to get some sleep," Charlie said to him. They had climbed the hill and dug in twice during their sleepless night, and Charlie didn't figure on a restful time to come.

"I'm okay," Ridley said; he didn't look like he'd be dozing any time soon.

"Back in five." Charlie stepped out of the trench with his carbine and, crouching, crossed over to the Bren gun trench.

Powell was alert, the Bren laid out on the parapet in front of him. Muller had a cigarette dangling from the corner of his mouth, while Frenchy slouched in the end of the trench, arms folded and eyes shut.

"What do you figure, Charlie?" Powell said.

"I figure we're ready."

"Lots of Chinese down there. They all going after the Diggers?"

"For now, anyway."

"Hope they aren't circling around behind us."

Frenchy stirred. "There's a happy thought."

"The Aussies are holding them up," Charlie said. In quiet moments they could hear the ongoing battle on Hill 504, the Australians still in the thick of it.

Muller took a last puff and stubbed out his cigarette on the parapet, flicking the remaining butt out front. "Come and pick that up, Mao, or whatever your fuckin' name is." He gestured to Powell and took the Bren. "My turn." He checked it over, laid it out on the parapet, propped it up on its bipod.

Powell kept staring out front.

"Better relax while you can," Charlie said.

Powell's Happy Valley grin had faded. "I just want to get this over with," he said. "I'm hoping for a picture next time we get mail."

"Bet you wish you were back in the pokey," Frenchy said. "Instead of waiting here for the Chinese to drop by."

"Give me this any day." Powell's grin was back. "As you well know, lance corporal, having been in Big Jim's cells yourself."

Charlie went over to check on Woody and Dunstan. Woody was alert, scanning the near horizon. "Those guys make me nervous, Charlie," he said, inclining his head. Barely visible down the steep slope the zombie-like ROKs—refugees or survivors or deserters, whatever they were—continued to trickle past.

"Don't worry about them, Woody," he said. "We just have to worry about the Chinese." He tried to grin but felt like it came out lopsided.

"That's just what I was thinking," Woody said. "If the ROKs can climb the hill, so can anyone else."

Charlie made his way back to the trench he shared with Ridley, Woody's words ringing in his head. The long day had moved on, and they went to a hundred percent stand-to. All was quiet to the front, but to the right on the valley bottom Charlie could see the oncoming Chinese. And way to the right, the limit of his vision blocked after that by the topography of Hill 677, the Australians continued to be pounded. American aircraft appeared from time to time, dropping bombs wherever they spotted a group of Chinese. A new plane came in from the west, a US Navy Corsair, skimming above the river, its engine shrieking. Charlie looked away and checked the hillside in front of him.

"Holy shit," Frenchy said.

Charlie swung around. Frenchy had climbed high ground behind their trenches so he could see Hill 504 and the Aussies. Charlie followed his gaze, just in time to see a wide swath of the hill burst into the hideous yellow flames and black smoke of burning napalm. "My god," he said. "The Aussies've been bombed."

"Friendly fire," Frenchy said.

Charlie felt sick, like he'd been slammed in the gut. During their two-month-long slog north, from hill to hill, they had come across bodies of men who had been napalmed. Black, twisted bodies—but Chinese bodies, enemies who hours before might well have been shooting at them. Easy to rationalize, to cheer their death.

Not their comrades, their brothers in arms, the Australians. They, like the Patricias, were a battalion in a Commonwealth brigade, a small piece in a huge board game played by outside forces. Men of flesh and blood, enveloped by burning napalm.

Charlie visited the trenches again, where he explained what he and Frenchy had seen. There were no comments, the men shocked at the suddenness with which the Australians' luck had changed.

Charlie tried not to flinch when he heard an aircraft in the distance.

The platoon was silent. Waiting.

—

Ridley said, "Gettin' dark."

Charlie jumped. "Yeah." Settle down, Charlie, he thought. He hadn't heard a peep out of Ridley for hours.

"Never heard it this quiet."

Charlie didn't respond, but Ridley was right. The Australian battle on Hill 504 was over. The Aussies had withdrawn, their position overrun. The ominous silence spoke louder than words to Charlie: the Chinese are everywhere. You're alone.

Common knowledge said nighttime was when the Chinese attacked, but they'd taken on the Aussies during daylight. Charlie's mouth was dry. He took a slug of water.

A distant machine gun rattled. The men of 13 Platoon froze. In the near darkness Charlie sensed Ridley turn toward him, as if about to speak. The gunfire sounded much closer than anything heard so far during the Australians' fight. The distant thump of mortar bomb explosions merged with machine gun fire. Chinese? Who was shooting? It sounded like it came from the other side of their hill, far to the east.

"Eyes all around, boys," Charlie said, fearful of being distracted, forcing himself to concentrate on the slope in front of them.

Activity behind him and to the right caught Charlie's attention in the dim light. A bent figure moved from trench to trench in the 10 Platoon position, pausing for a few moments at each. A short time later Lieutenant Levy strode across the fifty yards from 10 Platoon's trenches to where Charlie waited.

Levy crouched and spoke in a hoarse whisper. "That firing you hear is B Company and the Mortar Platoon. Captain Mills got word by radio that headquarters is under heavy attack." Levy gave Charlie a querulous look.

Cripes, thought Charlie. I must look scared.

"They're counting on us. If we go down, everybody goes down."

Charlie nodded, his throat dry.

"Last thing," Levy said. "Fix bayonets."

Levy went back the way he had come, clutching his Tommy gun, his semi-crouched figure silhouetted for a brief moment on the skyline.

Charlie crept to his trenches and passed on Levy's remarks. The chorus of clicks as the riflemen snapped on their spike bayonets scared him as much as anything had.

Later, close to midnight, a brilliant half-moon provided sporadic clear visibility interrupted by clouds moving across the sky, their undersides lit by the occasional flash of artillery. Charlie, crouched in his and Ridley's trench, shifted to avoid cramping up.

Their trench wouldn't have satisfied Sergeant Price, but it was the best they could do, barely three feet at its deepest. Charlie could look out of it even when sitting if he stretched.

Moonlight came and went as the clouds thickened. Charlie could make out a hill to the west, almost as high as they were on 677. Distances were hard to judge, but it was perhaps a mile away. To the north jagged peaks and hills marched and faded from sight, in all likelihood occupied by the Chinese. At their backs was D Company Headquarters, with its vital radio links to Battalion HQ and Big Jim Stone.

Only yards away to his front left Charlie could see the Bren on its tripod in front of Muller, who looked alert even from behind. Frenchy and Powell were there too, facing outward. He looked right to the northern-most arm of the trenches' V-formation. Woody and Dunstan, both steady, weapons on the parapet in front of them, their length extended by bayonets. Beside him Ridley crouched, leaning on his forearms, rifle extended.

When he had visited the other members of the platoon they greeted his recitation of the situation passed on by Levy with stoic silence. Except for Muller, who seemed to have recovered from his earlier jitters. But his words kept Charlie on edge, when he said with apparent satisfaction, "We're gonna be next."

CHAPTER 29

An earlier breeze rattled the dead grass on top of their hill, but it had died away. It was after midnight, and very dark. The troops were silent, waiting; no chatter, not even the click of inserted ammo clips or scrape of shovels to lend a touch of the familiar.

Ridley leaned toward Charlie. "What—"

Charlie put his hand on Ridley's shoulder. He had heard something indistinct, very faint. Like a snake in a pile of dry leaves.

There was a loud pop and the hillside was illuminated in a bright, eye-shattering white light. A flare arced high overhead and began to drift downward. A deafening chorus of bugles, shouts, and gunfire erupted. Figures rose from down the slope, charging toward them, bathed in the intense light of the flare.

Charlie swung the carbine to his shoulder. How the hell did they get so close?

"Rapid fire," he shouted, the report of his shot drowned out by the explosion of sound. The attackers screamed, flares of automatic fire from their burp guns rippling across their front. Ridley yelled an indistinct curse, working his bolt. Charlie aimed, his hands shaking so hard he couldn't settle on a target. Slow down, slow down, make it count. He took a deep breath and snugged the butt of his .30 into his shoulder, aimed at a running figure, and fired.

Charlie guessed fifty Chinese were half-way up the slope in front of them, closing fast. The Bren stuttered a deadly torrent of fire. Charlie kept firing. His magazine was empty, and he jammed in a fresh one, selecting automatic fire on his carbine. The first line of attackers broke like an ocean wave against rocks, mowed down by the Bren and rifle fire. A dozen came on, straight at Charlie and Ridley at the apex of the V of trenches.

"Grenade, Ridley, grenade," he shouted, and shouted it again, counting on the men in the other trenches to hear it and take cover. Bullets whizzed around him and spattered in the loose gravel in front of the trench. Out of the corner of his eye he saw Ridley rip a grenade from his webbing, pull the pin, and toss it.

Charlie shot again from the hip and threw himself down as Ridley's grenade exploded, the ear-splitting concussive noise lost in the roar of battle.

When he looked up there were no Chinese on their feet. One was trying to bring his burp gun to bear. Charlie took aim and shot him. Bodies were scattered in front of their trenches. The dead lay still, and the wounded tried to crawl away.

"Cease fire," Charlie shouted. "Reload, boys. Woody, you and Dunstan okay?"

"Piece of cake, Charlie," Dunstan shouted back. "All okay here."

Frenchy checked in. He, Muller and Powell were fine, and reported they had lots of ammunition left. They were taking advantage of the break in the action to refill the numerous Bren mag empties lying in the bottom of their trench.

"We were lucky," Charlie said. "Their flare helped us, not them." And thank God we were down in our trenches, with the enemy charging across open ground.

"Bastards know where we are now," Frenchy said, his voice low.

Charlie heard something close behind him. It was Sergeant Malloy, over from 10 Platoon.

"Any casualties, corporal?"

"We're all okay."

"Here," Malloy said. "Just in case." He pushed a bag with a dozen or more grenades in Charlie's direction. "A present courtesy of the riceburners. Gotta like those guys. Minor wounds in 10. Stay awake, boys," he added, before heading back to his own platoon.

The relative calm lasted only a few minutes. Ten Platoon was under attack again, the roar of a fierce battle reverberating with rifle and Bren gunfire, shouts and screams. From the east came the rattle of a Vickers medium machine gun, explosions of mortar bombs. Charlie glanced in that direction and was about to remind his section to look to their front, when the Bren stuttered into action. It was firing on a bearing of two o'clock, and when Charlie looked he saw movement there in the semidarkness. The flash and sharp blast of an artillery round erupted downslope, silhouetting a mass of Chinese running up the hill.

Pinpoints of small-arms fire erupted across a broad front, the Chinese coming on without a flare this time. Charlie felt calm, firing as fast as he could aim. Within seconds he stopped trying to aim, firing from the hip, kneeling in the trench, exposed.

"Too God damn many of them," Frenchy yelled, his voice somehow cutting through the noise, Charlie catching a glimpse of Powell jamming a new mag onto the Bren.

Charlie jerked a grenade from his belt and pulled the pin. "Down!" he yelled, "grenade, grenade." He released the clip, counted to three, and threw it.

The grenade exploded, and now there were only a handful of the enemy on their feet. The Bren fired, and Charlie swung his weapon up, shooting at a figure that attempted to turn away but was too slow. The distant artillery, located somewhere far to the rear, kept firing, the rounds exploding down the hill in front of them and off to the right, in front of 10 Platoon.

The platoon's rifle fire became more desultory. No more targets presented themselves, but incoming small arms bullets and some machine gun tracers continued to spray overhead and kick up dirt and pebbles from their front parapets.

Away to their right, 10 Platoon was still in the thick of it, machine guns and rifles firing. Inserting itself into the roar of battle was a loud, clear voice, shouting in what sounded to Charlie like Chinese, coming from 10 Platoon's location. Christ, were they overrun? Charlie leapt to his feet, forgetting the risk, knowing that if 10 Platoon fell it would be the end of them all. He could make out their trenches, still manned, still fighting. Puzzled, he dropped back down into cover.

He glanced left, taking in Frenchy, who was leaning over Muller and the Bren, pointing something out. Powell reached up to change magazines.

Charlie saw movement among the bodies scattered in front of the Bren trench. He shouted a warning and shot, just as one of the Chinese wounded fired a round.

Powell jerked back into the trench and dropped out of sight.

Charlie squeezed off two more shots and the burp gun fell from the soldier's hands.

Ridley shouted, "Look out, corporal."

Charlie swung around. Three Chinese had run past Dunstan and Woody and were coming fast at him and Ridley from their right front. Ridley shot the closest, who fell hard, face down. Charlie squeezed off two quick shots at the next figure, who stumbled, took two more steps, and fell. The third man was on Ridley, bayonet extended. Ridley tried to push the man's rifle to the side at the last instant and thrust his own rifle forward. Charlie couldn't shoot, Ridley blocking his view. The attacker and Ridley crashed back into the trench, the Chinese on top, trying to wrest his rifle out of Ridley's grip, his body semi-upright in an unnatural position. Charlie swung the butt of his carbine twice, bashing him on the head. He stopped moving.

Charlie gasped for breath. The Bren was firing, but a quick glance and Charlie saw no immediate threat. Dropping his carbine, he grabbed the Chinese and pulled him off Ridley, who groaned and got to his knees. Ridley jerked at his rifle, and Charlie realized the dead soldier was still impaled on Ridley's bayonet.

The man's skull was shattered, blood and fluid dripping to the bottom of the trench. Charlie and Ridley lifted the body out of the trench and pushed it a few feet to where it tumbled down a short incline.

The firing stopped. Ridley grimaced. He pulled up his sleeve, exposing a slash on the inner surface of his bicep. "Shit," he said.

There was a constant trickle of blood. Between the two of them they pressed a medicated pad on it and taped it tight.

Ridley picked up the Chinese soldier's rifle with his good arm and flung it behind the trench. "He won't need that anymore."

Catching his breath, Charlie looked at the other trenches. Woody peered out of his, but he couldn't see Dunstan. In the Bren trench, Frenchy was on the automatic gun. He squeezed off three single shots. No one else was visible.

CHAPTER 30

Charlie took his carbine and trotted over to the Bren trench. Frenchy was keeping a sharp eye out. Muller crouched, tending to Powell.

"How bad is it?" Charlie asked.

Muller glanced up. "The kid's luck is holding," he said, and turned back to the wounded man. "Went right through."

Powell managed a wry twist of his pinched lips. "I don't feel very lucky."

Muller had cut away Powell's tunic from the left side of his neck to his shoulder and peeled the layers of clothing open. Powell clenched his jaw, his facial muscles working.

"Can you hold this, Charlie?"

Charlie reached behind Powell's back to press on an antiseptic pad that Muller had placed. Muller stripped adhesive tape off a roll and used it to fasten the pad to Powell's back. He then slapped a quick patch on a small entry wound near Powell's collarbone.

Behind Charlie, Frenchy said, "Here they come again." He fired a short burst, followed by another.

"Powell, you have to hold on here," Charlie said. "We'll get you out as soon as we can."

"I'm fine."

Ridley was manning the rear trench by himself, rifle aimed. Charlie said a silent prayer and sprinted back to his trench.

He swung up his weapon and peered into the darkness. Bugles and whistles erupted as the Chinese came on again. Somewhere past 10 Platoon a Vickers machine gun hammered. Charlie aimed and fired. Ridley's wound wasn't slowing him any.

"Ridley. You're checked out on the Bren, right?"

"Yep."

"Go up to Frenchy's trench and relieve Powell. He's wounded. Send him back here if he can make it."

"You want me to stay there?"

"Yes. Go!"

Ridley crawled out and scuttled to the Bren trench. Charlie saw him settle in beside Muller, who was back on the gun as number one, with Frenchy directing fire. They had the Bren firing a steady series of short bursts. An ear-splitting clap reminded Charlie the artillery was still in the fight.

Powell was trying to climb out of his trench but was having trouble. Charlie raced forward. He boosted the wounded man up, grabbed him by his good arm, and supported him back to Charlie's own trench. Powell was white-faced, blood that looked black in the limited light soaking the bandages Muller had applied.

Charlie heard footsteps behind him. A runner. "Sergeant Malloy said he saw someone needed evac."

"Damn right. Just in the nick of time." Charlie helped Powell to his feet, and with the runner's help half lifted him out of the trench. Powell groaned as the runner grabbed his good arm and draped it over his shoulder. Charlie snatched up his carbine. When he glanced back both men were gone.

Bodies were scattered across the sloping ledge in front 13 Platoon's position. Spouts of dirt erupted here and there, and some nearly spent bullets ricocheted off rocks the defenders had thrown up when they dug their trenches. The sporadic fire appeared to be from a distant automatic weapon. Its obvious purpose was to keep the defenders cowering in their trenches while assault troops wormed their way forward among the dead. From that range it would be plain bad luck if any of them were to catch a slug. Let leaders like Big Jim Stone pace back and forth on the skyline under fire. Charlie saw no necessity to do the same, and made sure the platoon stayed as low as possible.

"Corporal!"

Woody's voice. Must be serious to call him 'corporal'.

"It's Dunstan," Woody said. "I think he's out of it."

If Dunstan was down, Woody was alone in his trench.

Charlie checked the slope. The Chinese were working their way up but keeping low, having abandoned their frontal, full-on charge for now. Charlie watched one man squirm forward, and took two aimed shots. The man lay still, but others kept coming.

From Charlie's left, the Bren crew kept up a steady series of bursts.

Slinging his carbine over his shoulder, Charlie scooped up his bag of .30 calibre rounds and another of grenades. He crouched and ran forward, sliding down into Woody's trench.

Dunstan lay unmoving on his side, facing the stony front wall of the trench. His balaclava was blood-soaked, and what Charlie could see of his face was the colour of old marble. Charlie felt his neck for a pulse and couldn't find it, Dunstan's skin clammy.

"Is he…"

"Yes." Charlie looked at Woody, who was kneeling in the shallow trench, looking forward.

Woody shot at something, cycled his bolt action, shot, and shot again, his movements jerky.

Charlie put a hand on Woody's shoulder. "Take it easy, Woody. Slow down."

Woody drew a deep breath. "I'm okay," he said.

Another wave of grey-brown enemy soldiers reared up and came on. The Bren stuttered into life. He and Woody fired, Woody under control.

Charlie changed magazines, thinking to himself the Chinese were too close. He reached for a grenade, then realized the enemy was being hit by something besides 13 Platoon's feeble firepower. From behind him came the rapid bang of automatic fire. Lying prone on the high ground that separated them from 10 Platoon was Lieutenant Levy, firing steady bursts with his Thompson.

The attack slowed. Between aimed shots Charlie looked and saw that Levy had gone back to the 10 Platoon trenches.

"Shit, the Bren's had it," Frenchy shouted.

"What?"

"Took a round or some shrapnel or something right on the loading slot. Magazine's jammed, can't get it out."

Charlie thought a minute. Frenchy, Muller and Ridley in their trench. "You all have rifles?"

"Yeah, we've got Powell's."

Three rifles in one trench, Woody's rifle and his own carbine in the other. It would have to do.

"Heads up, 13. Coming over." Charlie recognized Levy's voice as the lieutenant scuttled across the skyline and crouched down beside him.

"Only five of you?" Levy's Thompson dangled in his right hand.

"Yes, sir. And our Bren just went south."

"I'll see if we can dig you up another one when things quieten down."

An artillery round cracked, sounding like it had hit a few hundred yards down the slope. Levy didn't even look that way. "Good work so far," he said. "We have to hold on. If the Chinese keep coming I may have to call in closer artillery fire."

Closer? Charlie thought.

Levy looked him in the eye. "You'll want to be in your trenches with your heads down." Levy ran back toward the 10 Platoon trenches.

In the relative quiet Charlie heard a Chinese voice again, sounding like it was urging its troops on. The shouted words were interrupted by a scream coming from well down the hill. Seconds later it was as if a dam burst in front of 13 Platoon, shadowy figures erupting from the very ground itself, the noise of gunfire, shouts, and bugles pounding at the defenders.

Bullets zipped over their heads as they crouched in their shallow trenches. All five were aiming and firing. Charlie shot at a figure wielding a burp gun thirty yards in front of him. The man fell, and another one scooped up the fallen gun. Woody shot him.

The Chinese were closer. Charlie barely aimed, firing single shots, trying to save ammo. He emptied his magazine and jammed in a fresh one. "Woody, get a grenade ready. Grenades!" he shouted above the noise to the men in the other trench.

It was almost too late. Woody was ready. "Throw it, throw it," Charlie said, and fired another round. Woody was on his knees, head and shoulders above ground level, as he tossed his grenade. Behind him loomed a dark figure, swinging a rifle like a club. Charlie shot him but the rifle kept coming, clunking into Woody's head before Charlie shot again, knocking the man down.

Charlie ducked and snatched at a grenade from the bottom of the trench, pulled the pin, and flung it out. The rifle fire from Frenchy's trench stopped. The incomprehensible screams of the Chinese were close, bullets slamming into the back of the trench above Charlie's crouching back. The grenades exploded.

Charlie peered out. The closest Chinese were down on the ground. A handful came on, perhaps forty yards away, with dozens running up the hill behind them. 13 Platoon's pitiful fire-power couldn't stop them. He could hear the Vickers, firing from somewhere beyond 10 Platoon, busy there.

An artillery shell burst in the air down the slope, perhaps three hundred yards away. A second one followed, then a third and fourth. A figure closed fast toward Frenchy's trench. Charlie blasted two quick shots and took him down. Someone in the Bren trench threw a grenade. Charlie ducked again and threw a grenade of his own, yelling at Woody to get down, the nearest Chinese only yards away.

The artillery explosions were coming faster. Charlie reared up and shot from the hip as bullets whistled by him. There was a horrendous crash as a round exploded two hundred yards away, followed by another one even closer. Chinese bodies were thrown into the air, but still others came on. All three men in Frenchy's trench had .303s at their shoulders, rapid fire, feeding in fresh clips.

What a time for the Bren to pack it in, Charlie thought. It might be the difference between living and dying. He shot at a man twenty feet away, not even aiming. A terrific explosion rocked him. Artillery rounds, one after the other, seconds apart.

"Everybody down," Charlie screamed. He threw another grenade, and made himself as small as possible, his nose up against Woody's boot. In the corner of his eye he saw a sliver of sky above the top of the trench, and wondered if he'd see death coming. A bayonet, maybe a bullet. He saw only the flashes of the barrage, the noise pounding, unbearable. He covered his head with his arms.

The ear-splitting crash of twenty-five-pounder shells reached a crescendo and stayed there, explosion on explosion fractions of a second apart. The ground shook.

The sheer terror of lying in a hole in the ground while random forces beyond his control decided whether he would live or die constituted an unspeakable horror of its own. During their early training at Camp Wainwright an instructor told them men in proper trenches could only be killed by an artillery round that exploded directly on them. A matter of luck. Surely, in this barely adequate trench on a Korean hill his had run out.

A prayer, no words, just thoughts, that he might live another minute, another second. On and on it went, for hours it seemed.

The noise was unbearable, one explosion running into another. Against all reason they came closer. Surely the next one must be a direct hit. Earth and rocks rained down on him.

Charlie had read accounts of trench warfare and artillery barrages in his father's war, but he never thought he'd live it.

Terrified, his senses numbed, but he sensed a change. The barrage eased.

He crouched on his haunches, dizzy, ears ringing. Raising his head above the lip of the trench he saw bodies of Chinese soldiers scattered at random over the open slope in front of them. He counted and stopped at twenty, letting it go at that.

Across the way he could see movement in 10 Platoon's area. Lieutenant Levy dashed from one of his platoon's trenches to another, their occupants' heads popping up, the men no doubt also numbed by the artillery barrage. Like prairie dogs emerging from their burrows after a lightening storm.

From downslope came a banging and rattling noise. Small-arms fire erupted, bullets ricocheting off shale and rocks in front of and behind Charlie's crew. It wasn't only the Patricias that realized the artillery had ceased. Spectral figures rose to their feet and charged, coming from God knew where. 13 Platoon's rifles barked, an irregular tattoo. Charlie switched to auto, only his carbine able to do more than a single shot at a time.

Off to his right Charlie could hear 10 Platoon, fully engaged, Brens stuttering. The enemy kept coming, absorbing the bullets, falling, others running between the bodies, closing fast.

Charlie scooped up a grenade, pulled the pin and flung it, snatching up another. Across the way Frenchy hurled a grenade while Ridley and Muller kept firing their .303s. An artillery round crashed, followed by another, exploding just over the crest of the downslope in front of them. Charlie sensed shrapnel zipping overhead, and saw Chinese bodies flung into the air.

He crouched and shouted, "Get down, get down." Woody was down beside him. He threw another grenade and snatched a look out as soon as it exploded. A Chinese soldier ran hard toward the Bren trench. Charlie took aim and shot hm, then ducked down.

The artillery kept on coming, some of the explosions even more shattering than others. For a time he counted the rounds, which at first were a second or two apart, but they came faster and faster, a blur of concussive blasts that ran together. His mind veered away. If he were a Gunner, could he distinguish? Mortar rounds, twenty-five pounders, American 105 millimetres, 155s? On and on it went, his eardrums reverberating, his very body sore from the concussive blasts.

He felt he could take no more and caught himself about to straighten up. But the Chinese were out there and must be dying by the drove. Only one thing could be worse than what the troops were going through as they hunkered down in their trenches, and that would be to be out on the open slope with the Chinese.

It almost didn't register at first, the easing of the fusillade, the explosions coming less often and at last stopping.

He cautiously peered out. Nothing moved. Charlie's ears rang, adding to feelings of dizziness and unreality.

CHAPTER 31

A runner dropped into his and Woody's trench, sent by Levy to check on casualties. Charlie responded, and the runner left, returning with three more men. They lifted Dunstan's body from the trench and carried him off on a stretcher.

Charlie's ears still rang, but he heard Woody mumble something. Woody crouched in the trench, cradling his head in his hands. "Man, my head is killing me."

"I don't doubt it. I heard the clunk when you were clubbed, even with all that racket going on."

Woody picked up his rifle to lay it with great care onto the parapet where he could get at it in hurry, though he didn't look like he was going to hurry at anything soon.

They were into full daylight. Sporadic rifle and machine gun fire came their way.

"Where's Dunstan?" Woody said.

"Dunstan?" Charlie looked at Woody. "He's… are you okay?"

Woody looked around. "Where is he?"

Charlie laid a hand on Woody's shoulder. "You took a good bang on the head, Woody."

Woody looked at him, wide-eyed, his lips moving, nothing coming out.

"Dunstan's dead. He's been carried out."

"Really? Dunstan?" he said, his voice rising.

Charlie nodded, and eased the rifle, which Woody'd picked up, out of his hands.

"Relax, Woody. It'll come back to you."

Charlie hoped Sergeant Malloy or Lieutenant Levy or somebody from 10 Platoon would come by. Woody should be back with the walking wounded.

"They killed Dunstan?" Woody made nervous gestures with his hands, rubbing them together, his head jerking.

Charlie ignored him, and after a few minutes Woody quieted down.

"Tell him to shut up."

Charlie leaned on his elbows, binoculars in hand. He lowered them. "What?"

"That groaning. Where's it coming from?"

Charlie's hearing was still fuzzy, but now that Woody mentioned it, he could hear a low moan coming from somewhere in front of them. Is that what Woody was on about? Raising the glasses to his eyes, he scanned the near horizon. Nothing moved. He could hear it clearer now. Laboured breathing, a rasping groan that started and stopped. Woody was sitting in the bottom of their trench, knees up, leaning his head against the end wall, his eyes shut.

"Charlie," Frenchy shouted from his trench. "We might've fixed it."

The Bren! "What was it?"

"The loading slot. We can make it work. Straightened it with a bayonet. Permission to test-fire it."

"Hold on. We'd better tell Lieutenant Levy that's what we're doing. We don't want him calling in the bloody artillery again."

Charlie was about to run over to speak to Levy in person when Woody sat bolt upright, scrambled out of the trench, and rushed forward.

Charlie ran after him. A bullet whined past his ear.

"Shut up. Shut up," Woody yelled as a machine gun opened up from long range. He stopped and looked down as Charlie caught up to him. In front of Woody was a Chinese soldier, his padded coat open, blood soaking his chest. A gaping neck wound had bled out over the ground. His eyes were open but glazed, his breathing laboured. With every breath he gave a frightful groan.

Woody planted his feet either side of the soldier, grabbed his coat with both hands and jerked him into a sitting position. "I said shut the hell up!" Woody stepped to the downhill side, pulled hard, and sent the wounded man rolling and tumbling down the steep incline.

Woody's eyes were blazing, his face drained of colour. He swayed on his feet. "That's for Dunstan," he said.

Bullets ricocheted off a rock a yard away. Charlie grabbed Woody and hauled him back to their trench.

Charlie took stock. Powell wounded, Dunstan dead. Woody walking wounded. That left him, Muller, Frenchy, and Ridley. "How's the head, Woody?"

Woody turned toward him. "What?"

He looked confused, but at least he wasn't asking about Dunstan anymore. "Stand down, Woody," he said. "I've got it." They had the Bren and extra rifles, left behind by absent comrades. A handful of grenades. Ammunition was another story.

Sergeant Malloy was over from 10 Platoon again. "Things are tough over there," he said. "We're down to a few .303 rounds each, a couple of grenades. Then it's bayonets."

Charlie took a quick inventory of his .30 calibre rounds for the carbine. Twenty total.

"Sergeant, who was talking Chinese? Sounded like it came from 10 Platoon," Charlie said.

Malloy laughed. "Lieutenant Levy. Turns out he knows Chinese. He drove the Reds nuts. He said that Chinese guy who was doing all the shouting at us called him the son of a turtle!" Malloy glanced over his shoulder, and his voice dropped. "One of our boys yelled at Levy to shut the fuck up—he was just making them mad." Malloy shook his head. "Didn't seem to bother him." He chuckled and headed back to his own platoon.

It was broad daylight, with a layer of cloud obscuring the sun but visibility good. Frenchy busied himself gathering a small pile of spare Bren magazines, discovering 30 or so .303 rounds that he consolidated into a couple of magazines. "That's it for us," he said. "Hope to hell the Chinese haven't figured out how low we are on ammunition."

"We'll probably see another attack tonight," Charlie said, thinking it might be their last one. The Australians withdrawn.

The ROK's shattered and bugged out. The Patricias stood alone atop Hill 677, surviving so far on guts and determination, with a grateful bow in the direction of the New Zealand artillery. They may have run out of luck.

The five of them tensed as a distant light machine gun sprayed bullets over their heads onto the low ridge at their backs. Charlie glanced that way to see Lieutenant Levy dodging left and right, running toward them to jump into Charlie's trench.

"Sergeant Malloy tells me 13 Platoon is on the ball," he said. "Everything okay?"

"Yes, sir." Levy counted on them to protect his flank. 13 Platoon had followed Levy, and he'd looked after them. Charlie knew they'd stand fast. There was nowhere to go. Levy left them to it, dashing back to his own platoon. This time the machine gun was silent.

"Maybe they're short of ammo too," Frenchy said.

"They won't let that stop them," Muller said, with a nod toward where the Chinese dead still lay. "They don't care how many we kill, they keep coming."

They fell silent. Besides the shortage of ammunition, they were down to the last of their emergency rations and had little water left. Charlie glanced at each of his men. Frenchy was peering down the hill, the Bren close by, a spare magazine beside it. A couple of feet away, Muller sat relaxed in the bottom of the trench, smoking a cigarette, ready for anything. Ridley looked out, his rifle propped on the parapet. In the trench with Charlie Woody was silent, his face blank.

"You okay, Woody?"

Woody turned to him. After a moment he said, "Sure."

Charlie had it in the back of his mind that the Chinese were unlikely to attack in the daylight hours, when American air cover was available to protect the defenders. Nighttime, though, would be a different story. They had survived one night's desperate defence of Hill 677. Could they do it again?

—

Charlie thought he saw movement down one of the gullies that radiated from their position. He called Ridley over.

"Cover us," he said to Frenchy. He and Ridley crawled forward. A figure in the padded uniform of the Red Chinese darted from cover on one side of the gully across it and out of sight. Nothing moved for five minutes. What were the Chinese up to? A second man dashed across the gully. When the third one appeared, both he and Ridley fired. The soldier stumbled but disappeared from view.

"Jesus, is this an attack?"

Charlie thought a moment. "Could be, but more likely a patrol to see if we're still here."

For ten minutes they lay still, scanning the steep slope below them, but saw no further evidence of the enemy. They turned and crawled back to their trenches, where Frenchy, Muller and Woody crouched.

They waited.

Chapter 32

I000 hours. 13 Platoon was at fifty percent stand-to, with soldiers off watch keeping their heads down and out of sight as best they could in their shallow trenches. Long-range rifle and sporadic machine gun rounds kept their nerves on edge.

Excited voices drifted over from 10 Platoon. "Keep a sharp eye forward," Charlie said to Woody as he peered at 10 Platoon's area. Was an attack under way?

He stood up and took a few steps onto the ridge behind them. Something to the east had 10 Platoon buzzing. In the direction of the far-flung A, B, and C Companies an aircraft hung in the sky. A fat-bodied twin-engine plane turned toward them. It dropped lower, looking like it would plough into the ridge where Charlie stood, then grew larger and angled upward. Ground fire from the Chinese in the valley had no effect on its regal passage. It roared overhead. Charlie was able to make out a pilot peering down at him as it swooped by.

From the back of the Flying Boxcar small objects appeared and were backdropped by blossoming parachutes, which just managed to slow the fall of their loads as they plummeted the short distance to earth. The men of 13 Platoon watched, open-mouthed. A wooden crate crashed to the ground in front of them, followed by a second one that skidded and broke open, nearly dumping its contents down the slope.

Charlie snatched up the Bren to provide cover if necessary. "Go for it, boys," he shouted, as Frenchy, Muller and Ridley dashed to recover the unbroken crate and the loose C-rations, water, and .303 ammunition that had spilled from the damaged one.

"Well thank God," Muller said. He did a little jig, before hurrying up with an armful of water containers. "Or maybe the

US Air Force." He, Frenchy and Ridley soon had the supplies up to the trenches, the remaining box broken open, ammunition passed out. They reloaded their magazines before falling on the rations and water.

Charlie crossed to where Sergeant Malloy was coordinating 10 Platoon's similar blessings from the sky and returned with a bag of grenades. The odds of surviving more attacks had ramped up, and what's more, the Chinese would be aware the Patricias were resupplied.

Frenchy came over to where Charlie and Woody manned the right-hand trench. "You know what I think? I think we beat the bastards."

"I don't know," Charlie said. "They're still out there."

"Cheer up, corp." Frenchy gave Charlie a jab. "We've got the ammo, we've got the high ground. We showed we can take it."

"You're right. We *can* hold this hill," Charlie said, taking in the scattered detritus of the battle so far. Frenchy's enthusiasm was infectious. Even from a distance Lieutenant Levy's 10 Platoon looked more relaxed.

Was it true—they'd won a victory, not just another hill in a long series of running battles? The ROKs suffered a defeat, and the Australians had withdrawn. But the Patricias held.

Levy himself, Thompson still cradled in his right arm, came over to 10 Platoon's ledge and squatted in the open ground between their trenches.

"Orders from Tactical HQ," he said. "The battalion is to turn over our position to an American battle group tomorrow. We're being relieved."

Now Charlie believed it. He looked around at Frenchy, Muller, and Ridley, who were alert and ready for action but grinning in spite of the terrors they'd suffered, the men they'd lost. A buoyant feeling of triumph bubbled up in spite of his misgivings, but he looked at Woody, who sat by himself in a corner of his trench. Maybe later Charlie would allow himself to be celebrate, but not yet.

But he was proud of the battalion, even more proud of the men of 13 Platoon.

"Back to Happy Valley, sir?"

"No. We're withdrawing toward Seoul, and the Battle Group will cover us then follow behind."

"You mean we're letting the Chinese have the hill?" Frenchy said.

Levy gave him a look that brooked no come-back. "Those are our orders from Brigade. We're pulling back to consolidate the United Nations line."

—

On April 26 Charlie led his section off their forward position in single file, five yards behind 10 Platoon. Shellholes left by the 25-pounders pocked the hilltop and its slopes. Brass casings carpeted the ground, thicker where the machine guns had been sited. Ammunition boxes, broken crates, food and water containers littered the earth. They left behind their pitiful trenches, the whole scene looking like deranged monsters had played a violent game.

It reminded Charlie of something. A sharp image of the aftermath of the Canoe River crash and its wrecked railcars flitted across his mind. He'd been lucky then too, missing the Gunners' train. There had been similar loss of life, both events part of the ugly panoply of war. He shook his head.

The line of men wound up over the ridge that had been behind 10 Platoon, a line of men that included the survivors of 13 and 10 but preceded by 11 and 12 Platoons, men who had been forced to withdraw then recovered their ground and held. It passed close to where the company commander had positioned himself out of sight of the fighting platoons. From where he had passed on 10 Platoon Officer's call for direct fire on his own trenches, Levy's final desperate move that killed the Chinese attacks.

Crossing the high ground, Charlie glanced back one last time at the torn earth, the trenches that nature would soon fill, the scattered shell holes that marched to the very lips of the trenches. Another few steps and their abandoned trenches disappeared behind the height of land.

Some of the ammunition and supplies the men had carried up the hill had been replaced by the airdrop, but the weight of Charlie's pack felt almost negligible. The way down was barely recognizable as the slope they'd climbed in the darkness three days before, plagued by fog, confusion, and their own fears and doubts.

To the east Charlie could see Hill 504, where the Australians had given ground under a ferocious attack. How quiet it looked at the moment, occupied by Chinese troops keeping their heads down, watching for marauding American aircraft.

—

A, B, and C Companies had all pulled up stakes ahead of them, part of the single file of men making their way off Hill 677, *their* hill. Down off the heights, Charlie could see where Stone had located his Tactical Headquarters. The site was nearly deserted, leaving behind torn-up earth from the passage of trucks and half-tracks. There were multiple holes in the ground where vehicles had been dug in. A couple of jeeps and a truck remained. Fires had blazed in the grass and brush, set alight by exploding munitions, leaving scorch marks on the rough landscape.

Woody was in line behind Charlie. He walked erratically, sometimes on Charlie's heels, at others dropping back, attracting Muller's attention. "Take it easy, Woody. We're all going to get there at the same time."

Woody had said almost nothing since he pitched the enemy soldier down the slope. Charlie wasn't sure he realized, even now, that Dunstan was no longer with them. Muller kept reminding Woody to maintain a proper distance. Ridley followed, with Frenchy bringing up the rear, happy to be on the move, as they all were.

The long line of men passed within a hundred yards of a handful of soldiers loading up jeeps and a 6x6 truck. The soldiers stopped their activities and watched, perhaps drawn by the spectacle of the last of the rifle companies filing past.

One of the men walked over at an angle to intercept the line of riflemen. Charlie didn't pay any attention until he spoke. "Corporal Black."

Charlie missed a step, amazed to see Lieutenant Toogood, sporting a vivid scar on his forehead. "Didn't expect to see you here, sir."

"Almost didn't make it," Togood said. "Hello Woody, Private Muller. You too, Frenchy." He nodded at Ridley, a stranger.

The men responded, and Toogood fell in step with Charlie. He had heard about Sergeant Price's wound, and that his own replacement, Strachan, was no longer around. He asked about Powell and Dunstan.

"I heard good things about the platoon," he said after a moment.

"The boys did well," Charlie said. He stepped out of line. He and Toogood watched as the rest of 13 Platoon passed.

"Lieutenant Levy kept an eye on you, did he?"

"He did, sir. Sorry you missed it."

"Thank you, corporal." Toogood looked away, nodding at the retreating line of men. "You'd better catch up."

Charlie saluted, and Lieutenant Toogood returned it.

Charlie turned and hurried to overtake Frenchy.

The track up which they'd climbed three days before was well worn. They could have made much better time but for the need to stay in line. Sergeant Malloy didn't want Charlie stepping on his heels, no matter how good Charlie felt.

2 Section, 13 Platoon, followed D Company toward whatever lay ahead. Five men. Charlie wondered how long they'd be together. Woody was in trouble, whether he realized it or not, from whatever reality he was functioning in. Ridley, their new guy, was a good soldier after a hard start. Muller and Frenchy had proved themselves yet again.

Gone was steady Dunstan, his body spirited away on a stretcher. Dunstan, whom Charlie met aboard the *Private Joe*, a veteran of their abortive foray in Yokohama and many hills since. Powell, freckled kid from Medicine Hat, who almost drank himself to death but was now wounded, perhaps on his way home to his new family.

There was a lot of swagger in the Patricias' body language. Grizzled, tired, and grimy, they came down off their hill.

CHAPTER 33

They dug in three times in three days on the move south and west in the general direction of Seoul. Those three days were memorable for the weather that accompanied them, the rain so heavy it felt like the skies had split wide open. On the morning of the fourth day Charlie joined Muller, Ridley and Frenchy where they stood and stretched under a brilliant sky, their sodden clothing steaming in the sunlight.

The war news, what there was of it that filtered through, was not good. At the same time that the Patricias defeated a major Chinese attack at Hill 677, the 1st Battalion Gloucestershire Regiment, which belonged to the 29th British Commonwealth Brigade, had been annihilated when the communists attacked across the Imjin River.

Charlie didn't know how many Chinese had broken through on the Glosters, but he had heard that the Australians and Canadians had been attacked by at least one division, upwards of 5,000 men. The 700 Patricias had accounted for many of them.

A day after they withdrew from Hill 677 Woody disappeared. Charlie tracked him down to the A Echelon medical tent. He was morose and complaining of a ferocious headache. The medics wanted to keep him for a while. Charlie wondered if he'd see him again this side of the Pacific.

Blinking in the unexpected sunlight, Charlie had a sinking feeling that what was left of 2 Section 13 Platoon was scattering like quicksilver dropped on a tile floor.

A runner appeared from battalion headquarters with written orders. "You got a Ridley here?"

Charlie nodded, and Ridley stepped forward, taking a sheet of paper from the runner and glancing at it. "Shit," he said.

Without another word he jammed a couple of loose items into his pack, shouldered it, and picked up his rifle.

"Where you off to?" Charlie said.

"B Company. Guess I'll be a replacement there, now."

"Yeah. But they're getting a good one."

"Thanks, corporal." Ridley looked up at Charlie and squared his shoulders. "For everything." He nodded at Frenchy and Muller and walked off in search of B Company.

A jeep came for Charlie. The driver dropped him off outside what turned out to be an abandoned schoolhouse. Inside, the battalion adjutant sat at a cluttered table. Apart from him, the room was bare but for a pile of undersized chairs and desks in one corner. Charlie wondered where the children were now.

"Not much left of 13 Platoon," the adjutant said, looking up at him.

Charlie didn't like to dwell on it. Too many men, gone. "No sir."

"You men need a break. Hell, we all need a break. R and R sometime soon; you're due. But for now, C Company needs a corporal and a couple of men. I'm assigning you and Lance Corporal Accardo and Private Muller to 7 Platoon. They're due to cross the Imjin River two days from now, and we have to fill in some gaps in personnel. Report to Lieutenant Lund."

"What about 13 Platoon, sir? Couldn't we get some replacements?"

The adjutant stared back at Charlie. "13 Platoon never existed, not really, corporal." He snorted. "They're forgotten already." He glanced down at his desk, picked up a document, put it down again. "You have your orders."

"So who do you know in 7 Platoon, Charlie?"

Leaning back against his pack, Charlie sat on an exposed boulder, his carbine across his lap. Frenchy and Muller were almost ready.

"Not sure. There won't be many of the guys left that I knew there, back in Wainwright."

Those that he knew, and were still there—would he recognize them? They will have gone from raw recruits to hardened veterans in their brief months in Korea. And what would they see when he turned up? He was no longer the nervous teenager who had, wide-eyed, boarded the train in Vancouver bound for the unknown. He was a corporal in a rifle company, for better or worse.

He wished he'd been able to talk to his dad one last time. But the letter would have to do. One day he'd be home, where he could get to know Wanda again, and spend time with his mother, Harry, and Jackie.

"Feeling nostalgic, Charlie?"

"Cripes no," he said. Frenchy could think whatever he liked. He jumped up and shrugged into his pack. "Let's go."

CHAPTER 34

November 1951. The assembled men had been summoned in a hurry. They wore rumpled khaki uniforms, a mixture of British, American, and Canadian accoutrements; on their heads were winter lined or peaked caps or balaclavas or even a regulation beret or two. Standing easy in the foreground was a lieutenant-colonel with Canada flashes on his shoulder. He was Big Jim Stone to his troops when they were in a good mood and there was no brass in sight.

Forewarned by the thump of helicopter blades, their second-in-command called the men to attention and, saluting, reported to Stone, who ordered, "At ease."

A helicopter sprang into view, rising above a nearby ridge and clattering its way overhead. Stone bawled over the noise, "Ten-shun!"

Descending, the helo's propwash blew dust and grit into the faces of the men. One man's cap flew off, but he knew enough to ignore it. Stone, a handful of officers, and a couple-of-hundred-odd Canadian soldiers waited.

A staff officer swung the helicopter's door open, jumped out, and stood aside for three-star general James Van Fleet, United States Army. Van Fleet climbed down and crouched, his immaculate uniform a contrast to those of the Patricias. Holding his braid-covered cap, he made his way to where Stone waited.

As the helicopter's rotors slowed and died, Van Fleet read part of a document to the troops. Charlie didn't catch much of it, but did hear "…2nd Battalion Princess Patricia's Canadian Light Infantry… they stood their ground in resolute defiance of the enemy… and by their achievements they have brought distinguished credit on themselves, their homelands, and all freedom-loving nations."

The general spoke a few more words, followed by a hand-shake with Stone and a flurry of salutes.

Minutes after alighting, Van Fleet returned to the helicopter which whisked him away to his next task.

The document from which the general read resides today in the PPCLI museum in Calgary, the only US Presidential Citation ever publicly presented to a Canadian unit. It is represented by a blue bar with a gold background on the uniform of every member of the Second Battalion Princess Patricia's Canadian Light Infantry.

Afterword

Lieutenant-Colonel "Big Jim" Stone was born in England but came to Canada as a young man in 1927. He lived for a while in the Peace River district, making a living as a farmer and forest ranger. When war broke out in 1939 he enlisted in the Loyal Edmonton Regiment and served in their campaigns in Italy and Northwest Europe, ending the war in the Netherlands. During his time with the "Loyal Eddies" he occupied every rank, from private to lieutenant-colonel and in command of the regiment. In the course of World War II he earned the Distinguished Service Order twice as well as the Military Cross.

He returned to civilian pursuits, although staying active in the Reserve Army in 1948 and '49. Recruited for the Special Force to command 2PPCLI by Brigadier Rockingham, he was a brilliant choice. A hard task-master but a superb leader, his courage and initiative are considered unsurpassed.

In Korea, as Commanding Officer of 2PPCLI, Stone is given much credit for his brilliant defense on Hill 677.

Like many strong leaders, he had his weaknesses. Many who served under Stone labelled him hypocritical because he maintained that the men of the Special Force were volunteers, and so unworthy of medals, even as he accepted a third DSO for himself. There is some suggestion that he refused a medal for Lieutenant Michael Levy because of anti-Semitic prejudice, although that seems unlikely as he later appointed Levy his Intelligence Officer. In addition, Levy did not practise Judaism and his family rejects that suggestion. Stone did see fit to award a medal to Captain Mills, while ignoring Levy.

Stone went on to serve as Chief Instructor for the Royal Canadian School of Infantry and, later, head of the army's

Provost Corps (Military Police). Not without an emotional side
to his character, he founded the Military Police Fund for Blind
Children after losing a daughter to cancer of the eye, for which
he was awarded the Order of Canada.

Even those veterans who served in Korea with Stone and
note his faults will admit he was a "soldier's soldier," a superb
leader and tactician.

LIEUTENANT MICHAEL LEVY, 1925–2007

To say Michael George Levy had an adventurous life would
be an understatement. Born in Bombay, when he was an infant
his family moved to Shanghai, where his father worked as a clerk.
Levy grew up surrounded by Chinese culture and language.

After Shanghai fell to the Japanese in World War II, 17-year-
old Michael Levy was interned in Pootung, and later transferred
to Lunghwa (featured in the movie "Empire of the Sun") from
which he escaped with four companions. Making his way across
occupied China, he reached Kunming, and was flown "over the
Hump" by the RAF. Once safe in India he joined the British
Army, which trained him and parachuted him into Malaya as a
member of the Special Operations Executive Force 136. (Once
again, Levy's life attracted Hollywood, the actions of Force 136
featured in "Bridge On the River Kwai.") Mentioned in
Dispatches, Levy was discharged from the British Army in 1948
as a captain.

Levy's comrades behind the lines in Malaya were Chinese
Canadians originally from Vancouver; because of them, he opted
to move there, but it seems civilian life didn't hold the attractions
that service did. When the Korean War broke out, Levy volunteered for the Special Force and found himself in Korea with
2PPCLI, first as 10 Platoon Commander and, later, Intelligence
Officer.

On Hill 677 10 Platoon was exposed, along with the other
D Company platoons, to an extremely heavy attack by the
People's Liberation Army. Described later as suicide attacks, the
Chinese threatened to overwhelm the defenders' rifles and Bren

guns. Levy, in a move both desperate and courageous, called down friendly fire from artillery and mortars ("Danger close" in army parlance) to within yards of his own trenches, not once but over an extended period. Later analysis showed more than 4,000 rounds were directed at his location. In spite of this, and attesting to the quality of Levy's leadership, 10 Platoon suffered no fatalities in the battle.

Subsequent histories for years indicated the source of the order to call in direct fire on 10 Platoon's position was given by D Company Commander Wally Mills, but in fact Captain Mills' role regarding the "Danger Close" was to relay Lieutenant Levy's requests for direct fire.

Michael Levy stayed in the army after Korea, remaining with PPCLI during peacetime assignments in Germany, Vietnam, Cyprus, and the United States, retiring with the rank of major in 1974. His later career included work with federal Departments of External Affairs and Public Works, retiring in 1986.

A fellow Patricia and veteran of Kapyong, Hub Gray, made it his business to correct the record on what Mike Levy had accomplished on Hill 677. D Company's acting commander, Wally Mills, had been awarded the Military Cross following the battle, while Levy went unrecognized.

As a result of the efforts of Gray and others, Levy, long since retired from the army, received special recognition. In 2003 Governor-General Adrienne Clarkson granted a personal Coat of Arms to Michael George Levy in recognition of his service during the Korean War. His accompanying motto: "I have prevailed."

BRIGADIER-GENERAL JOHN MEREDITH ROCKINGHAM, 1911–1987
Brigadier "Rocky" Rockingham had an excellent record as a leader in the Second War. When war was declared in 1939 he was a reserve lieutenant in the 1st Battalion Canadian Scottish Regiment in Victoria, BC. By 1941 he was a major with the Royal Hamilton Light Infantry, going on to command the regiment and earn a Distinguished Service Order. From there he was

promoted to brigadier and commanded a brigade, crossing the Rhine and earning a Bar to his DSO.

The peacetime army wasn't for Rockingham. In the summer of 1950 he worked as superintendent of Pacific Stage Lines, a BC bus company. When he received a telephone call asking him to return to the colours and head up the Special Force, he was in the middle of a negotiating meeting with the drivers' union. The meeting was terminated and he found himself a very busy man, in command of the 25th Canadian Infantry Brigade.

Rockingham's first task in command of Canada's Special Force was to choose the leadership of the three battalions that would be at the centre of his brigade. For 2PPCLI he sought out and recruited James Riley Stone, whose wartime record paralleled his own.

Known as a hands-on leader, Rockingham anticipated spending time supervising the ongoing training of his three battalions. The changing face of the war, however, resulted in the Patricias arriving in Korea in December 1950, instead of training at Fort Lewis, Washington State, with the RCRs and the VanDoos. The result was that LCol Stone and his 2PPCLI saw Rockingham only on occasional flying visits until after their epic battle at Kapyong.

"Rocky" remained in the army after his Korea service, retiring in 1966. Doubtless his time commanding the 25th Brigade was one of the highlights of his career. As he observed later, he was "not particularly keen about soldiering when there is no fighting involved."

LIEUTENANT RONALD BIRCH TOOGOOD, 1928-2008

Ron Toogood applied for a transfer to Canada's active army before his short term commission ran out. Following acceptance he parlayed his one year of university math and physics into a career in the artillery. Retiring as a lieutenant colonel, he would often remark that he always felt he owed a debt of gratitude to the Gunners in Korea. He died a vigorous 80-year-old, the scar on his forehead still a subject of interest to his great-grandchildren.

CAPTAIN MURRAY EDWARDS, 1920-

Murray Edwards was raised in the US but came north to join the Queen's Own Rifles in 1942. After basic training in Canada he was posted to England, promoted to sergeant, and ultimately commissioned in February 1944. Following the war he was discharged, but signed up with 2PPCLI and the Special Force as a lieutenant in 1950.

In Korea, Murray fought as a platoon commander, then was promoted in short order to captain and Quartermaster. He took great pride in making sure the battalion was well-equipped, freeing-up much in the way of American arms and supplies through channels both official and otherwise.

Following service in Korea Captain, later Major, Edwards took jump (parachute) training. His career took him to Europe and UN-connected service in Cyprus, New York, and Palestine. He retired from the regular army in 1969, continuing in a training role with cadets until 1984. Murray Edwards died in 2023 in Victoria at the age of 103.

SERGEANT TOMMY PRINCE, 1915-1977

Although only mentioned briefly in *The Forgotten*, Tommy Prince inspired my characters as he did his comrades in real life.

Born in a tent in Manitoba, Prince was one of 11 children of an Ojibwe family. He was an excellent marksman and tracker, skills taught by his father. He attended and survived a residential school, then applied to join the Canadian military several times but was rejected. In June 1940 his application was at last successful.

Initially assigned to the engineers, by 1942 he was a sergeant with the Canadian Parachute Battalion. A later posting saw him in the 1st Special Service Force, the "Devil's Brigade," where he served with American troops as well as Canadians. (He was portrayed as "Chief" in the movie of the same name.)

In Anzio, Italy, Prince scouted on his own to a dangerous location behind enemy lines. He stayed for three days in an abandoned house close to an enemy artillery position, sending valuable intelligence back to his unit. As if that wasn't enough, he repaired a broken communication wire under the noses of the enemy, pretending to be a peasant tending his crops. A similar exploit in France resulted in the award of the Military Medal from King George VI. He was also decorated by the US, with the award of a Silver Star.

Discharged in 1945, Prince was active in lobbying for Indigenous rights but struggled with unemployment and discrimination.

When the Korean War broke out and Canada set up the Special Force, Prince rejoined with his former rank of sergeant and served with 2PPCLI. The Battle of Kapyong saw him with A Company. Later, he led many patrols into enemy territory; according to one comrade, Tommy Prince continued his tradition of making exceedingly dangerous patrols. Returning home to Canada due to physical problems, he returned to Korea for a second tour and, later, a new injury in 1952.

Honourably discharged from the army in 1954, Prince married and had a family. He continued to support Indigenous affairs, at one point explaining, "All my life I had wanted to do something to help my people recover their good name. I wanted to show they were as good as any white man."

Tommy Prince fell on hard times and died in 1977 in Winnipeg. He was buried with full military honours in a service that included First Nations comrades chanting the "Death of a Warrior." Princess Patricias served as pallbearers. The service was attended by more than 500 people, among whom were Manitoba's lieutenant governor and the consuls of France, Italy, and the US.

SERGEANT RICHARD PRICE, 1915-1993

Richard Price joined the army in 1938, and during the Second World War was promoted to sergeant. Much to his chagrin he trained others for action while remaining in Canada, quitting the army in frustration in 1946. His knowledge was again valued in 1950, and he rejoined with his old rank. Price's leg wound haunted him throughout the balance of his career although he stayed in the forces. He retired as a major with a display of medals the envy of many a senior officer.

CORPORAL CHARLIE BLACK, 1931–2006

Charlie Black married his sweetheart Wanda within a year of his discharge from the Army in 1951. He went on with his education and made a career of teaching high school and later at a community college. A long-time member of the Royal Canadian Legion, Charlie also took part in veterans' events with fellow Korean veterans. He died surrounded by his family. An interesting side note is that when the men of 2PPCLI saw the *Private Joe P Martinez* waiting to take them home from Korea, Charlie and a handful of others refused to go on board. They were flown home in style by the RCAF.

PRIVATE ROBERT POWELL, 1933–2011

Robert Powell recovered from his wound, but not until his time in the Special Force had run out. He was discharged home to Medicine Hat, where he married the mother of his daughter. They lived a happy life; Robert pursued a career in banking and died with his family around him.

LANCE CORPORAL FRANCO "FRENCHY" ACCARDO, 1929–

Accardo was among those who, like Charlie Black, staged a minor mutiny when they were ordered to again board *Private Joe P Martinez*. At some point between refusing the trip home on board *Private Joe* and reporting for the alternative flight on an RCAF North Star, "Frenchy" disappeared. He was sought by the Canadian provost corps and UN military police but was never located. He is listed as Missing in Action.

PRIVATE MICHAEL MULLER, 1930–1951

Two-and-a-half months after 2PPCLI's epic battle on Hill 677, Michael Muller was killed by machine gun fire when ambushed on a patrol, his body recovered two days later. He left behind his parents and two sisters in Red Deer, Alberta.

Private John Ridley, 1932–

John Ridley lives in Cornwall, Ontario. He made a career of the Canadian Army, retiring with the rank of Lieutenant Colonel. He belongs to several veterans' organizations, and maintained a correspondence with Charlie Black throughout the latter's life. He served as an honourary pallbearer at Charlie's funeral.

Canoe River

November 21st, 1950. The train designated Passenger Extra 3538 West, hauled on its trip toward the Pacific by the steam locomotive bearing that number, had rattled its way across the prairies. Smoke from the engine's stack streaming behind it, 3558 started up the eastern slopes of the Rocky Mountains. Seventeen carriages trailed behind.

In the wider world the Korean War had broken out five months before. Louis St. Laurent was prime minister of Canada, and Mike Pearson was his Minister of External Affairs. St. Laurent and Pearson had been kept hopping by mixed signals from Washington and Lake Success, home of the fledgling United Nations. In the White House Harry Truman had troubles of his own. Legendary American hero General Douglas MacArthur, ensconced in Tokyo as Commander-in-Chief, UN Command, called the shots in Korea that should have been the president's or the Unite Nations' prerogative.

Canada's Minister of Defence, Brooke Claxton, had opened the floodgates to volunteers for a Special Force for Korea, and the men in the train reflected the success of the recruitment campaign. The 2nd Regiment Royal Canadian Horse Artillery, like their infantry comrades, were a mixed bag of World War II veterans who reenlisted, regular army Gunners, and barely trained volunteers. The steel undercarriages and wooden frames of the cars carried 315 men and 23 officers of 2RCHA.

This may have been the furthest west some of the soldiers had ever been. They may have craned their necks to look at the scenery. They may have reset their watches for the time change.

Perhaps the train felt like it was moving faster as it crossed the continental divide and started down the long grade to the Pacific Ocean, the nearby rivers flowing west and south. The men were on their way to a great adventure; they'd turn back the communists, they'd fight for their country as their fathers and older brothers had in the previous war.

The men played cards or dozed, or boasted about the girls they'd left behind, or thought about their mothers who had waved good-bye. 3538 picked up speed, rushing the young men toward futures bright with excitement and occasional twinges of trepidation.

At precisely 10:35 am the train accordioned, its engine smashed to pieces, the engineer and fireman dead. Passenger cars stood on end and crashed down on each other or tumbled into the river alongside. Steam flashed, scalding to death many of the already injured trapped in the first two cars.

Bewildered and shocked survivors struggled to rescue the wounded and dying. Joining them were passengers and surviving crew from the eastbound CNR *Continental Limited* that hit them head on. By good fortune a doctor was among the *Continental's* passengers, who suffered only a few minor injuries.

Within hours a rescue train arrived from Edmonton, and was soon loaded with recovered bodies, the injured, and the lucky uninjured. The latter were carried back to Camp Wainwright, to regroup and once again entrain on their trip to Korea on November 29th.

Hours after the collision oil burst into flame, igniting the now-kindling wooden carriages, incinerating urecovered bodies still trapped in the wreckage.

The butcher's bill from the crash was 17 killed and some 50 injured. Both the train crews lost their engineers and firemen, making the total killed 21. The fatalities and bad injuries were concentrated in the lead cars, while soldiers housed toward the end of the train experienced a mild buffeting.

WHAT WENT WRONG?

A young telegraphist at the CN station at Red Path, a stop on the route through the Rockies, handed the troop train's crew instructions that read, "[Troop train] meet [Continental] and [a second train] at Gosnell," a siding well to the west. Unfortunately the message omitted the words "at Cedarside," which were included in the dispatcher's original message to Red Path. The result was that the troop train barrelled right past the Cedarside siding, where it should have waited, and rounded a sharp bend to crash into the oncoming *Continental*.

Twenty-two-year-old telegraphist Jack Atherton was charged with manslaughter for the death of the trainmen, and the case seemed airtight. Luckily for him a woman ill with leukemia followed the story in the newspapers and drew it to her husband's attention. John Diefenbaker, MP and lawyer, took the case on, not without difficulty. He wasn't a member of the British Columbia bar. He wrote the necessary exam, paid the fee out of his own pocket, and took on the trial in Prince George.

Edna Diefenbaker died before the trial, which had attracted national attention. Diefenbaker presented a defence that pitted the establishment Canadian National Railway against the low man on the totem pole, Jack Atherton. Diefenbaker also took advantage of possible bias by the jurors against army brass as represented by the prosecutor, whom Diefenbaker referred to as "Colonel" at every opportunity. The jury deliberated forty minutes and acquitted. Atherton later described his lawyer as "the greatest man in Canada," which, along with the spectacular victory in court, may have contributed to Diefenbaker, "Dief the Chief," becoming Canada's 13th prime minister in 1957.

ACKNOWLEDGMENTS

As always, heartfelt thanks to Patricia Sandberg, fellow writer, artist, and wife, and the rest of my family for their constant encouragement.

For *The Forgotten*, I'm deeply indebted to veterans John R. Bishop and Murray Edwards for their generosity in speaking to me and sharing their memoirs. Former Princess Patricia's Light Infantrymen and others who contributed and encouraged me include Ted Adye, Jack Bates, Gordon E. Brown, Bruce Dickey, Colonel (Ret'd) Keith Maxwell, Judy Moss, Brigadier-General (Ret'd) Ray Romses, and James Stanton—many thanks to you all. Published works such as John Bishop's *The King's Bishop* and Hub Gray's *Beyond the Danger Close* proved invaluable resources. Much gratitude as well to the Michael Levy family for sharing stories, mementoes, and photos.

Much thanks to Damian Tarnopolsky for his invaluable comments and a structural review, and also to the Rainwriters, the very accomplished writers in my longstanding critique group, for their suggestions and encouragement.

Finally, let me say what a thrill it was when Chris Needham, publisher at Now Or Never, said, after seeing the manuscript, "We like this story!"

Robert publishes a newsletter called *Forces With History* every two weeks, where he writes about Canada's armed forces both historical and modern. To receive *Forces With History* contact him via email, and he'll be glad to send it to you. He is available to speak to interested groups about Canada's World War I cavalry, submarines, Canada's Korean War, and other topics.

Robert is on Linkedin at linkedin.com/in/robertwmackay/ and Facebook at facebook.com/bob.mackay.50. He can be contacted at robert@robertwmackay.ca.

"I've just finished my first read of your excellent new book. It was a delight to read. You've captured the essence of the life of an infantryman. Your dialogue is perfect; your soldiers speak like real infantry grunts. You have done a great service to all who served in Korea, the PPCLI and the Special Force. Canadians should read this novel to understand how the citizens of this great land respond in times of crisis."
~ James B. Stanton, recipient of the Minister of Veterans Affairs Commendation

"This book is a soldier's story of courage, hardship, professionalism, and dedication to duty; it's a gripping read from Canada's forgotten war in Korea. I served in the Regiment that provides the setting for this novel of Canada's first soldiers to fight in that conflict and knew many of the veterans of the time. This tale rings true and is tribute to those who fought so well under great peril. We will remember them."
~ Colonel [Retired] Keith Maxwell, Officer in the Order of Military Merit

"*The Forgotten* is a meticulously well researched novel about Canadian soldiers from the 2nd Battalion, Princess Patricia's Canadian Light Infantry who served in the first year of the Korean War 1950-1951. Most importantly, it focuses on the Battle of Kapyong that highlights the courage, perseverance and sacrifice of Canadian soldiers in combat that resulted in the single instance of a Canadian unit being awarded a US Presidential Unit Citation for "outstanding heroism and exceptionally meritorious conduct." The author is to be commended for this riveting narrative that brings alive the sensation that you are actually there serving alongside the soldiers in 13 Platoon. This book is highly recommended."
~ Major [Retired] Bertram C. Frandsen, CD, PhD